ABOUT THIS BOOK

Lost in Time by Tish Thawer

Three sister witches escape the Salem witch trials when the eldest casts a spell that sends their souls forward in time. Separated by unknown forces, their soul journeys place them into new lives, causing two of the three Howe sisters to end up in an unforgiving mountain range in the early 1700s, where they come face-to-face with a native tribe living in a secluded box canyon. Forced to shift their focus from their lost sibling, the girls quickly realize they've been trapped in a time loop and now must face the tribe whose end goal remains to be seen.

Dawn of the Witch Hunters by Morgan Wylie

Witch hunter Marie Blackstone has always planned to follow in her mother's ways, learning to control her power and live at peace with their coven neighbors. Dante Blackstone has craved power from a young age. After the death of his and Marie's mother, his hatred for the witches grows into madness. Seeking freedom from her brother's vendetta, Marie joins other supernatural beings as they set out in search of a new home and a new way of life. But he won't let her go easily—even if that means eradicating any witch who gets in his way.

Redemption's End by Eric R. Asher

Gregory and Charlotte left their lives as pirates behind to huddle in a tinker's shop, building fantastic creations powered by steam and aether. Fifteen hundred miles inland from the ocean they once called home, they seek a quieter, safer way of life in the mountains of the Colorado territory. Fixing their neighbors' watches, creating beautiful and unique gifts, and helping to protect the burgeoning town is how they hope to make up for their past life of misdeeds. Becoming a target of a crazed fae was not part of the plan.

LEGENDS OF HAVENWOOD FALLS VOLUME ONE

A LEGENDS OF HAVENWOOD FALLS COLLECTION

TISH THAWER   MORGAN WYLIE   ERIC R. ASHER

LEGENDS OF HAVENWOOD FALLS BOOKS

Lost in Time by Tish Thawer

Dawn of the Witch Hunters by Morgan Wylie

Redemption's End by Eric R. Asher

Trapped Within a Wish by Brynn Myers

Blood and Damnation by Belinda Boring

Fated Beginnings by E.J. Fechenda (September 2018)

Emeline by Katie M. John (October 2018)

Released From a Curse by Brynn Myers (November 2018)

More books releasing on a monthly basis

Also try the signature New Adult/Adult series, Havenwood Falls, and the YA series, Havenwood Falls High

Stay up to date at www.HavenwoodFalls.com

Subscribe to our reader group and receive free stories and more!

LOST IN TIME

TISH THAWER

HAVENWOOD FALLS

LEGENDS

LOST IN TIME

TISH THAWER

ALSO BY TISH THAWER

The Rose Trilogy:

Scent of a White Rose (Book #1)

Roses & Thorns (Book #1.5)

Blood of a Red Rose (Book #2)

Death of a Black Rose (Book #3)

The Women of Purgatory Trilogy:

Raven's Breath (Book #1)

Dark Abigail (Book #2)

The Witches of BlackBrook Series:

The Witches of BlackBrook (Book #1)

The Daughters of Maine (Book #2)

The Ovialell Series:

Aradia Awakens (Book #1)

Dark Seeds (Book #1.5 – A short-story novella)

Prophecy's Child (An Ovialell Short Story)

The Rise of Rae (An Ovialell Short Story)

Shay and the Box of Nye (An Ovialell Short Story)

Behind the Veil (An Ovialell Omnibus)

Additional Works

Magical Bullet Journal & Planner

Handler

Fairy Tale Confessions

Dance With Me (A Short Story
originally featured in Fairy Tale Confessions)

Losing It: A Collection of V-Cards

Christmas Lites II

"Return us to our journey's end, find our sister, lost again. Use the bond that unites the three, as we will it, so mote it be."
— Tish Thawer

PROLOGUE

*I*PSWICH, MASSACHUSETTS – 1693

OUR SOUL JOURNEYS begin ~ Kara Howe

KARA

Kenna and I held tightly to Jeremiah as we watched Karina being pulled through the crowd. She was whipped around and tied to the stake, her long auburn hair lashing her face as she looked out over a sea of hateful faces who would love nothing more than to see her burn. With no solid proof, Governor Danforth announced her conviction and cast a torch at her feet. Flames rose, flickering closer and closer to her shoes and blackening the bottom of her cotton petticoat and apron as she struggled against the ropes holding her in place.

Karina, please. Use your magic to escape. Using our magical bond, I sent my deepest wish into Karina's mind as tears streaked down my face. Karina's only reply: a simple, peace-filled smile and the building of magic in the air.

My auburn hair—a perfect match to both my sisters'—fell forward from beneath my white coif and covered my freckled face. Bowing my head, I listened to Karina's inner plea to the goddess. Kenna, Jeremiah, and I all closed our eyes and surrendered to Karina's spell pulling our souls forward through time. Surrounded by wind and fire, we escaped this unbearable life of wrongful convictions as our astral bodies spun wildly into the starry night. Sparking against one another, we recognized each other's magic and knew Karina had just saved us all.

Opening my eyes, I took in the unfamiliar space but quickly understood how the soul journeys now worked. Solidified into my new lifetime, information flowed into my mind, filling in details of the person I would now be living as. I looked around the room and saw two others—a man and a younger woman—standing directly across from me. Thankfully, I was fully cognizant that despite their outward appearance, it was actually Jeremiah and Kenna who remained with me. I quickly glanced around at the rest of the room, and my heart clenched as I realized, however, Karina was not.

CHAPTER 1

$\mathcal{O}$PEN TERRITORY—June 1703

OUR SECOND SOUL JOURNEY. Karina was not found in our previous lifetime. After her initial spell, we were all pulled to Salem a few years in the future, but were unable to locate her there. It took months of using our magic to even pinpoint her, but shortly after that, her signature was permanently lost. She had died and jumped again, and we were not far behind. Hopefully this time, we will have better luck. ~ Kara Howe

KARA

I woke within the safety of what appeared to be a large covered wagon. A thick, dingy canvas stretched tight over hickory bows flexed above my head. I sat up, fully entrenched in my newest lifetime, and rubbed my eyes as the memory dump that accompanied this soul journey quickly informed me that Kenna and I were the daughters of a fur trader—Jeremiah.

"Girls, are you all right?" Jeremiah called from the other side of the wagon.

"Yes. I'm all right," I replied, then looked to my little sister, who now wore the face of a young Spanish beauty. She had dark almond-shaped eyes and a cascade of dark flowing hair. "Kenna, are you well?"

"Yes, I am fine." Kenna sat up from beneath a bundle of covers made of skins and furs and adjusted her heavy coat and the raccoon-tail hat that sat upon her head. "But what in the world am I wearing?"

She twisted the end of her hair around her finger and stared down at her clothes, clearly distraught over the current fashions.

Jeremiah, now a Spanish fur trader named Lorenzo Vargas, sat up and adjusted the suspenders under his thick wool coat, then tugged at his newly acquired beard.

"It seems I'm a fur trader, and you two are my twin girls," he explained, confirming the answers I had already received.

Pausing for only a moment as more information filtered in, I quickly continued, "It's late spring, and we are in the open territory of a massive mountain range that has recently been claimed by Juan de Ulibarri of the Spanish conquistadors."

"Are we in danger?" Kenna's head snapped up—the curl of dark hair still wrapped around her index finger—and addressed the one thing that remained a constant pull upon her soul: our family's safety.

"No. We are safe," I confirmed, as the last filaments of information seeped into my consciousness. "Apparently, our family is one of the 'approved' traders still allowed into the villages."

"Excellent. At least that is one less concern." Kenna squared her shoulders and released the lock of hair. Uncinching the ties that let in a blast of frigid mountain air, she moved to exit the back of the wagon. "You two rest while I scan the area and put our protection spells in place. We will begin our search for Karina in the morning."

She shivered, pulling down her fur cap, and then stepped out into the pitch-black night.

Jeremiah and I exchanged nods, knowing we were in good hands, then settled back into the warmth of our own fur coverings.

CHIEF AQUAKAWWA

Scents of sage, mugwort, and a hint of copal wafted from the fire as I sat with my shaman in the center of our village. Mountains surrounded us on all sides, rising into the horizon and backlit against a starlit sky.

"A change has arrived," my shaman said in our native tongue. His weathered face and gray-tinged braids hung low as he focused intently on the smoke rising from the burning embers.

I turned and glanced around the village, but found nothing out of place. "The family teepees remain tightly arranged within the box canyon from winter. I see no change," I replied.

"You will. When the trader and his family come from the west, do not send them away." The shaman rose from the log he had been seated upon and turned to leave, stopping with just one last thing to say. "Do this, and our tribe will no longer face the threat of war, be it from the Comanche or the white man."

The elder shuffled off, and when he was no longer in view, I turned back to the fire and cupped the smoke in my hands, inhaling deeply. A haze washed over me, and I closed my eyes, allowing myself to become lost in thought as the history of our tribe played out in within my mind.

Peace for my people had always been a struggle in the changing landscape around us. Our lineage came from the larger Ute population that occupied much of the extended territory nearby, but our smaller offshoot tribe now maintained our home in the box canyon we had found during one of our southern hunting expeditions.

"There is something special about this land," my shaman had said at the time, and he was right. Rugged mountains boxed us in, and a great waterfall fed into the ponds and rivers below, providing life-sustaining resources and seclusion from the outside world—until recently.

Invading tribes threatened from the east, and the rapid movements of the Spaniards heading north in recent years had forced me to choose whether to relocate with the majority of the Ute people, or to stay behind and defend our village alone.

I made the decision quickly. Ever since, we had defended our traditional way of life in the quiet solace of this canyon and would continue to protect ourselves and the joy we had found within this special place.

I opened my eyes and sat quietly, watching the flames dance upon the air, and thought about what my shaman had said. If his vision came to pass, we would face a beautiful future no longer threatened by war. I rose from the log and looked upon the teepees scattered throughout the village, my focus settling on that of my own family dwelling. I hoped this trader and *his* family would be able to find us soon.

CHAPTER 2

KARA

I woke, bouncing roughly to and fro as the wagon lurched forward. Jeremiah must have risen before either of us girls and set off on the trail this trader had been traveling over for the last few weeks. I sat up and rubbed my head, foreign dark hair cascading over my shoulders. It would take some time to get used to not seeing the red locks my sisters and I normally shared. Our names in this lifetime were Lorenzo, Catalina, and Clara Vargas, the latter being myself. As twins, Kenna and I looked exactly the same—tan skin, brown eyes, long black hair, and in our early twenties with curvier figures than either of us were used to. We would continue in this lifetime living as the Vargas family with all their knowledge and memories, but it was through the magic of our soul journeys that we were now in control and cognizant contributors to it all.

Pushing from beneath the blankets, I climbed through the front opening to join Jeremiah on the loosely fashioned hardwood bench that sat in front of the tarp.

"Wow!" I gasped. Two large oxen, strapped and reined, strained to pull the wagon across the rough terrain. "That was unexpected."

Jeremiah huffed out a laugh. "Yes, oxen are far more capable of pulling the weight of a wagon this size and all its contents than horses would be. At least for our purposes."

"What is our purpose here? Do you know of the trader's destination yet?" I asked.

"Yes. It seems he was heading toward a secluded canyon where trade with the local Indian chief has already been approved. Though," Jeremiah scratched his beard, "he's never dealt with them before and seems a bit nervous about it."

"Well, from the information our soul journey has provided, I think that is a normal reaction for these parts in this particular time. Do you think we will be able to start looking for Karina soon?" I prompted, anxious again to start the search for our lost sister.

"Yes. Once we are safe within the village, we will finalize our business and then begin our search for Karina on the way back out. Spring is upon us, but this high up in the mountains, the temperatures still drop below freezing at night, which will make the pass we are meant to take a treacherous mess. We will need to be in and out as quickly as possible."

I nodded in understanding and continued to bounce along in my seat as the sun rose over the distant mountains. The landscape here was wild and untamed compared to our previous locale of Salem, Massachusetts, but it was shockingly beautiful. Evergreens surrounded us, glistening with a coat of frost in the late spring morning, while cragged mountains and snow-covered peaks reached far into the bright blue sky. I blew out a breath and squealed at the tiny plumes of frozen air that escaped past my lips.

"Damn, it's cold," Kenna muttered in lieu of a morning greeting as she squeezed her way between us on the plank seat.

"That it is, little sister. Shall we do something about it?" I lifted my brows as magic played in my eyes.

Jeremiah reached across and grabbed my wrist. "No. Do not use magic out here in the open. The trials of our time may not have been heard of here, and we need to keep it that way. I will not risk exposing ourselves in an unfamiliar land."

I looked at Kenna, who had begun to twirl her hair again, and nodded at them both.

"You are right, of course." I patted Jeremiah's hand with my free one.

Kenna scooted closer, sliding under the fur that was draped across my legs, adding to our shared warmth. "If we are not going to practice magic out in the open, then how are we going to search for Karina? The last time, it took a lot of magic performed under the moon to even find a trace of her location," she asked.

"Yes, Kenna, I am aware of that too," Jeremiah replied in a smooth, even tone. "But like I have explained to Kara, we will finish our business with the Indian chief and be on our way as quickly as possible. Once we are back down the pass, it is my hope that we can make camp for the summer in a secluded area where we can cast our spells without reprisal. But, until I know where that might be, we need to keep up appearances. Understand?"

"Certainly." Kenna dipped her chin, giving Jeremiah a clipped nod as she continued to spin the thick strand of her hair.

We rode together in silence for another half mile or so before Kenna spoke again. "Speaking of appearances, I think this is the first time I have ever seen you with a full beard."

She winked at Jeremiah, a wide smile spreading across her face. Jeremiah shifted in his seat, the apples of his cheeks flushing a light red.

"Yes, it is going to take some getting used to for me as well." He gave it another scratch. "At least I have some built-in fur to help keep me warm," he teased, clearly happy his reprimand had not dampened Kenna's spirits.

Kenna and Jeremiah laughed, and I giggled at the sound, grateful that Karina's original spell had saved us all and started us on our continual soul journeys. Despite her absence—and the multiple lives we would be forced to live while continuing our search for her—at least we three would always be together.

With my heart a little lighter, I continued to make observations as the sights around me developed under the sun's morning rays. A thick layer of pine needles and dark leaves covered the forest floor beneath the evergreens, while chirping chipmunks raced through their limbs above. However, after another two hours of bouncing along the rough path and taking in the breathtaking views, it was Kenna's stomach that captured my attention.

"Goodness gracious, was that your stomach that just growled?" I whipped my head in her direction.

"Yes. I'm so sorry. Clearly, working our protections last night has sapped my energy and left me completely famished." She turned to Jeremiah. "If we can stop soon, I can prepare us something to eat. I believe I saw a small box-stove and some supplies in the back corner of the wagon."

"Wonderful. Let me get past this next bend, and I will look for a place to stop."

Kenna and I shifted our weight and climbed back through the canvas and into the rear of the wagon as Jeremiah continued to work the handbrake, guiding the oxen through the muddy terrain. After one final turn around a tight curve in the ascending trail, Jeremiah yanked hard on the reins, bringing us to a sudden stop. Pots and pans clattered around us, and we both yelped at the abruptness.

"What in the world are you trying to do, kill . . ." My words trailed off as I peeked my head back out the front of the wagon and found our path blocked by savages.

CHAPTER 3

CHIEF AQUAKAWWA

*T*he crunching of dirt and rocks reached my ears as the clatter of a wagon approached. I looked to my shaman and received a confirming nod, signaling these were the traders we had been waiting for. I motioned to my tribesmen and we mounted our horses. The beads and feathers in the manes of our fierce and noble creatures drifted silently on the wind as we rode forward to intercept our guests. My anticipation reached its peak as iron-rimmed wheels ground their way around the last bend in the trail.

I gave a whistle and then led my men to the entrance of the canyon, quickly blocking the wagon's path. The male had a full beard and fine clothes, but it was the dark-headed woman who had emerged from the wagon that captured my attention.

"Maiku." I lifted my hand in welcome, curious if she would understand our native tongue.

She leaned toward the man I assumed to be her father and whispered in his ear, then returned my greeting fluently. "Hello. We are the Vargas family and were sent with approval to trade with your tribe."

I smiled widely, pleased to know they had studied our native language in preparation for their trip. It was a sign of great respect. "I am Chief Aquakawwa of the Ute people. We have been expecting you. Please follow me."

I motioned my men ahead, then led the family to the northernmost point in the village, where my shaman had already set up a teepee and a hitching post for their animals. The skins for the dwelling had come from our winter stores, but my shaman had assured me it would be for a "grand and wonderful cause."

The man climbed down from his perch and tied up the oxen, releasing them from the wagon's tongue, while the girl returned to the back of the wagon, disappearing from my sight.

Still sitting astride my war-painted horse, I provided the man with instructions. "Get settled, then come to the main dwelling in the center of our village as the sun begins to set. All here are aware of your visit, and I assure your safety. You are my welcomed guests."

The man stood still as my men and I rode off in a flurry of flying dirt and pounding hooves.

KARA

As soon as the natives were out of sight, Jeremiah motioned for us to join him. Pulling back the flap of the teepee, I walked inside and gasped.

"Look at all of this!" Turning in circles, I took in the beautifully dyed clothing and moccasins laid out across handmade quilts. There were also coiled containers sealed with pitch for water storage, and weapons made of stone and wood, including bows and arrows, flint knives, arrow heads, and throwing sticks, all scattered around our new lodging. Digging sticks, weed beaters, tools, and more baskets, plus metates and manos for food preparation, lined one whole area, as if we'd be expected to stay for the spring harvest. "It is all so beautiful."

"Yes, it is. The tribeswomen are highly skilled, and their goods are very sought after. It is the reason we are here," Jeremiah explained, thanks to Lorenzo's knowledge.

Kenna ran her hand over a beaded dress lying on one of the beds, then frowned. "Are we supposed to put these on?"

Jeremiah shrugged. "The chief didn't specify, but I think it would be a show of respect if we did. But first, let us gather our supplies and fix a bite to eat while we wait for tonight's gathering."

I nodded in agreement, then led Kenna outside, filling our afternoon with the menial chores of emptying the wagon, cooking lunch, cleaning, and organizing our supplies. Once done, we each took turns behind the small fur-draped partition, donning our new attire, then waited outside for Jeremiah to do the same.

"All set." Jeremiah emerged from the teepee in a pair of dyed pants, a matching beaded vest, and a heavy fur draping slung over his shoulders which would help fight the dropping temperature at night. "The chief said to make our way to the main dwelling." He gestured to the worn footpath in front of us, then took the lead, pounding softly ahead in his fur-lined moccasins.

"I hope they have prepared some sort of meal, because I am *still* starving." Kenna rubbed her stomach, trying to inject some playfulness into her words.

"I'm sure they have. I smell some sort of roasted meat coming from up ahead," I replied, pointing toward our destination.

Kenna reached for a strand of hair and closed her eyes, twisting it around her finger as she inhaled deeply. "Oh, thank goodness. I wonder what else they have planned?"

Drums sounded at that exact moment, bringing an ominous end to our short walk. Jeremiah pulled back the flap of the main dwelling, and the pounding beat intensified, rattling our chests as we walked inside the oversized teepee. Smoke drifted from a fire pit in the center, while members of the tribe—fully dressed in elaborate headdresses and face paint—sat around the perimeter of the gathering. Chief Aquakawwa stood, and the drums fell silent.

"Welcome, friends. Please sit." He pointed to the blanket-covered log closest to the fire and waited for us to take our seats. "We welcome you into our village and celebrate with the Ute Bear Dance. This celebration traditionally marks the *beginning* of spring, but tonight we perform it in honor of you and your timely arrival." The drums picked up again and dancers moved into formation.

Shuffling feet wove intricate patterns into the dirt floor as the natives chanted and moved to the beat. Jeremiah and Kenna sat quietly, enjoying the show. I, however, found the chief and the older man whispering in the corner far more interesting.

A small bowl, filled with herbs and fragments of things I could not see, popped and hissed under the smoke of his long pipe. The elder continued to blow on the ingredients until they burst into flames, their smoke mixing with the main fire's as it spiraled up and out through the teepee's vaulted opening. Magic tingled along my skin, and I squinted, trying to read the words forming on the elder's lips. Unfortunately, from this distance, all remained unclear. At the song's crescendo, the dancers released a shout and gave a final stomp, standing tall and effectively blocking my view until the chief rose and dismissed them back to their seats.

"Spring is a time of awakening and rejuvenation. As the bear emerges from his long winter's nap, we too shall spend the season re-embracing our customs, holding tight to tribal traditions in preparation for the battle ahead." The chief opened his arms wide, motioning to the entire room, which sent the fringe hanging down from the sleeves of his shirt swinging wildly back and forth. "The constant struggle against Mother Nature's turning seasons is not the only thing we must prepare for; other forces still threaten to change our way of life."

Jeremiah, Kenna, and I all shifted uncomfortably when the chief's gaze fell upon us.

"Our new visitors are the only traders allowed within this village, and with them comes a chance for us to secure our place in the future as this land continues to change. But make no mistake, our traditions will stand, and tonight, we will begin this successful union with the customary exchanging of gifts." The chief motioned for Jeremiah to rise.

Jeremiah nervously looked back at Kenna and me, and then stood. Thankfully, my sister was quick in preparing a protection spell that she sent to us both—just in case things went askew.

"Tonight, in celebration of the upcoming Strawberry Moon, we give thanks to the protective spirits of the land. As we make this exchange, know your gift will be offered as payment to the spirits, so that they may protect and grant us prosperity in the upcoming harvests." Chief Aquakawwa reached behind him then presented Jeremiah with a stack of thick furs and skins.

Jeremiah bowed in acceptance and handed them off to Kenna, who had already cast another spell to conjure up a suitable gift in exchange. Taking the chief's offering, she handed Jeremiah a burlap-wrapped jar, its lid tied tightly with twine.

"Please accept this gift of our healing salve. It will soothe and heal any injury that may befall you," Jeremiah repeated the words that Kenna had obviously spoken into his mind.

Chief Aquakawwa took the jar and nodded, signaling the exchange was a fitting one. "The spirits are appeased. Let us eat."

A dull roar filled the teepee as the women of the tribe brought forth the meal they had prepared. Steaming bowls of meat, corn, and wild onions were presented to the chief and shaman first, then to Jeremiah and us girls. Wild raspberry, gooseberry, and what I thought to be buffalo-berry had been gathered and could be eaten raw but had also been mashed and strained to serve as our drink. Everything was fresh and delicious, though different from what we were used to. Thankfully, the Vargas family were familiar with the native fare, and their memories continued to serve as the perfect bridge between our cultural differences. This was the beauty of Karina's original spell, which allowed us to transition smoothly into each new lifetime we would have to live.

I ate in silence, enjoying the food, but kept a watchful eye on the shaman throughout the meal. After the grumblings of our stomachs were curbed, the chief announced the celebration's end, and all began to return to their homes—all except the shaman. I rose slowly from my seat and watched as he continued to mutter and fiddle with the bowl of ingredients in his lap. The chief must have noticed my hesitation, because he stepped in front of me and held out his arm, pointing to the main exit, his fringe swinging wildly again.

I smiled and left with my family, my stomach roiling as it filled with questions and concerns.

CHAPTER 4

KARA

*C*hief Aquakawwa followed us out, escorting us all the way back to our teepee.

"Thank you again for your gift. A healing salve will be most useful to my tribe. As for our official trade negotiations, they are set to take place in two days' time." The chief bowed his head, his long black braids falling forward as he stared at the ground, then turned to leave without another word.

Once inside, Kenna and I took turns discarding our heavy dresses, changing instead into the lightweight nightclothes the Vargas girls were used to wearing. Though with the temperatures still dropping at night, a fur draping would be required over our cotton petticoats to fight against the bone-numbing chill in the air.

"That was . . . interesting," Kenna said as she climbed into the warmth of her cot.

"Yes, I agree," I replied, finding my way under the blankets as Jeremiah stoked the fire in the center of the room. "Did you notice the shaman chanting during their dance? I hope I wasn't the only one who felt something was off."

"No, I didn't notice. But then again, I was concentrating on the chief," Jeremiah replied. "He seems eager to welcome us and accept our trade, but there was something intense in the way he discusses their history and traditions."

"I agree," I continued. "We need to be careful here. The rise of magic was distinct during their dance, and I think the shaman was attempting to cast some sort of spell."

"Were you able to identify what the root of it was?" Kenna asked.

I shook my head, still getting used to her Latin features and habits, instead of her usual light-skinned, red-haired self. "No. I could not see his ingredients or hear the chant he seemed to be whispering. Either way, I think tomorrow we should try to get back into that tent."

Kenna nodded and Jeremiah agreed, finally crawling into his own bed and drawing the fur coverings up to his neck.

KARA

Pots and pans rattled in the wagon as we bounced along the rough terrain in the foreign mountain-scape our soul journey had brought us to. Jeremiah must have woken before either of us girls and . . .

"Ouch!" I grabbed my head, rubbing small circles against the sharp pain that shot through my temples. With the pressure slightly relieved, I climbed through the front opening and joined Jeremiah on the wooden bench. "Oh my! How unexpected," I exclaimed, shaking my head against the lingering sting.

"Yes, oxen are far more capable of pulling the weight of a wagon this size . . ." Jeremiah paused and ran a hand over the back of his neck.

I looked to the sky, taking in the scenery as the morning rays lit up the snow-covered peaks.

"Have we been here before?" I asked, frustrated at the strange nagging feeling in my head.

"No. I do not think so." Jeremiah continued to rub the back of his neck. "It seems we are heading toward a secluded canyon, where trade with the local Indian chief has already been approved."

Another sunburst of pain shot through my temples. I leaned back against the canvas of the wagon and took a deep breath. The wild landscape surrounding us was breathtaking. I concentrated on the tops of the evergreens as they reached far into the sky, glistening with a coat of frost in the late spring morning.

"Damn, it's cold." Kenna squeezed her way out the opening, dragging with her a heavy fur, and flopped between us on the board.

"That it is, little sister." I lifted the edge of the blanket and scooted over, making room as she draped it across our legs.

"Speaking of appearances . . ." Kenna started—though no one had been speaking of anything of the sort. She smiled and pointed at Jeremiah's beard.

Jeremiah yanked at the scruff on his chin. "Yes. I know. It will definitely take some getting used to . . ."

"But at least you have some built-in fur to help keep you warm," Kenna finished for him.

Jeremiah shook his head, rubbing his neck again. "How did you know I was going to say those exact words?"

"I . . . do not know," Kenna gasped. Claiming a piece of her hair between her fingers, she looked around nervously and continued to make observations at the sights around us. "I wonder why the Vargas family never came this far south before?"

I looked between the two, confused and feeling severely off-kilter myself.

Jeremiah tilted his head up to the sky and replied, "I honestly don't think *any* outsiders have ventured this far into the region before."

We all fell silent and listened as the sounds of the forest continued to wake around us—the crunch of snow under unknown hooves, the chattering of animals racing through the trees, and songs from the wind whipping between the boughs overhead. It was all so unbelievably peaceful—if one could block out the distracting clatter of the wagon.

I snapped my head toward Kenna as a loud grumble sounded from her direction.

"Goodness gracious, was that your stomach that just growled?" I asked.

"Yes. I'm sorry. Clearly . . ." She paused, pinching the bridge of her nose. "I think I am in need of a good breakfast. If we can stop, I can whip us up something to eat. I think there are some supplies in the back of the wagon."

"Let me get past this next bend, and I will look for a place to pull off," Jeremiah quickly replied.

I shifted my weight and followed Kenna back into the wagon as Jeremiah worked the handbrake to guide the oxen through the muddy terrain. Suddenly, he must have yanked hard on the reins, because pots and pans rattled around us as we came to a sudden stop.

"What in the world . . ." My words trailed off as I peeked back out the front of the wagon and found our path blocked by savages.

CHAPTER 5

KARA

"Maiku!" An Indian astride a large painted horse raised his hand and addressed me directly in his native tongue.

I leaned toward Jeremiah and whispered, "Give me just a moment," then I cast a quick language spell that would encompass us all:

"Language yours, language mine, bridge the gap and intertwine. Understood, shall we be, as I will it, so mote it be."

With the spell in place, I understood and returned the man's greeting. "Hello. We are the Vargas family and were sent with approval to trade with your tribe."

"I am Chief Aquakawwa. We have been expecting you. Please follow me."

The chief motioned his men ahead, then led us to the northernmost point in the village, where a beautifully painted teepee had already been erected. There was also a hitching post for our oxen and from the looks of the smoke rising out the top of the structure, a fire already built within.

Jeremiah climbed from his perch and tied up our animals, releasing them from the wagon's tongue while Kenna and I remained hidden in the back.

Still astride his horse, the chief dismissed his men and provided Jeremiah with instructions. "Get settled, then come to the main dwelling in the center of our village once the sun begins to set. All here are aware of your visit, and I can assure your safety. You are my welcomed guests."

I peeked through the front opening and saw Jeremiah nod in understanding with a clenched jaw. He stood still with his arms crossed over his chest as the chief and his men rode off. Once they were out of sight, he waved us down.

Kenna and I climbed from the wagon and quickly entered the teepee. I pulled back the flap and walked inside, gasping as another sharp pain shot through my head. Rubbing my temples, I stood awestruck, taken aback by the scene.

"Look at all of these beautiful wares."

"Indeed." Jeremiah frowned as he circled the room. "The tribeswomen are highly skilled . . ." His words trailed off, and he ran a hand through his hair, stopping to rub at the back of his neck again.

"Are we supposed to put these on?" Kenna asked, pointing to a beaded dress laid out across a cot.

"The chief did not specify, but I think it would be a show of respect if we did." Jeremiah shrugged. "But first, let us gather our supplies and fix a bite to eat while we wait for tonight's gathering."

Agreeing, Kenna and I set ourselves to task. We unloaded the wagon, sorted and cleaned our supplies, then prepared a small lunch before taking turns behind the fur-draped partition to don our new attire.

"All set." Jeremiah emerged from the teepee in a pair of dyed pants, a matching beaded vest, and a thick fur slung over his shoulders. "The chief said to make our way to the main dwelling." He gestured to the worn footpath in front of us, taking the lead but stumbling slightly.

"Are you okay?" Kenna asked, grabbing him by the elbow.

"Yes. I'm fine, but obviously, this trip has taken a toll. Hopefully, they will have prepared some sort of meal, because I think a little more nourishment would do us all some good."

I looked back at Kenna with my brows drawn tight, not wanting to alert Jeremiah to my concern as we continued on.

"I'm sure they have." Kenna sniffed the air. "I smell some sort of roasted meat coming from that direction."

Jeremiah drew in a deep breath and closed his eyes. "Smells good. I wonder what else they have planned?"

Drums sounded at that exact moment, bringing an ominous end to our short walk. The pounding beat grew in intensity as Jeremiah pulled back the flap of the oversized teepee. Smoke drifted from a fire pit in the center, while members of the tribe—fully dressed in elaborate headdresses and face paint—sat around the perimeter of the gathering. Chief Aquakawwa stood, and the drums fell silent.

"Welcome, friends. Please sit."

Jeremiah, Kenna, and I walked forward and took seats upon the blanket-covered log closest to the fire. I reached for Kenna, who had dropped her head and pinched the bridge of her nose as soon as she was seated.

"Are *you* all right?" I whispered.

She closed her eyes and shook her head but did not respond as the chief began to speak.

"Tonight, we welcome you into our village and celebrate your arrival with the Ute Bear Dance. This celebration traditionally marks the *beginning* of spring, but today we perform it to honor you and your timely arrival." The drums picked up again and dancers moved into formation.

Kenna lifted her head, seemingly recovered, and sat quietly next to Jeremiah, twirling her hair as they enjoyed the show. I, however, was drawn to the chief and the older man whispering in the corner. Herbs popped and hissed in a small bowl as the elder blew smoke over it from his long pipe. The dancers' movements faded into my periphery as I stared intently at the ingredients until they burst into flames. Pain shot through my head and magic crawled across my skin. Squinting against the throb in my temples, I focused on the shaman again, trying to make out the words forming on his lips. Unfortunately, from this distance, I simply could not. At the song's crescendo, the dancers released a shout and gave a final stomp, standing tall and effectively blocking my view until the chief rose and dismissed them back to their seats.

"Spring is a time of awakening and rejuvenation. As the bear emerges from his long winter's nap, we too shall spend the season re-embracing our customs and . . ."

"AHHH!"

Chief Aquakawwa's words petered off as I grabbed my head and screamed.

KARA

I woke to the sounds of arguing outside of our teepee.

"What is happening to her? What did your shaman do?" Jeremiah's huff was distinct and familiar, while Chief Aquakawwa's voice remained low, yet audible.

"I assure you, nothing is amiss. The herbs our shaman uses are nothing out of the ordinary and are used to cleanse and purify our ritual space. Nothing more. I am sure your daughter is just worn out from her long journey. Please rest, and we can discuss more in the morning."

I remained quiet and listened to the chief shuffle away, but sat up when Kenna and Jeremiah reentered through the thick flap covering the door.

"What happened?" I asked.

"You screamed, then lost consciousness during the welcome celebration," Jeremiah explained.

"Oh my goodness! Did I offend the chief?"

"No. That was *all* me," Kenna snapped, kicking her moccasins into the corner. Silence hung in the air as she disappeared behind the changing screen, reemerging in her nightclothes and claiming a seat at the end of my bed. "Do you remember anything about what happened?"

I lay back down, massaging my temples as I thought back. "I remember arriving, cleaning out the wagon, having lunch, organizing the supplies here in the teepee . . ." I paused, looking at the tools and weapons against the far wall. "Then walking to the gathering, the dance starting, and . . ."

"And . . . ?" Kenna prompted, reaching for a thick swath of her hair.

"And . . . magic!"

"Yes! I knew it." Kenna bounced from the cot and walked to where the baskets and bowls were stacked between two support beams. "Look at these. Do you not remember them being clean and new when we arrived?" She held them out for Jeremiah and me to see. Frayed threads hung from the baskets, and scrapes from vigorous cleaning marred the bowls, inside and out. "How did they become like this in a matter of *hours*?"

I gasped. "What are you saying?"

"I am saying, something is not right here, and we need to be careful. I asked the chief to explain what the shaman was chanting during the dance, and well . . . as you may have heard, everything is supposedly *fine* and nothing is *amiss*." Kenna walked to her own cot and crawled beneath the covers, frantically spinning a curl between her fingers. "But I do not believe him. We need to remain alert."

CHAPTER 6

KARA

*P*ots and pans rattled around me as I woke within the covered wagon. Jeremiah must have risen before either of us girls and set off on the trail this trader had been traveling over for the last few weeks. We were the Vargas family in this lifetime, and . . .

"Ahhhh!" A scream tore from Jeremiah at the front of the wagon.

I jumped up and pushed out the opening, scrambling to claim the reins and yanking the oxen to a stop as Kenna burst through the tarp with a small pistol in hand. "What is wrong?"

Jeremiah fisted his hair and began rocking back and forth.

"I do not know." I yanked the handbrake into place. "Help me get him inside so I can scan him," I instructed.

Kenna placed her hands under Jeremiah's shoulders and pulled, while I lifted his legs and pushed him back into the safety of the wagon bed.

"God and Goddess hear my plea, through your vision let me see. Reveal to us the wrongness here, allowing me to cure those dear."

Visions of disjointed scenes filled my head: Indian celebrations, meals being shared, the three of us working the fields in a summer that had yet to come, friends becoming family through native customs, all set against the wild landscape in a canyon surrounded by mountains on all sides. Some things seemed the same, while others were slightly different, yet all were somehow looped together.

I tried to focus on the images, pinpointing their origin, and suddenly my magic wavered, but not before I caught sight of one last thing . . . a shaman burying an item under three beds in a grand teepee.

"Oh no!" I pulled back my hands, severing the connection.

"What is it? What is wrong with him?" Kenna pleaded, dabbing his forehead with a damp towel.

"There is nothing wrong with him . . . *yet*."

"What on earth do you speak of? Look at him!"

"What I am saying is, whatever is affecting him has not happened yet . . . *or* has already happened before. I do not understand it all, but I think time is being manipulated around us." Kenna stared at me wide-eyed as I continued to explain. "What is clear, however, is that something happened—or *happens*—once we arrive in the Indian village. I believe it is the catalyst for this entire situation."

"Should we rather not go?" Kenna posed the obvious question.

I shrugged, unsure. "I do not know. Whatever this time spell is, it has already been cast upon us, so at this point, I am not sure it would even matter."

"Then, how exactly do we figure that out?" She reached for the end of her thick raven hair.

I thought for a moment, recalling what I had seen. "Well, we could either continue to the village with the awareness we now possess and try to find the objects I saw in my vision, *or* we could stay here and not arrive today as planned, to see if that changes anything. Unfortunately, if I'm right, that means everything may just start over again tomorrow, leaving us to hopefully figure it out once more." I took the rag from Kenna's hand and dabbed Jeremiah's brow. "Personally, I say we continue on as planned, use this knowledge to discover the root of the spell, and put a stop to it as soon as possible."

Kenna nodded, pushing back to sit against the canvas of the far wall. "I agree. Once Jeremiah is well, let us continue on as though nothing has changed."

I smiled, thankful for her unwavering bravery and strength. "I am not sure what the items are, but I know they are buried under each of the beds, so as soon as we reach the teepee, we will need to dig them up."

"This whole thing gives me the jitters." Kenna cringed. "Entering an unknown village, yet knowing we are already familiar with these people, and they with us . . . what if we mess up and say the wrong thing? Will that not make it clear we are aware of their spell?"

I reached out and took my little sister's hand. "We just have to act as we usually would and say whatever comes to mind. I am certain that, however many times we have re-started this loop, it all works out the same in the end, or else it would not be continuing as it has. Honestly, I think what rattles me the most is not knowing how many times we have actually been reset."

Kenna shivered and rubbed her arms. "Oh my, when you put it like that . . . it is definitely not something I want to think about."

Jeremiah moaned, reclaiming our attention. "What happened?" He sat up, holding his head.

"You fell ill, in a way, and I had to cast a spell to find out what was affecting you," I quickly explained.

"And . . ."

"*And*, I discovered that we have all been caught in a time loop cast by the tribe's shaman."

Jeremiah took the damp cloth from my hand and ran it over the back of his neck.

"You are certain?" he asked calmly. Like the rest of us, he was completely used to magic and mayhem continually affecting our lives.

"Yes. The more we discussed it, the clearer things became to us both. Like distant memories—moments of past or already lived events —and feelings about people and families we have yet to meet. But most importantly, there are three cursed objects placed under the beds in the teepee we will be assigned to, which are maintaining this loop." I paused, dreading my next question. "Have either of you felt Karina or had a desire to find her?" They both shook their heads, confirming my suspicions. "I think our quest has somehow been blocked by the shaman's spell, and more likely than not, it is affecting our memories as well."

Jeremiah nodded and tossed the rag atop a stack of pans in the back corner. "Then let's not dally. The sooner we arrive and get to the bottom of this, the sooner we can get back to wherever it is we're truly supposed to be and find Karina."

Without another word, Jeremiah climbed back through the front opening, reclaimed the reins and released the handbrake.

Kenna and I remained in the back, taking in the wild landscape through the hole in the tarp. The sun crept over the distant mountains once again, revealing the same snow-covered peaks I had seen in my vision. The evergreens reaching far into the sky now seemed familiar, glistening with a coat of frost in the late spring morning. I pulled my jacket further up my neck to combat the chill in the air as Jeremiah continued to work the oxen around the final curve in the ascending trail. Yanking hard on the reins, he brought us to a sudden stop, shifting the pots and pans in a cacophony of motion. Neither Kenna nor I made a peep, however, because we both knew what was coming next.

CHAPTER 7

KARA

"$\mathcal{M}$aiku!" The chief spoke directly to me again, offering his usual greeting in his native tongue.

I cast my language spell again and replied, knowing my words were correct and matched the others I had previously spoken in this situation. "Hello. We are the Vargas family and have been approved to trade with your tribe."

"I am Chief Aquakawwa. We have been expecting you. Please follow me." The chief motioned his men ahead, and then led us to the northernmost point in the village, just like before. Jeremiah and I exchanged nervous glances as he climbed from his perch and tied up the oxen, releasing them from the wagon's tongue.

"Get settled, then come to the main dwelling in the center of our village once the sun begins to set. All here are aware of your visit, and I can assure your safety. You are my welcomed guests."

Jeremiah crossed his arms and nodded to the chief, standing still until he and his men rode from sight. Not waiting for him to call us down this time, Kenna and I raced into the teepee and immediately scoured the earth under each of our beds.

"Kenna, grab some of those tools." I pointed to a pile of digger sticks and stone trowels lying against the far wall.

"Here." Kenna handed us each something to further our progress and returned to her designated spot, working furiously until she had a long tract of upturned dirt in front of her, despite the smudges it created on her cotton petticoat and stockings.

"Did you find anything?" Jeremiah asked, settling back on his knees.

"No, not yet. Did you?" I replied.

"No. How about you?" Jeremiah lifted his chin at Kenna.

"Nothing here, either." Kenna threw her digging stick to the ground. "Damn it! The shaman must have moved them this time around."

Jeremiah turned to me. "You said these objects are feeding this loop, correct? So they must be here somewhere," he deduced.

"Yes. That's right." I pushed to my feet, removing my ragged wool coat. "Look around. Search for anything that appears to be out of the ordinary."

Kenna stood with a huff. "Everything here is out of the ordinary. Look at all of this!" Turning in circles, she pointed out the beautifully dyed clothing and handmade items littering the space. "How do we determine what is *out of the ordinary*?"

I walked to meet her in the middle of the dwelling and took both her hands in my own. "With a spell, of course. That should make things a little easier, don't you think?"

Magic sparked in her eyes and tingled between our joined fingers as I cast a quick spell.

"Goddess of old, lend us your sight, open our eyes, to see as you might. Through altered time, unveil unto me, hidden objects, so mote it be."

A gust of wind blew through the flap of the teepee, lifting our hair and drawing us all outside. A tiny shimmer of light sparkled before us, leading the way on a swirl of chilled breeze. Following its path, we crept toward the back of the teepee, then bent down as the spark settled in a pile of leaves at the base of the structure.

"Here." I pointed, pushing away the leaves to reveal a mound of freshly dug dirt.

Jeremiah shooed me and Kenna to the side, protective as always. "Let me."

With his roughly crafted spade, he dug into the fresh loam, tossing tiny piles to the side until he uncovered a tightly wrapped object. It was sealed within a skin and bound by twine with bones and feathers weaved into its knot.

"I think we found what we are looking for," he surmised.

I moved forward, grabbing Jeremiah by the arm.

"Do not touch it." Reaching out, I closed my eyes and held both hands slightly above the object, scanning for any ill intent. I concentrated, letting my magic read the energy that was used to forge the talisman. "The magic here definitely has pure roots, but it has been tainted for a darker purpose."

"Well, that's not good," Kenna stated the obvious. "What do we do?"

"I am not certain at the moment. We need to understand what this is. We need more time to determine what kind of spell was cast before we can create a counter-spell of our own to negate its power. With all that being said, I am terrified that when we go to sleep, this whole damn loop will start all over again."

"And back to square one we go." Jeremiah stood and crossed his arms.

"Exactly." I lifted a brow.

"Goodness me. Then let us get it inside so we can get started," Kenna prompted, clearly eager to get to the bottom of this as quickly as possible.

I nodded and leaned forward, whispering a quick protection spell, then grabbed the package gently by its edges.

Sneaking quietly back to the front, we all ducked inside, then sat crossed-legged on the ground with the bundle resting in front of us. I slowly unwrapped the package, carefully sliding the bone and feather from the twine, then gingerly plucked at the edges and pulled back the exterior skin.

Each of us gasped and stared at three glowing stones hidden within. One was a ruby, pulsing bright red; one, a rose quartz, shining a beautiful pink; and the last, an amethyst, radiating a deep violet glow.

"That was not what I was expecting," Jeremiah confessed.

"Nor I." I leaned forward, placing my hands above the stones, and began another chant.

"Stones of earth, stone of old, rid yourself of your evil goal. Cleansed by the goddess and her servants three, as we will it, so mote it be."

When nothing happened, I nodded to Kenna and Jeremiah who immediately joined in, intoning the spell two more times.

Energy whipped around the room, stirring on an unseen breeze until it reached its crescendo. Tendrils of magic in the color of each individual stone rose in sparkling strands as they lifted into a vortex. I concentrated on the push and pull of the tainted native magic, and finally, the spell snapped, turning all three strands instantly black. Charred dust floated to the ground, and the room immediately settled.

"Wow. So it is done?" Kenna asked. "The spell is broken?"

"I am not sure. I guess we will have to wait and see if things reset in the morning." I shrugged.

"Should we do a remembering spell, just in case?" Jeremiah suggested.

I nodded in agreement and reached out to join our hands. The tingle of magic that remained from the spell we had just worked burst forth past my lips, shooting light out of the roof as my chant took flight.

"Remember now, remember us three, today, tomorrow, and forever need be. If time resets, our magic trumps thee, straight from the goddess, so mote it be."

I smiled. "There. That should do it." I released their hands and took a deep breath, grounding myself and releasing any residual magic back into the earth to safely dissipate.

"Should we dress for their dinner now?" Kenna prompted, twirling her hair.

"Yes, I suppose the best thing we can do is continue the evening as if nothing has changed." I reached forward and picked up the stones. Energy pulsed from within them, calling out to each of us specifically. Following the energy, I handed the ruby to Jeremiah, the amethyst to Kenna, and kept the rose quartz for myself. "Let's keep these with us, though. I do not want to chance the shaman getting his hands on them and recharging them in any way."

Kenna and Jeremiah tucked the stones into their pockets and moved off to dress for the evening, while I whispered one last request to the goddess.

"Goddess of love, goddess of light, protect all those I love this night. Allow us triumph over any threats to thee, as I will it, so mote it be."

PHAEDRA

I pulled my wings in tight, landing in the nearest tree as I stared at a bright light that had just burst from the top of a teepee in the canyon below. Magic filled the air, and I shivered. This was true power, born of something greater—something divine, and not the usual earth-based magic the natives practiced here. After all my wandering alone, it was their traditions and magic that drew me to the area originally, but now, something had changed, and I would not be leaving until I knew exactly what.

CHAPTER 8

KARA

"*A*ll set," Jeremiah called out as he emerged from the teepee in a pair of dyed pants, a matching beaded vest, and with a thick fur slung over his shoulders. He gestured to the worn footpath in front of us and took the lead without a single misstep. "Here we go again."

"Are we all good?" I asked, holding up my stone before dropping it into a small skin pouch I had tied to my side.

Jeremiah and Kenna both held up their stones, each clutching them tightly as we started down the path. I drew in a deep breath. "Smells good. Let us enjoy the food but be sure to maintain vigilance. Do you both remember what happens in there?"

"Yes. I've already produced the salve for the gift exchange." Kenna patted the small jar tucked into the folds of her dress.

"Yes. I remember, but what do we do if things go awry? What if the shaman realizes we have broken his spell?" Jeremiah asked.

The drums sounded at that exact moment, bringing *another* ominous end to our short walk.

"I guess we will just have to wait and see." I shrugged.

Jeremiah pulled back the flap of the oversized teepee, and the pounding beat of the drums assaulted us again. Smoke drifted from a fire pit in the center, while members of the tribe were dressed in their elaborate headdresses and seated around the perimeter of the gathering just as before. Chief Aquakawwa stood, and the drums fell silent.

"Welcome, friends. Please sit."

Jeremiah, Kenna, and I walked forward and took our seats upon the blanket-covered log.

"Tonight, we welcome you into our village and celebrate your arrival with the Ute Bear Dance . . ." The drums picked up again, and dancers moved into formation as the chief's words trailed off.

We all sat quietly, straining to appear interested in the show. But just as before, my focus flickered nervously back and forth between the dancers, the chief, and the shaman. I squinted and watched as he continued to work his spell. Frustrated, he blew a third puff of smoke over the herbs in his small bowl, but the ingredients remained benign. No flames rolled, and the magic I had felt before never began to rise. The shaman's head snapped up and caught my eye.

"He knows," I whispered.

Holding his stare, I sat still while Kenna quickly chanted a spell of her own.

"Words on the wind, float to us three, allow us to hear any plans to harm thee."

A puff of smoke escaped the fire, as if a dragon had just released a breath that carried Kenna's words toward the heavens. We all quickly turned back to the dancers, keeping the shaman and chief visible in our periphery. However, when the shaman stood to speak to the chief, his voice now drifted clearly to our ears.

"The spell has been broken. We no longer have the witch's magic to protect us here. The time loop is at its end." The shaman turned, then exited out the back of the teepee, leaving us surrounded by warriors when the chief raised his fist to stop the celebration.

PHAEDRA

Balanced on the lodge poles of the nearest teepee, I watched as the tribe's shaman scurried away from the gathering being held below. Hurriedly, he shuffled down the path and walked straight toward the dwelling the newcomers had just recently left. Ripping back the flap, he entered unimpeded. I glided to the top of the structure with a pump of my snow-white wings, and then peered down through the top flap to continue my investigation.

The shaman was frantic, tossing clothes and furs, upending their beds, and throwing tools and dishes against the far walls. Finally, out of breath, he stood in the middle of the room and began to chant and shake his rattle. The sounds of the beads, feathers, and bones raked through the air like claws ripping at the sky. Tainted magic radiated up and out of the opening, blasting me to the ground as I covered my ears in pain.

KARA

Jeremiah stood in front of us, arms crossed over his chest.

"What is the meaning of this?" he asked, taking in the warriors surrounding us.

Surprisingly, Chief Aquakawwa pushed through the men, waving them off and dismissing the entire crowd. "Return to your homes. There will be no feast tonight."

All the natives shuffled to leave, casting curious glares in our direction—some worried, some sad, and even some angry.

"I am sorry," the chief offered. "It is clear you now know what my shaman has done."

I stepped around Jeremiah, pulling Kenna close to my side. "We know we have been trapped in a time loop but are unsure how or why." My words were short and direct but left no room for misinterpretation. I wanted an explanation, and I would not be leaving without one.

Chief Aquakawwa gestured for us to retake our seats, folding himself to the ground in front of the fire. "I will explain the best I can."

With protection spells at the ready, we all sat and listened intently.

"A few years ago, the Ute and Comanche began negotiations to ensure peace between our two powerful tribes that controlled the southwestern plains. However, peace talks were interrupted, and since then, war has threatened us all." The chief shifted uncomfortably on the ground. "When our shaman sensed your arrival, your well of magic called to him, and the idea of utilizing your power to safeguard our tribe took root in his heart." He met my eyes with an intense gaze. "I did not understand his true purpose at the time, but once I saw his spell working, I had no idea how to break it." He lowered his chin. "Nor did I want to." Shaking his head and freeing his guilt, he looked up at us and continued. "He protected our home and people, and as chief, that is my one and only goal. I had no idea he would have to siphon your magic to do so, and for that, I am sorry."

"What do you mean, siphon our magic?" Kenna snapped, sparks playing at her fingertips.

"While trapped in the time loop, your memories were lost. You have not performed magic in all the seasons you have been here, and without it, your powers have started to drain. Only when your minds fully break free do you regain full access to it and can you start casting again."

"Wait. How many *seasons* has it been, and why do we not remember the rest of our time spent here?" I asked, desperate to obtain as much information as possible.

The chief took a deep breath. "Your lives here progress normally until you begin to recall other memories, at which point, the shaman resets the loop to start again, wiping all your previous experiences from your mind." He swallowed hard. "It has been three seasons."

Kenna jumped up. "What? We have been stuck in this loop for nine months?"

I stood and grabbed Kenna by the arm, trying to calm her while I explained as much as I understood.

"Yes. It is why we are remembering the others of the tribe and working in the fields during the summer." I turned to the chief. "From what you have explained, I assume we only *reset* whenever our memories break free, which brings us back to this initial starting point each time, correct?"

Chief Aquakawwa pushed to stand, addressing us each and spouting his apologies. "Lorenzo, Clara, Catalina. I am sorry, but yes, that is correct. Once it begins again, the rest of us are also pulled in, and as I have explained, I had no knowledge of how to break the spell."

Kenna yanked her arm from my grasp and strode to the opening of the teepee and tore back its opening. "Well, we did break the spell, and now, we're going to make sure this never happens again." She jerked her chin at Jeremiah and me. "Come on. We have a shaman to find."

CHAPTER 9

KARA

*R*acing from the teepee, Kenna pounded down the path that would lead us back to our assigned dwelling. She stopped dead in her tracks, however, when she caught sight of two wolves stalking around a prone figure lying on the ground directly in front of us.

"Go on, get out of here!" Jeremiah shouted at the wolves, pushing past us and waving his arms in the air.

"No. Wait." I grabbed him and walked forward. "These are not normal wolves, and that *isn't* a person wrapped in white coverings."

Kenna joined me, and I immediately felt it when she sensed the same magic I had. I looked around, making sure we were alone, and quickly cast a spell.

"Cloak us now, from mortal sight. Hide their vision, though try they might. Allow us to talk safely within, protect this haven as we greet new friends."

46

A shimmering bubble burst forth, encapsulating us all within it. Under the protective dome, our true selves became visible instead of the Vargas façades we currently wore.

"Hello. We are the Howe witches from Salem, Massachusetts, and have been brought here through our soul journeys. Is the angel going to be well?" I asked, fully aware of the divine being lying before us.

The three of us remained still as the two wolves began to shake. They shed their pelts within seconds, reclaiming their true form, standing naked before us, completely unabashed.

"Greetings," the male replied with a tilt of his head. "We are Ric and Gaby Kasun. And yes, I think she will be fine."

Gaby, a stunning woman with long black hair, silver-gray eyes, and an exotic oval jaw line, bent down and ran a hand over one of the angel's snow-white wings.

Stirring slowly, the delicate angel rose from the ground. Stark white hair fell over her beautiful, yet sullen face, while crystalline blue eyes roamed over each of us from between the strands. There was a sadness about her that somehow darkened the space in which she stood.

"Hello, my name is Phaedra." She smiled kindly at us all, but her voice rang with a sadness that had me clutching my chest as we all introduced ourselves again. "I was drawn here by your magic." She nodded to Kenna and me. "But after witnessing the shaman's attempt to reclaim his power, I was knocked to the ground."

"You saw the shaman here? He did this to you?" Jeremiah asked.

"Yes. He ransacked your teepee, obviously looking for something, but when he did not find it, he cast another spell, which was tainted and forceful. Its off-balance resonance knocked me from my perch above."

Ric Kasun, standing broad-shouldered and at least six four, looked up at the top of the lodge poles sticking out of our teepee and shook his head. Black hair, silvery-blue eyes, and a slight scruff along his jaw painted the picture of a hardened mountain man, yet his concern for the situation rang with the sincerity of a true protector. "Sounds like we need to find this shaman before he hurts anyone else."

"Our thoughts exactly," Kenna replied, then with a swipe of her hand, clothed the Kasuns.

Phaedra and the Kasuns followed us into our teepee, and we began our preparations.

"I could take flight and look for him in the surrounding forest," Phaedra offered.

"Not to offend, but we have been here for a very long time and know the territory well. It would be quicker for us to shift and track him through the woods," Gaby stated flatly, pulling on the hem of the cotton shirt Kenna had produced without asking.

Clearly dejected, Phaedra lowered her head. "You are probably right. Besides, I never fly low enough for people to see me, so looking for him visually would be a waste of time."

Jeremiah shifted next to me, and knowing him as I did, I could tell from the look on his face he would not want the angel to feel unneeded in the situation, so it was no surprise when he piped up again. "No, but you could take to the sky and see if you sense any further use of his tainted magic."

This earned him a quick nod and a small smile from the petite beauty.

"Of course. I could do that," Phaedra replied.

Jeremiah smiled and returned his attention to the Kasuns. "If you have been here that long, have you ever had dealings with this tribe before?"

"No." Gaby reached for her mate's hand. "Ric's mother and our last alpha, Adele, sacrificed her life to get the pack out of Croatia and the blood feud that threatened our family there. She sent us here, to this specific territory in the New World, where we've remained disguised as a roving native tribe. We've spent our time fostering peace with everyone we have encountered in the surrounding areas."

"While that sounds fantastic, and I am so grateful we have met, can we get down to business?" Kenna interrupted. "We need to locate the shaman as quickly as possible and strip him of his power, so let's have Phaedra take to the skies, and you and Ric track him through the forest. Whoever finds him first, simply crush this in your hand, and we will be brought straight to you." She held out what appeared to be two small pieces of fruit.

"What?" I asked.

"Yes. I have charged them with a locator spell. Once they are crushed, I will draw upon the magic of this land to transport us there."

"No. That is not what I mean. What I mean is, *what are you saying* —that you want to strip him of his power? How can we do that to someone whose magical traditions run so deep?"

"Kara. We need to make sure he does not inflict this time loop on us or anyone else *ever* again," Kenna replied matter-of-factly, extending me her hand.

I shook my head and pushed to stand. "I know we are only visitors here, pulled out of our lives and time, but after all we have learned about the natives in the nine months we have lived among them, you are okay with stripping them of their ancestral magic?" I pushed her hand away. "Because now that I can remember our time here, I'm not sure I am comfortable with that plan."

Kenna stood still, shocked and staring at me as I turned and stomped outside.

"I will go talk to her," I heard Jeremiah offer.

"Let me." Gaby's voice drifted from behind me, then called out, "Kara, wait . . . please?"

I stopped a few feet away but did not turn around. Staring out at the surrounding forest, I remained quiet, knowing I would be forced to listen to whatever the alpha wolf had to say.

"I understand your concern. I, too, would normally fight against your sister's plan. Unfortunately, there is a greater good at play here. Once a shaman's magic becomes tainted such as this, things will only worsen. I have seen it before. His spells will cause the tribe to suffer, and any and all prosperity bestowed upon them will start to fade away as a punishment for his actions." She laid a hand gently on my shoulder. "If you want to truly save these people, you will need to do this."

"I know. The threefold law." I wiped a tear from my cheek and followed Gaby back inside, but continued to contemplate an alternative as I struggled to look my baby sister in the eye.

SHAMAN

"No one understands," I mumbled, cutting a trail through the forest and slipping on the remaining ice and snow still gathered in the shadows of the massive evergreens. I trudged over rocks and stumps, fleeing the village, and listened for the rumble that would announce the Great Falls up ahead.

Dropping almost three hundred feet from a dip in the cliff above, the falls poured into a large pond, surrounded by boulders where the canyon met the base of the mountain. Its power and beauty left all who ventured here with an overwhelming sense of magic and peace.

Rounding one final corner of the trail, the pond came into view, its churning water easing my despair. Kneeling, I gave thanks to Great Spirit—the creator of things including the mountains, rivers, people, and animals—and poured out my soul. "Great Spirit, I call to thee. Allow my magic to take root again to protect our tribe from the outside world. Keep us safe within our haven and help maintain the spell I placed upon the witches. My intent was not to harm, only to protect. I did this for my chief and our people, and no one was hurt by my actions. They are out of their time; nothing will be affected by their absence. The witches lived happy lives here until their memories resurfaced. I do not know what went wrong. I reset the time loop, and everything had fallen back into place . . . until now. How did they break through my spell? I need your help, Great Spirit. It is said you created all things when you grew bored with life in the sky and drilled a hole through which to see the world below. I ask that you see me now and hear my plea."

Blood spilled as I pulled my knife across the neck of the rabbit I had brought along as my sacrifice. Its thick life force dripped onto the ground, cutting a trail through the rotted leaves and creeping its way toward the water's edge.

I sucked in a breath, shocked when the water in the pool recoiled from its banks. The blood turned to inky wisps and evaporated into thin air as a great sigh resonated from the sky. I closed my eyes as a powerful wind blew into my face—no doubt a message that my request had been heard. With my hope restored, I opened my arms wide and waited to be blessed by the Great Spirit.

CHAPTER 10

PHAEDRA

*J*took to the sky and flew in circles above the clouds as I focused on the energy radiating from the forest below. Every living thing cast a unique signature, so it did not take long for me to sense where something was wrong. Soaring to the highest point in the area, I pinpointed the shaman and flew down in a great gust with a pull of my wings. Landing on a large boulder next to the base of the Great Falls, I called out, "Shaman! You have tainted the magic of your people, and for that you will now be punished."

Just as the red piece of fruit materialized in my hand, the shaman disappeared.

SHAMAN

Surrounded by clouds, I smiled widely as a heavenly scene formed before me. Stark white teepees as far as the eye could see lined a beautiful valley—lush with green hills, flowering trees, and bubbling waterfalls and rivers. Smoke rose from a large sweat lodge at the center of the scene, piercing my senses with the smell of sage, cedar, and sweet grass. It was then I realized that I was in the Sky World, the realm of the Great Spirit.

Shuffling forward as quickly as my old legs would allow, I walked to the dwelling and entered with my head bowed in reverence. "Great Senawahv, thank you for hearing and listening to my plea, and for allowing me to visit your heavenly realm. I am greatly honored."

Another heavy sigh drifted to my ears, this one of sorrow and disappointment. I moved to lift my head but found myself held in place, unable to gaze upon the Great Creator. Suddenly, I was forced to my knees, and the Great Spirit's voice boomed, filling the space.

"Tainted magic, devious plots, and the spilling of innocent life will never be rewarded by me. Only your good intentions are saving you this day. However, you *will* face punishment, albeit not by my hand. Return now and plead your case, for your future rests with those from the past."

The surrounding vision faded into the clouds, and I found myself back in the main teepee of our village, standing directly in front of my chief.

PHAEDRA

I spun around, looking for where the shaman had gone, then took to the sky and continued to glide over the Great Falls. I spotted the Kasuns stalking toward the water from the forest and quickly returned to the ground, landing again on the large boulder.

"I had him. He was there," I pointed, "but then he just . . . disappeared."

With teeth bared, the Kasuns combed the area, sniffing and rifling through underbrush near the river's edge. Shifting into her human form, Gaby quickly announced, "He killed something right here."

"If he has resorted to killing, then stripping him of his magic may not be enough of a punishment," Ric added, after shifting to join her.

I snapped my wings closed and stalked toward the wolves. "I do not like the idea of killing."

"Nor do we, but you saw it with your own eyes—you said he disappeared, which means his powers are growing. He has to be stopped," Ric replied.

"I am not sure that is a decision any of *us* should make. The decision should remain with the witches he has cursed." I pushed into the sky, hovering over the wolves. "Let's return to the village and let them know he has escaped."

CHAPTER 11

CHIEF AQUAKAWWA

"Chief. I . . . I have been returned to explain . . ." Shock muddled my shaman's words.

I spun to face him—the man I'd trusted with the welfare of my people since the formation of our tribe. "How dare you return to this sacred place! You have put all our people in danger with your selfish works, and now you are being hunted."

"Hunted? By whom?" he asked, clearly unaware of what had transpired here.

"Who do you think?" I snapped. "The witches you have cursed will find you soon enough, and there is nothing I can do to stop them." I walked forward and laid a hand on his shoulder. "You have brought this on yourself, old friend, and unfortunately, we are now all in line to pay for your mistakes."

"No!" he shouted, shrugging off my hand and stomping to the raised platform where he traditionally worked his magic spells. "The Great Spirit told me I could return and plead my case—to explain that my intentions were pure." He pulled his medicine bowl into his lap and dumped in a handful of herbs, his brow wrinkled in concentration.

"Perhaps that would have made a difference before you killed an innocent living thing," a voice sounded from the opening. I turned to see a woman and man stalking forward. Without another word, their bodies shook, and suddenly a pair of wolves replaced their human forms.

"Great Spirit!" I stumbled backward, turning toward my shaman. "He has sent his hounds to collect your soul."

"Stop!" another voice echoed from the doorway.

I sank to my knees and whispered, *"The White Woman . . ."*

"Yes, you see, a gift! The Great Spirit sends me an angel from above," my shaman called out, still clinging to the hope of redemption.

The White Woman stepped forward. "No. I am not from your Great Spirit, nor do I come bearing a gift—only a message, and a sentiment I am sure your Great Spirit shares. Your magic *was* the gift, given to you by Mother Earth, and you have ruined it, placing your tribe at risk through your selfish deeds. You know as well as I that when power is used to harm in *any* way, there is always a price to be paid."

My shaman shook his head, fighting back his fear and desperation as he struggled to complete his spell.

The White Woman lifted her hand, producing a piece of fruit, then crushed it between her fingers. "It is time for you to face those you have cursed."

I crouched low, remaining still, as the wolves crept closer to my shaman. Suddenly, a bright light appeared in the center of the teepee, and all three witches stepped out of what seemed to be a tear in the air.

With a flick of her wrist, Catalina turned my shaman's entire bowl to dust. "You have ripped us from our time, cursing us as you siphoned our magic, and doomed your people in the process. For this, you will pay."

Clara stepped in front of her sister. "Are we really doing this? Are you sure there is no other way?"

"He killed a rabbit in the forest," the White Woman interjected.

Lorenzo's gaze snapped to me. "I thought all living things were cherished by your people."

"They are." I lowered my head, silently giving them permission to proceed.

"The Kasuns believe he should suffer the same fate." The White Woman lifted her chin at the wolves as a tear shimmered down her cheek.

Shifting back to their human forms, the wolves remained stoic and unapologetic. "As I told Kara," the female wolf lifted her chin, "I have witnessed this before. Once a shaman's magic becomes tainted, things will only grow worse. Livestock will start to die, crops will no longer produce, even illness may threaten the tribe. It is in everyone's best interest to end the . . . threat."

Silence filled the teepee as the inevitable sank in.

Slowly, Lorenzo and the male wolf moved toward my shaman, and there was nothing I could do to stop them.

"Wait. There has to be another way. Can you do a spell to cure him?" the White Woman pleaded. "Use your magic to heal his?"

Lorenzo reached out to the male wolf, grabbing him by the arm. "Hold on. That just might work."

Catalina released a tendril of her dark hair and turned to her sister, taking her hands in her own. "I'm willing to try, but if it doesn't work, we put an end to this. Agreed?"

"Agreed," Clara replied, a small smile lighting her eyes. "This will take some time, though, so I suggest we all prepare for a long night." She turned to me, those same piercing eyes that first caught my attention softening as she bowed her head. "Chief Aquakawwa, I hate to ask, but may we have that meal now?"

I looked at my shaman being held in place on his knees. Although facing punishment, he was still safe and sound. So, with a sharp nod, I exited the teepee, happy to provide sustenance to those willing to save his life.

KARA

With everyone fully clothed again—thanks to Kenna—and all with full stomachs—thanks to the chief—Jeremiah and Ric cleared the plates of dried meat and fresh vegetables off to the side, as Phaedra and Gaby positioned the shaman's body on the ground near the fire. I had cast a sleeping spell upon him in order to make his aura more pliable to the work we would be doing here tonight. However, we were now on our third attempt, and my hands were beginning to shake.

I spread them over the shaman's body again and tried my next spell.

"Heal the heart, heal the mind. Combine our magics over time. Reverse the darkness rooted in he, as I will it, so mote it be."

Damn it! Nothing. I threw the small charm bag clenched in my fist to the ground, spilling the herbs from within.

"Let's try the stones," Kenna suggested, retrieving the amethyst from her pocket.

Holding out her hand, she waited for Jeremiah's ruby, then bent down to add both to the rose quartz already resting in my palm.

I stared at the stones, suddenly entranced. "No. I do not think that is a good idea."

A vision filled my mind, pulling me out of time again. People, dressed in what looked to be costumes of some sort, milled around a quaint little town filled with colorful tents in brilliant shades of red and green, while a kaleidoscope of brightly colored signs advertised Tarot readings, palm readings, and psychic interventions.

"Why? What do you see?" Kenna asked.

I closed my eyes and focused on the three women filling my mind's eye, the most prominent a redhead who looked strikingly like our mother. She held a stone within her hand, and her heart ached to help lovers who had also been ripped out of their time. "My family . . . in need. Here . . . in this canyon . . . but different. In a different time." I shook my head, freeing myself from the vision, and stared intently into my sister's eyes. "We cannot use the stones for this."

"Okay. We will think of something else." Kenna spoke softly, knowing not to question my visions.

"Why do you think your magic's not working?" Gaby asked.

"I am not sure." I stood and shook out my tired arms.

"Perhaps he needs to be awake after all," Jeremiah suggested.

"Perhaps, but honestly, I fear it is just too late. I think his magic is leaving him, and there is nothing left for us to heal." I brushed off the front and back of my dingy skirt and began to pace.

"Or maybe it's his spirit that is fighting you," the chief interrupted from the corner. "As an elder and a shaman, he possesses powerful protection magic. His inner bear may be fighting to survive."

"That is a really good point," I conceded. "All right, let's wake him up."

CHAPTER 12

KARA

*W*ar cries tore through the village, piercing the air as pounding hooves and battle drums sounded outside.

"What is happening?" Kenna shouted.

"The Comanche! We are under attack!" Chief Aquakawwa pulled a hatchet from his belt and ran out of the teepee and straight into the fray.

Ric Kasun poked his head out the opening, but quickly pulled the heavy flap closed, securing the entrance with the cross beams that lay on the ground next to the door. "Looks like the outside world has finally come crashing back in."

"What do you mean?" Phaedra asked, wrapping her snow-white wings around herself and sliding as far away as possible from the chaos outside.

"While the tribe and witches have been stuck in their time loop, the outside world continued to turn. The Comanche have no doubt been searching the area for this village, only to find it once the spell was broken," Ric quickly explained his theory to the entire crowd.

"This cannot be happening right now!" Kenna threw her arms in the air.

"Well, it is. Which means we have an immediate problem to deal with if we all want to survive the night." Gaby nodded to her husband as smoke began to seep across the ground. "They are going to burn this village down. We need to split up."

"Wait. You are not going to help them?" Jeremiah asked. "I thought you spent your time fighting for peace across these lands."

"Fighting for peace, yes. Not for blood."

Flames made their way under the thick skin of the structure. "Go now, while you still have a chance. If we do not find you again, just know it was a pleasure meeting you all." Gaby and Ric shifted into their wolf forms and slid out the back opening, blending smoothly into the night.

"Well, isn't that just great!" Kenna threw her hands in the air.

"Gaby is right. It is not our place to interfere with their history." Phaedra turned to follow the Kasuns, but stopped and stared at me with her sad eyes. "I have been wandering a long time, and know that love is the only thing that truly can make a difference." She nodded toward the pink stone still lying in my hand. "Follow your heart, and you will find a way."

I stared, blankly, as Phaedra pulled her wings in tight and slipped through the back flap, taking flight the moment the night engulfed her.

Thick poles crashed to the ground as fire ate up the sides of the canvas.

"Come on," Jeremiah yelled, heaving the shaman's body over his shoulder. "We have to get out of here. The teepee is coming down."

Left with no other choice, we followed Jeremiah out the back opening and crept into the nearby trees.

Screams of war and shrieks of terror raked through the air, shredding the calm that usually layered this peaceful canyon. Thundering horses stampeded through the village, tromping over burned homes and broken bodies. Blood-coated hatchets and knives flew into soft flesh, only to be yanked out and cast through the air again and again.

Plastered to the ground and hidden in a ditch, Jeremiah, Kenna, and I caught glimpses of the chief and other warriors of the Ute tribe fighting valiantly, slaying numerous Comanche as they defended their homes. But in the end, it was not enough, and we were forced to watch helplessly as the entire tribe was slaughtered.

KARA

The warmth of the morning sun woke me first. We were still alive and safe within the hidden ditch, thanks to our protective cloaking spell. I shivered and reached out to wake Jeremiah and Kenna. "I do not see anyone. I think it is over."

Jeremiah held up his hand, signaling for me to stay quiet while he rose and evaluated the area. He was no more than ten steps away when Phaedra landed directly in front of him, her white wings spread wide, making for one hell of an entrance. "It is safe. They have all returned to their own territory."

Jeremiah waved us forward then returned his attention to the angel. "I am surprised you came back. Are you all right?"

"Why?"

"You seemed . . . distraught about what we have to do, and again when you were speaking to Kara about love. Is that why you always seem so sad? Did you lose someone close to you?"

With a huff, she shot into the sky without another word.

"What did you say to her?" I nudged his shoulder.

"Obviously, the wrong thing." He shook his head. "Come on, we need to get the shaman and finish this."

"Finish what?" Ric called out from behind us. "Everyone is gone."

He walked forward to meet Gaby, who was already standing over the shaman's body where it still lay within the ditch.

I knelt down next to the shaman, easing him awake. "You are right. And that is another problem we have to fix."

CHAPTER 13

KARA

"*A*re you sure you want to do this?" Gaby asked.

"Yes. The angel was right. I have to follow my heart, and I *know* if we do it this way, balance will be restored." I smiled at the alpha wolf, then nodded at Jeremiah, signaling we were ready to go.

Taking the shaman by the arm, Jeremiah waited as the rest of us joined him. Kenna, the last to step forward, smiled at me and with a wave of her hand, produced another split in space. Stepping through, we all emerged at the base of the Great Falls, finding Phaedra already waiting atop a giant boulder.

"I am glad you have joined us again." I smiled.

"I am glad you followed your heart," she retorted.

Jeremiah cast another sleeping spell upon the shaman, then carefully laid his body near the pond's edge. Reaching into his pocket, Jeremiah handed me his ruby. "If you are sure."

"I am." I held out my hand to Kenna and accepted her amethyst next.

Finally retrieving the rose quartz from my own pocket, I hiked up my skirt and knelt beside the shaman and began. "Ruby, for contentment and peace." Leaning forward, I placed the red stone on the ground above the shaman's head. "Amethyst to guard against self-deception." Reaching across him, I placed the amethyst in his left hand. "And rose quartz . . . for love." Closing my eyes, I gently pressed the rose quartz into the palm of his right and recast the remembering spell I had used before, this time including the Kasuns and Phaedra.

> *"Remember now, remember us six, today, tomorrow, and forever be fixed.*
> *If time resets, our magic trumps thee, straight from the goddess, so mote*
> *it be."*

A snap of magic sealed my words in place, and it was time to prepare for the next phase of my plan.

"Jeremiah, you kneel above him there," I pointed to the shaman's head, "and Kenna, you next to his left hand, by your stone." Kenna nodded and moved into place across from me. The Kasuns shifted into their wolf forms and lay peacefully on the ground next to the pond, just below the shaman's feet and out of the way, while Phaedra stood still upon the boulder.

With everyone present and all in place, I began the spell that would take us back to the beginning of it all.

> *"Forged by magic, old and true, reset the time loop again to renew.*
> *Activate the spell within, one last time to save our friends."*

KARA

Jeremiah must have woken before either of us girls and set off on the trail this trader had been traveling over for the last few weeks. Lorenzo, Catalina, and Clara Vargas were our names in this lifetime, and . . .

Kenna interrupted my thought as she jumped up, tossing furs and blankets into the air.

"It worked!" she cried out, startling the two large oxen pulling the wagon across the rough terrain.

"Yes, it seems so," Jeremiah replied from the front, yanking on the reins and pulling us to a stop as Kenna and I both pushed through the opening to join him.

"Do you both remember?" I asked.

"Yes. Everything." Kenna smiled and relayed the visions spilling into her mind—the same visions I'd had before when the spell previously broke. Celebrations, meals being shared, Jeremiah, me, and herself working the fields in a summer that had yet to come. Friends turned family through native customs, all set against the wild landscape in the box canyon they were all so desperate to protect . . . Everything poured back to her, exactly the same as it had been before.

"Me too," I added. "It is time to set things right."

Jeremiah snapped the leathers and released the handbrake, ready to finish our trek to the village.

We rode in silence as the sun crept over the distant mountains. Snow-covered peaks surrounded us again, while the evergreens still strained to reach far into the sky, glistening with a coat of frost in the late spring morning.

"You realize this will be the last time we see this magnificent landscape," Jeremiah stated as he pulled his jacket further up his neck to combat the chill in the air.

"You never know. Maybe one of our soul journeys will return us here at a later date." I shrugged, thinking back to what I had seen within my stone.

"Perhaps, but first, we have to finish this and get back to finding Karina," Kenna added. "I am still upset the memories of her were wiped from our minds by the shaman's spell."

"Me, too. His intentions still do not justify his actions, and maybe it was Karina who reached out and helped us to remember in the first place. Regardless, I know this is the right choice."

"Are we ready, then?" Jeremiah asked.

Kenna and I nodded in unison and climbed back into the wagon, preparing to once again play our parts. Pulling on the handbrake, Jeremiah guided the oxen around the final turn of the ascending trail. With a hand raised to greet our friends—alive again—he slowly pulled the wagon to a stop.

"Maiku!" The chief spoke directly to me as usual as I peeked my head out the front.

Muttering the language spell once more, I replied on cue, "Hello. We are the Vargas family and were sent with approval to trade with your tribe."

"I am Chief Aquakawwa. We have been expecting you. Please follow me." We followed the chief to our familiar structure with tight lips and wide smiles. "Get settled, then come to the main dwelling in the center of our village once the sun begins to set. All here are aware of your visit, and I can assure your safety. You are my welcomed guests," the chief instructed yet again.

Jeremiah nodded and helped us from the wagon, immediately leading us around the back of the teepee to retrieve the stones.

"It is all exactly the same." I grinned, pleased everything was going to plan. I bent down and whispered my protection spell again, then unearthed the package from beneath the pile of leaves, gently grabbing it by its edges and dusting off the dirt.

Walking back inside, we sat crossed-legged on the ground with the bundle resting in front of us, just as before. Slowly unwrapping the package, I carefully slid the bone and feather from the twine and pulled back the skin, revealing our stones within.

Again, the ruby pulsed a bright red, the rose quartz shone a beautiful pink, and the amethyst a deep violet.

"Stones of earth, stones of old, rid yourself of your evil goal. Cleansed by the goddess and her servants three, as we will it, so mote it be."

I signaled Kenna and Jeremiah to join in again, and we repeated the spell two more times.

The familiar energy whipped around the room, yanking the

tendrils of tainted magic high into the air. With one last push and pull of our power, the shaman's spell snapped, breaking the time loop once more.

"All set." I reached forward, fearlessly gathering the stones, and passed them out to each of us again. "Time for dinner?"

Kenna laughed and reached for a strand of her hair. "Yes, but this time, I am not wearing any of those itchy furs."

CHAPTER 14

KARA

*K*enna, Jeremiah, and I reached the oversized teepee before the drums even began to sound.

"Are you ready to do this?" Jeremiah asked.

Kenna and I stood resolute, both poised and prepared to face what we knew was coming next, then nodded for him to continue.

Pulling back the entrance flap, Jeremiah entered first, and we followed, this time dressed in our own travel-worn clothes. Chief Aquakawwa dropped a log in the fire pit, then stood to meet us with his brows drawn tight. "Friends, is something wrong? We have only begun to prepare for tonight's celebration."

"Cancel the celebration. We have come to warn you." I stepped forward, holding out my stone for the chief to see.

Jeremiah crossed his hands over his chest. "We know we have been trapped in a time loop, and understand why, but what *you* do not know, is now that the spell is broken, your entire village is in danger."

A shift from the back of the teepee drew everyone's attention before the chief had a chance to respond.

"What is the meaning of this?" the shaman asked, still clueless to the fact that his spell had been altered again.

"They know," Chief Aquakawwa replied.

"Wait!" I yelled as the shaman moved to run. "The Comanche are coming, poised outside your canyon, and they will wipe out your entire tribe later tonight if you do not let us help you."

"Help us?" the shaman questioned. "Why would you be willing to do such a thing, after what has been done?"

Kenna released a strand of her hair with a flick, stepping forward with a slight curl to her lip. "Because, despite the fact you siphoned our magic to trap us here, we understand that your intentions were true. Do you not trust *our* intentions? Perhaps you need a sign from the Great Spirit that we are telling the truth." Flicking her wrist, Kenna tore open a portal, and out walked Phaedra in all her bright, shining glory.

"The White Woman," Chief Aquakawwa whispered, dropping to his knees.

"Yes. I am here with a message from the Great Spirit. Trust these witches to aid your tribe, and accept your punishment along their side. Foolish were you to attempt such a feat, now fallen from grace, forever you'll be."

I smiled at the angel's delivery of our pre-planned speech, while Kenna kept her eye on the shaman to make sure he was buying our ruse.

Chief Aquakawwa rose and raced to his shaman's side. "Listen to their plea, for I will not let you doom the fate of our tribe."

Accepting his defeat, the shaman lowered himself to his knees. "I will do as the Great Spirit instructs."

"Now, tell us about the Comanche," the chief requested. Standing tall over his shaman, the chief listened as Jeremiah described the impending attack, and how we planned to stop it.

KARA

As the sun began to set, the flap of the teepee opened, and the rest of the tribe filtered in. Chief Aquakawwa raised his hands and quieted the gathering crowd.

"There will be no feast tonight, for there is a much more important task at hand. The Comanche have invaded our land, but with our new friends' warning, we have the time we need to flee the village."

Shocked gasps and angry voices rose at once.

"Why would we flee?" one of the warriors questioned.

"Because this fight not only affects our tribe, but the lives of others. So if we are to remain here, in the heart of this special place, we need to do things differently this time."

Jeremiah, Kenna, and I sat against the far wall behind the shaman, blocking any chance of his escape out the back exit. Phaedra had warned us, before she made her dramatic exit through Kenna's portal, that the shaman still should not be trusted. Sitting quietly while the chief rallied his people to our cause, I rolled the smooth pink stone in my hand.

"We need to hurry," I whispered to Jeremiah.

Jeremiah stood, knowing better than to question me. "Chief. It is time. Gather your people at the Great Falls and stay hidden until the White Woman appears to you again." Laying a hand on the chief's shoulder, Jeremiah leaned in and whispered the last part of his instructions so that only Aquakawwa could hear. "Be sure to not let the shaman out of your sight."

The chief nodded, then led his frustrated and confused tribe from the village and into the surrounding forest. As the last of the warriors fell from sight, Ric and Gaby Kasun emerged from the trees, clothed again with a flick of Kenna's wrist.

"You are sure about this?" Ric asked me, while shaking Jeremiah's hand. Gaby stepped forward and hugged both us girls.

"Yes. This is the way it has to be. Just follow the tribe, and make sure the shaman does not try to escape or cast any more spells. No one can be in the village at the time of the attack," I explained.

"Except for you, you mean." Gaby looked deep into my eyes. "And you are sure the illusion will work?"

I didn't bother replying, but instead, closed my eyes and cast the spell I had previously developed for this exact moment.

"Time will bend, and time will renew. Protected by us, through and through. Cast the illusion to put history in place, all moving forward with the Spirit's grace."

Nothing around us changed . . . until we walked outside.

Smoke billowed from the central cooking pit, wafting scents of savory meat and vegetables into the air as families roamed the trails between the teepees. Women and children layered in furs carried plates of food toward the gathering that was supposed to be taking place. Warriors dressed in their celebratory skins practiced the dance they would be performing later tonight. And all of it was a lie.

"Unbelievable." Gaby sighed.

I laughed. "Hopefully, it is *very* believable."

"Oh, it is," Ric replied, grabbing Gaby's hand. "We'll keep an eye on the shaman and make sure no one ventures back from the falls. Be safe."

"Thank you." Jeremiah lifted a hand, then turned to face me. "Do you think we are strong enough without Karina's magic to aid us?"

"I think we will have to be," I replied somberly.

"I wonder where she is in this lifetime? Do you think she is close by? Or have we been pulled so far out of time that our family connection has been severed?" Kenna wiped a tear from her cheek.

"I am not sure without doing our locator spells for her, and unfortunately, we simply do not have time." I patted my sister's hand. "But, as soon as this is all over, it is the first thing we will do. I promise."

War cries and the pounding beat of hooves tore through the village, bringing our discussion to an end.

"It is time." Jeremiah nodded and led us both around the back of the teepee and to the ditch in which we knew we would all be safe.

Watching the attack again was so very difficult. The burning structures were real homes being lost, but thankfully, the tribesmen, women, and children were only figments of reality, created specifically to be destroyed. With history back in line, the tribe would remain hidden in this special box canyon until they moved on by choice, or died out peacefully, for that was the one side effect of my spell. All magic had a price, and the tribe as a whole would still have to pay for the shaman and chief's deception, regardless of their good intentions. The shaman would be stripped of his magic, and the tribe would no longer be allowed to expand and grow.

"It's done," Jeremiah announced as the last Comanche warrior rode away from the village, spelled to never return.

"I will signal Phaedra." I whispered a quick spell, sending my words across the back of a breeze, straight to the angel's ears. "Now, let us conjure up the supplies, so they will be ready to rebuild."

Kenna and Jeremiah smiled, then moved into place as we prepared to cast the spell that would provide the necessary items for the tribe to reclaim their lives here within the canyon. Cupping our hands, we each held our respective stones while connecting to the tribal magic native to this land.

"God and Goddess, hear our plea, help provide for those in need. Supply what is needed, and nothing more, for the work of the tribesmen shall endure. So mote it be."

Our stones glowed, each in their vibrant hues as I finished the chant. The materials needed appeared in the center of the village, and a rush of magic blasted back into each of our chests.

Kenna gasped. "Wow! That was amazing. I haven't felt power like that since before we lost Karina."

I shook out my arms, trying to dissipate the buzzing energy running through my veins. "The tribe's magic is definitely powerful and combining it with ours seems to have heightened its reach."

Jeremiah stared at the stone in his hand as the red glow began to fade.

"It will need to be contained," he stated, stone-faced. His gaze snapped to mine. "I know we agreed to strip the shaman of his magic, but what is to stop someone else from tapping into this energy and creating another time loop or wreaking havoc in some other way?"

I looked at Kenna, who simply nodded, agreeing the risk was far too great to take.

CHAPTER 15

CHIEF AQUAKAWWA

The Great Falls glistened as the night sky filled with stars. Huddled with our families, my tribe and I gathered near its base, awaiting word of our beloved village.

Gasps of awe echoed through the crowd when the beautiful White Woman appeared atop a large boulder in front of us. "I bring word from the witches. The attack is over. You may return to your village, but beware, all has been lost. Provisions, however, will be provided for you to begin again."

I quieted the crowd. "Thank you and thank the Great Spirit for sparing our tribe."

The White Woman nodded, then approached my shaman, holding him back as I led my people into the forest. I made no move back toward them, nor had the need to inquire why, for I knew it was time for the shaman to face his punishment. Before they fell from my sight, however, the witches appeared through the trees, and I wondered if I would ever see my shaman again.

KARA

After completing the spell for the tribe's provisions, Kenna opened another portal that we all stepped through, emerging back at the Great Falls as planned.

"Everything all right?" Phaedra asked, still gripping the shaman's shoulder and playing her role of the *White Woman* perfectly.

Jeremiah nodded, moving closer to the edge of the water just as Gaby and Ric emerged from the forest, still in their human forms.

"Have you decided what you are going to do with him?" Ric asked, lifting a chin toward the kneeling shaman.

"Yes. We know what has to be done." I approached the shaman, who lowered his head, finally accepting his fate. "For abusing the ancient power of this land, he will now and forever be stripped of his tribal magic. Neither he nor anyone in this canyon will be able to wield its power without first proving their worth." I paused and looked between Ric, Gaby, and Phaedra. "But we will need your help to protect it."

Ric looked to Gaby and shrugged. "What can we do?"

"Our time here will come to an end sooner or later, at which point we will continue on our soul journeys and most likely never return here again. We need protectors to stay in this canyon and watch over the magic once we are gone."

Phaedra stepped closer, her sad eyes meeting mine. "I cannot promise to remain in the canyon at all times, but I will return often to maintain a watch over it. I hope that will be acceptable."

I smiled. "Having the *White Woman* drop in now and then would truly be a blessing."

Dipping her head shyly, Phaedra made her goodbyes, and in a display of power and grace, took to the sky and faded from view behind the clouds.

Turning again to the Kasuns, I asked, "Can we count on you, too?

You have protected this area for so long, it would be our hope that you would continue to do so, holding this secret in place."

Gaby stepped forward, her chin held high. "Of course. We will stay within the area and continue to protect the magic and people of this land." Shifting into their wolf forms, she and Ric moved to the water's edge, lying down, ready to witness as silent protectors.

Satisfied all would be well after we had gone, I gestured to Kenna and Jeremiah to take their places. "Then it is time."

The three of us surrounded the shaman, holding the stones in the palms of our hands. Closing our eyes, we pulled deeply on our pool of true magic from the goddess and allowed our powers to build. Each stone began to glow, radiating with the natives' magic as our energies combined.

"Siphon the magic from this man, protect the history and this land. Guarded by the dedicated three, concealed and linked, forever shall it be."

Repeating the chant three times, we stood still as ribbons of energy flowed from the shaman's aura and into each of our stones.

All three stones pulsed in our hands as we trapped the shaman's magic inside. Flinching, I looked down at my stone as it became hot against my palm. The perfect oval stone—a pale pink in its natural state—suddenly changed, its interior shifting to a milky white, like a cloud forming in its center.

"Why is yours now different?" Jeremiah asked as our spell came to an end.

I closed my eyes and held the stone against my heart, concentrating on the pull I'd felt from the first time I had touched it.

"Make your way to my daughter's hand, lending her guidance as fore-planned, give her this message, for she will know what to do, 'Time is fluid, fickle yet true.'"

I continued to whisper into the stone, leaving a message for a daughter I had yet to conceive.

Kenna gasped, openly shocked. "Well, that is an interesting development!"

Jeremiah moved to support the shaman who was still alive, yet clearly drained.

"A discussion for another time," he stated, helping the elder to his feet. "Let us finish this, so we can return him to the village and prepare to say our goodbyes."

Jeremiah nodded to Ric and Gaby, who stalked forward, standing behind the shaman as we moved into place to complete the last part of our spell.

Nearing the pond's edge, Jeremiah, Kenna, and I looked up at the Great Falls and gathered our magic once more. Holding our arms over the surface, the stones that now contained the shaman's power floated out of our hands and hovered in midair above the water.

"Magic stored safely within, encased for all time from beginning to end. Mixed with our power, by the witches three. Protect this new aether, so mote it be."

Kenna and I fell backwards as a massive shockwave blasted from the pond, sending a tube of water straight into the air. Jeremiah stumbled to keep his balance and raced to help us as we watched the water whip around the stones. Within the liquid vortex, bright bursts of pink, red, and purple shot into the swirling mass. Seconds later, the water wall dissipated in a rush, sucking the absorbed magic to the bottom of the pond with it, along with the stones. A stillness hung in the air as a silver tint blossomed just under the water's surface.

"The magic of this tribe, combined with that of our goddess, will now remain in the Great Falls for all time," I explained as I turned to face Ric and Gaby. "Protect it, for it will undoubtedly draw many others to the area."

Ric and Gaby lifted their snouts into the air, confirming their earlier promise, then ran into the surrounding evergreens.

"Let's go," Jeremiah prompted, taking the shaman gently by the arm.

Kenna shook her head, claiming a piece of hair between her fingers. "We will need to walk back to the village. My powers are too drained to tear another rip for us to use."

I placed an arm around my sister's shoulders and fell in line behind Jeremiah as he led the shaman through the thick forest.

"You know, the Utes harvest the inner bark of these pines for their healing compresses and teas." I pointed to the large ponderosas surrounding us, pinpointing the visible scars on the trunks. "Perhaps we could incorporate some of it into Karina's healing tea." I winked. "I think we could all use a magical boost after that."

Kenna smiled and pulled a knife from her thick wool coat, carefully taking just enough to aid in our healing. "Once our energy is restored, we need to discuss what just happened, and also how we are going to get back to our search for Karina."

"Do you not think we could live out our lives as the Vargas family while we search for her here?" Jeremiah asked from a few steps in front of us.

I dropped my head, not ready to discuss the facts of what I knew in my heart to be true. "I am sorry, but we need to return to our true soul journey as soon as possible because . . . Karina is not here." I reached for Kenna's hands again. "Not only did the shaman trap us in his time loop, but we have been diverted away from our original destination in time. If we stay here, we will lose an entire lifetime of searching for our sister."

Kenna stopped on the trail, pulling her hands from mine, and wrapped her arms around her middle. "What does that mean? How are we supposed to trigger our next soul journey, then?"

I took a deep breath and replied, "We will have to die."

CHAPTER 16

KARA

"Thank you for not killing him." Chief Aquakawwa bowed to us all, and then led the elder to the back of the temporary structure that had already been erected in the center of the village. "You are still my welcome guests here. Please stay as long as you like. A teepee will be ready for you within the hour."

"Thank you." Jeremiah tilted his head to the chief, then walked back to meet Kenna and me, where we stood waiting off to the side. "A place will be ready for us soon. Until then, I think we should find some utensils to brew that healing tea and discuss our plans."

A large fire pit had already been dug outside the gathering tent, where I quickly found three metal cups. "I am surprised they have such modern utensils."

"I'm sure they were traded for during the recent peace treaties." Jeremiah smiled as he poured the provided water into each cup, then waited for me to do my part.

Looking around to make sure we were not being watched, I opened the clasp on my poison ring—the one I wore at all times.

From journey to journey, it never wavered from my finger and held Karina's special blend of healing herbs that she had created long ago. Tipping the dried flakes from within, I filled each cup then snapped the metal closed.

"I miss her so much." Memories of our original lifetime together filled my mind as I stirred the tea.

"I know," Kenna replied. "So do I. But I promise, we will find her soon."

I sniffed the warm brew, its potent notes of angelica root, adder's-tongue, and burdock tickling my nose. "I hope so, but I wish it didn't have to be this way. I am not sure ending the Vargas's lives prematurely is something I can come to terms with."

"What other choice do we have? And how do we know they were not destined to freeze up here during their dealings with the tribe, or be killed in the Comanche raid anyway?" Jeremiah asked as delicately as possible. "I know it sounds cruel, but we cannot tell their future. However, we do know Karina will have one once we get out of here."

I jerked my chin in understanding, then sat quietly and sipped my tea.

As promised, within the next hour a teepee had been set up in the same location as our previous one. Kenna and I rushed inside, anxious to tuck in beneath the warmth of the furs and skins.

"Get some rest, and we will make a plan tomorrow." Jeremiah slid down to a pallet laid out on the ground and crawled beneath its coverings.

I tried to hide the soft sighs and tiny whimpers coming from my cries and heard Kenna doing the same. No further words were spoken as I fell asleep with both hope and dread in my heart as the reality of our plans continued to sink in.

Soft rays pierced through the tiny holes in the skin of the teepee, creating a dazzling grid of sunlight throughout. I could hear the tribesmen and women already hard at work outside, tightening up the seams and hauling supplies from here to there.

"Good morning," Jeremiah offered tentatively, probably unsure if I would be able to forgive him for what we had to do.

"Good morning." I rose slowly, stretching my arms and back, then walked toward Jeremiah, wrapping my arms around his middle. "Thank you for always looking out for us and putting Karina first."

He hugged me tightly. "Always."

"Okay, okay. Let me in here." Kenna joined in on the quick family hug, then pulled away, rubbing her stomach.

"So, food first, then plans?" she asked, flipping her long dark hair over her shoulder.

"Yes, please." I grabbed a large clay bowl from beside the door. "But first, let me go fetch some water for us to clean up with."

I pulled on my fur hat and exited the teepee, stepping immediately into the flurry of activity racing by outside. Horses pulling large lodge poles pounded near me, while women and children scurried about, gathering any remaining vegetables and berries they could find to restock their food supply. The efficiency with which the tribe had begun to rebuild brought a smile to my face as I made my way to the nearby stream. Bending down, I lowered the bowl into the frigid water and shivered.

"I am surprised to still see you here."

I looked up to find Phaedra standing on the opposite bank. "I could say the same for you." I smiled.

"Yes, well, I wanted to make sure that you truly did follow your heart."

"If you mean did I realize the stone was meant for my future daughter, then yes, I did." I stood. "It called to me from the first time I touched it, and being a rose quartz, it is no surprise the message was buried deep within my heart. I am not sure how or when it will happen, but I now know not to close myself off to future love. Thank you for that."

Phaedra dipped her eternally sullen head. "You are most welcome.

I hope you find what so many of us do not." With tears in her eyes, she shot into the sky, fading again into the white fluffy clouds.

Returning to the teepee, I poured some of the crystal-clear mountain water into the cooking pans, then used the rest to clean up and prepare for the hard conversation ahead.

After a quick breakfast, all three of us placed blankets on the ground and sat cross-legged around the small fire Jeremiah had built in the center of the structure. An uncomfortable silence thickened the air.

"I guess I will start," I began. "Before you ask, I have no idea how or why the crystal triggered the message for my daughter. I do not know who she is, or when she will be born, and have received no other information other than the words that came to me from the goddess."

"Do you know how she will get the stone, since it's currently resting at the bottom of the Great Falls pond?" Kenna asked.

"No, I do not. But I am sure other witches will occupy this village in the future and have no doubt that somehow, the stones will find their way to the surface again."

Kenna nodded and winked at me. "Wow! A daughter."

I lowered my head, smiling widely at the unexpected revelation as well.

"With that in mind, our future awaits, though I am not really sure how to approach this," Jeremiah confessed. "This situation is new, and unlike our previous two journeys, we have to contemplate cutting our lives short on purpose." He turned to face me directly. "Do you think this could affect how we travel to our next lifetime, or if by committing suicide, we risk ending our soul journeys here and now, leaving Karina to wander the centuries alone?" He asked the hard question I was sure none of us wanted to face.

I shifted nervously with my head still down and heard Kenna suck in and exhale a deep, exaggerated breath.

"Well, I suppose the first thing we discuss is whether we treat this as a human problem or a magical one," Kenna suggested.

I looked up, my interest piqued. "What do you mean?"

"I mean," she proceeded softly, "we could either take our lives in a multitude of ways like humans do, or we cast another spell that will do the job for us."

Cringing at the thought of taking my own life in *any* way, I pushed to stand. Pacing helped relieve the nervous energy building inside.

"Personally, I do not know of many ways in which to—" I paused, not wanting to use the word associated with such an act. "—accomplish this task, but I would think we could probably make it as simple and painless as possible if we combined the two."

I looked to Kenna and Jeremiah, who both shrugged, obviously unclear as to what I meant.

"For the human element, we could find some hemlock and grind it into our tea, and for the magical side, we can cast a spell that will speed up the process and carry us to our next journey as intended."

"That sounds relatively easy, but again, do you know if by doing this, are we risking the end of our journeys altogether? Besides, does hemlock even grow this high up in the mountains?" Kenna shifted uncomfortably on the ground, scooting closer to the fire in her ragged cotton dress, pulling tight the thick fur covering wrapped around her shoulders. This entire topic brought a chill to the air.

I bent down to warm my hands, answering the second part of her question first. "Yes. While we were at the falls, I noticed some growing in the low-lying area around the far side of the pond."

Jeremiah stood, shaking out, then folding his blanket. "I will retrieve the hemlock, while you two work on the spell."

I held up my hand to stop Jeremiah. "Wait a moment." Then, reaching out to Kenna, I wrapped my arms around her and pulled her close. "Before we begin, how about we contact the goddess and ask her permission to move forward with our plan? If she gives it, we will depart tonight. But if not, we will be stuck here for the natural course of our lives, leaving Karina to fend for herself, wherever she is, until it is time for us to travel again."

Kenna leaned into my shoulder, her small frame shaking as she struggled to hold back tears. "All right."

I held my little sister for a moment longer while she cried, releasing her frustration and fears into the universe, then dabbed her cheeks and positioned myself across from her as we prepared to call out to the goddess.

Holding my sister's hands, I closed my eyes and reached out with my thoughts. "Goddess above, hear our plea. We come to you for permission and guidance, and only with your love and approval will we move forward with our plan."

I didn't have to explain what was in our hearts or minds, for the goddess always knew.

Moments passed, until suddenly a wave of contentment fell over Kenna and me both, activating our heart chakras and radiating a soft glow within our auras.

Kenna's eyes snapped open and a smile stretched across her face. "She approves and understands."

"I had no doubt she would. Karina is the heart of this family, and without her, perhaps it is we who are truly lost." I rose to stand, relieved we would be continuing our soul journeys despite this strange and unfortunate setback, and then walked to retrieve a piece of parchment, a quill, and some ink from our supplies.

"Here." I handed a rough sketch to Jeremiah. "This is what you are looking for."

Jeremiah looked at the drawing, finding a tall, thin stem with small clusters of delicate flowers fanning out at the top. "Okay. I've got it. I will be back as soon as I can."

I turned to Kenna. "So, are you ready to create the spell that will return us to our true time?" I smiled, trying to stay positive despite my own fear.

Kenna reached for my hands, giving them a firm squeeze. "As a matter of fact, I am. I miss Karina too, and if this is what it takes to return us to our soul journey and put us back on the path to finding her, I am more than ready."

I stepped forward and drew her into hug. "Thank you for always being so strong."

"It is my job," Kenna teased, her confidence restored. "Now, let's get to work."

CHAPTER 17

KARA

Forty minutes later, Jeremiah returned with the hemlock in hand.

"Did you encounter any problems?" Kenna asked, always the protector.

"No. Did you?" He lifted a chin at all the gathered ingredients laid out before us.

"No. We are ready." I stepped forward, taking the hemlock from Jeremiah and mashing it into the three cups I had prepared.

"Should we look for the chief in order to say our goodbyes?" he asked.

"No need. I have asked that he join us here shortly," I replied.

Silence fell as we waited for the chief, each preparing ourselves privately.

"Friends," the chief called out as he entered our teepee, "you called for me? Is your dwelling not sufficient?"

Jeremiah offered his hand. "Everything is fine and much

appreciated, Chief. Thank you for your hospitality and for trusting us to save not only your tribe, but ourselves."

Chief Aquakawwa looked at me, then bowed his head. "You are leaving," he stated somberly.

"Yes. We will be returned to our time, and the Vargases will no longer exist in this one. They will need to be buried once the spell is cast," I explained.

Looking up, Chief Aquakawwa stood tall and lifted his hand, offering us a traditional farewell gesture. "I will return once the sun sets to confirm you are gone, then lay the family to rest. You have my word."

The chief turned and left, leaving us to proceed in peace.

Stepping forward, I passed out the cups, then motioned to the three blankets lying on the ground. "Lie down once you drink the tea. After that, Kenna and I will complete the chant, and . . . that is it."

Taking deep breaths, we each moved into position, sitting first as we raised our cups.

"Wait," Kenna interrupted, "I just . . . I want you to know I love you both so much."

Jeremiah smiled with tears in his eyes, obviously unable to speak past the lump in his throat.

"We love you, too." I smiled. "Now, let's go find our sister."

With confident nods, we all downed the tea, then lay back, ready to complete our spell. Reaching out to Kenna, I clasped her hand.

"Return us to our journey's end, find our sister, lost again. Use the bond that unites the three, as we will it, so mote it be."

Three more times we repeated the spell, falling silent as the death tea took its toll. We burst free of our mortal bodies, our energy signatures flying into the cosmos, confirming our spell had worked. Soon, we would be immersed in our new lives and able to continue our search for Karina.

CHIEF AQUAKAWWA

As the sun set, I reentered the teepee to gather the Vargas family and bury them as promised. The hair on my arms stood on end, a result, I was sure, from the remaining traces of magic lingering in the air.

Lifting my arms, I looked to the sky. "Be free, my friends, and know that our remaining time here will be spent well. Thank you for your sacrifice, and for protecting our way of life within this special place. We are the people of the land and will make sure to leave it as pristine as we found it when our time here comes to an end."

Howls sounded nearby as a single white feather drifted down from the opening above, landing directly at my feet. Weaving my way between their bodies, I sang our traditional farewell song and performed a final dance in honor of the witches who had given their lives for my tribe and our uniquely magical home.

EPILOGUE

PHAEDRA – 1786

I spotted Ric and Gaby poised on the cliff overlooking the village below. Landing softly next to them, I gazed down into the canyon we had all sworn to protect more than eighty years ago. "It's hard to see the last of them go."

Gaby and Ric remained silent as we watched the current Ute chief prepare the most recent dead. He had cut their hair and washed their bodies, wrapping them with skins and rope to prevent their ghosts from rising. Their homes were then burned, along with their personal belongings, then he buried them atop the ashes in rock-covered graves. Over the last fifty years, the canyon had transformed from a full and thriving village into an eerie, isolated burial ground, high within the mountains. I shivered, never truly getting used to the sight. Beautifully painted teepees had been reduced to ash, replaced by mound after mound of heavy rocks, marking the dead.

The chief—no longer with a tribe to rule—lay down beside the final grave, pulling stones atop his own body as he readied himself to join the Great Spirit as well. We had discussed his options and he promised me—the *White Woman*—that this was his preferred way to go. I watched as he swallowed the hemlock crushed within his fist and sent up a silent prayer when his chest ceased to rise and fall.

"Time will cleanse this special place, wiping away all that has been. The witches foretold there would be others to settle in the canyon here, and I for one plan to honor their wishes and keep it protected and as pure as it should be." I turned to face the Kasuns. "Will you remain, as promised?"

Gaby stepped forward, extending her hand. "Of course. We always keep our word. And while we do not plan to live within the canyon itself, we will remain in the area and protect its secret until our dying days."

I extended my wings, preparing to take flight, when Ric reached out to me. "Will we see you around as well?"

My eyes returned to the canyon below as I thought about the secret that I, alone, now held. A baby—the chief's newborn daughter, born before the witches' spell was cast, that I had smuggled to the nearest Ute village. I, too, had followed my heart, and she was currently alive and well, living safely within a tribe of her ancestors.

I pushed from the ground and hovered slightly above them. "Yes. I am certain you will."

OPEN TERRITORY – 1854

We found it. Our slice of heaven on earth. The pull of magic strengthened as soon as we crested the last mountain ridge, and now, we've finally arrived. This secluded box canyon will serve as our haven from the outside world. Surrounded by a thick wood of evergreens, it rings with the sound of a great waterfall in the distance. Now, it is time for us to get to work. Protections need to be cast and then building can begin.

We are home. ~ Anne-Marie Beaumont

ABOUT THE AUTHOR

Bestselling and award-winning author Tish Thawer writes paranormal romances for all ages. From her first paranormal cartoon, Isis, to the Twilight phenomenon, myth, magic, and superpowers have always held a special place in her heart.

Tish is known for her detailed world-building and magic-laced stories. She has received nominations for multiple RONE Awards (Reward of Novel Excellence), and Author of the Year (Fantasy, Dystopian, Mystery), as well as nominations and wins for Best Cover, and a Reader's Choice Award.

Tish has worked as a computer consultant, photographer, and graphic designer, is a columnist for Gliterary Girl media, and has bylines in RT Magazine and Literary Lunes Magazine. She resides in Arizona with her husband and three wonderful children.

You can find out more about Tish and all her titles by visiting www.TishThawer.com and subscribing to her newsletter at www.tishthawer.com/subscribe.

ACKNOWLEDGMENTS

Thank you to Kristie Cook for the invitation to join this wonderful world and family. I'm so honored to be here.

To my family: Whether together or separated by miles, Colorado will always be home. The memories we share of our lives there together will always be something I cherish. I love you all!

To Michele G. Miller and Kallie Ross Mathews: Thank you for allowing me to borrow your characters (Ric, Gaby, and Phaedra). They truly helped bring my story to life.

To all my Witches of BlackBrook fans: Thank you for following my Howe witches to Havenwood Falls, so we could finally discover why they were missing from Karina's timeline in Maine, 1703. ;)

DAWN OF THE WITCH HUNTERS

MORGAN WYLIE

A Legends of Havenwood Falls Novella

HAVENWOOD FALLS

LEGENDS

DAWN OF THE WITCH HUNTERS

USA TODAY BESTSELLING AUTHOR

MORGAN WYLIE

ALSO BY MORGAN WYLIE

YA FANTASY

Silent Orchids (Book 1)

Veiled Shadows (Book 2)

Daegan (Novella 2.5)

Fractured Darkness (Book 3)

Fading Light (Book 4)

The Sol-Lumieth (Forthcoming)

The Rise of the Paladin (An Alandria Short Story Prequel–Free with
Newsletter subscription)

YA PARANORMAL/SUPERNATURAL

HAILEY: The Necromancer (A Shadow Realm Novella 1)

JAX: The Doppelgänger (A Shadow Realm Novella 2)

WILLOW (A Shadow Realm Novella 3) (Forthcoming)

SOLANGE: (A Shadow Realm Novella 4) (Forthcoming)

NA/ADULT PARANORMAL ROMANCE

RYLEN (The Tangled Web Book 1)

MATHER (The Tangled Web Book 2)

JET (A Tangled Web Novella)

ENOCK (Forthcoming)

LUCIUS (Forthcoming)

ADDITIONAL COLLECTIONS

Reawakened (A Havenwood Falls High Novella)

To YOU the readers, whether this is your first introduction to Havenwood Falls or the Blackstone family of witch hunters, or if you are already an honorary member of the town like we all wish to be, I thank you for being here!

I hope you enjoy the origins of the Blackstone family and their epic adventure across the country, searching for the place we all long to be whether in the past or present . . . Havenwood Falls.

CHAPTER 1

THE EARLY YEARS

CENTRAL VIRGINIA ~ 1840

*B*arefoot, she walked the path padded with moss from her quaint cottage home to the outskirts of a neighboring village. Cessily Blackstone had a meeting with the leader of an unsuspecting coven of witches. She needed this meeting to offer her the answers she sought. Her time was running short, and she knew it. She could feel it in her bones. Since Sarah Stronghold—the leader about to meet her—had gifted her with the ability to sense not only witches near her but also black magic in her vicinity, Cessily could discern even more within herself. Something dark bubbled in her veins. The town doctor wasn't able to help her. She hadn't told her family yet—her five young children and her beloved husband, Hank— she couldn't imagine leaving them behind. Only time and a visit with the witches—her last resort—would tell.

The grass under her toes sent soothing shivers of joy up her legs, igniting a spring in her step. Though her outlook was grim, she couldn't help but feel the life and strength of the forest around her, longing for her to commune with it. Her long blond hair flowed behind her as she headed toward the meeting place. As she drew closer, the familiar tingling in her arms gained strength. Over time, she had learned to be at peace with the unusual sensations she knew were not human characteristics. Cessily had learned to control the deep desires to seek out and kill a witch—apparently an undesired side effect of the "gift" she had been given to protect her family.

She watched her children closely as they matured. Each had developed varying degrees of the same gift, passed down through her, but thankfully diluted by the joining of her human husband. Except for her second eldest, Rodney, who seemed to be fully human. Part of the gift she'd been given allowed her to sense others similar to her as well. Cessily did her best to keep the children away from the witches until they were ready, but the three eldest—LeAnna, Rodney, and Isaiah—knew of their heritage while the two youngest, Dante and Marie, were still in the dark.

"Cessily, welcome. It has been quite some time since we last spoke," a female voice came from the other side of a tree as Cessily passed by. With a smile on her face, a woman, possibly in her sixties, wearing a long brown but lightweight cloak with a hood over her head, stepped into the pathway. Tall and willowy, she held her chin high and her head proud.

Cessily stopped and inclined her head respectfully. "It has indeed. Thank you for meeting with me, Sarah."

"How can I be of service to you?"

"Is there a way to reverse the gift you bestowed on me?" Cessily sighed. "I mean no disrespect, but I am not sure it is having the intended effect as it is passed down to my children. They are reacting differently, each one."

Sarah frowned, but kept her eyes trained on Cessily, clearly debating something. "No, I'm afraid it is permanent, Cessily."

"Is there anything that can be done to help ease the strongest of the desires for my children? Please don't misunderstand. I am grateful for how you helped me long ago. But I fear for my children. If they are not able to control the gift as I have learned to do, they might let it get the best of them."

"I told you when I awakened this power within you that it would not be an easy road. It is more a responsibility than a gift. You must instruct your children the way I instructed you." Sarah's gaze searched Cessily's face. "What is it you're not telling me, Cessily?"

Cessily scratched at the back of her neck and turned her head slightly, as if listening to something.

"I don't have much time. I think I am dying, Sarah," she said, her voice lowered. "And I've seen darkness in a couple of my children as the gift awakens within them. I'm scared for them."

"Give me your hand," Sarah demanded, holding out her own palm face up. Cessily placed her hand palm up within Sarah's. Sarah studied it, drew her index finger along Cessily's life line, and frowned. A lone tear escaped one of her eyes. "It is true. I am sorry, Cessily."

"Is there anything you can do? Any magic that could delay my end? Anything?" Cessily pleaded, desperation escaping her tone. "I'm not ready to die," she whispered.

Sarah reached out her other hand and placed it tenderly against Cessily's cheek. "I am truly sorry. There is nothing I can do. It is the way of nature, and I cannot interfere, even if I could do something."

"I understand."

"There is more you need to understand . . . more I have not told you about your past, Cessily." Sarah's words were slow, hesitant, with a weight Cessily didn't comprehend.

"What is it?" Cessily frowned and tilted her head, watching Sarah struggle with something internally.

"This gift . . . this power you believe I gave you . . ."

"Yes?" Cessily was concerned. A strange sensation crept up her spine, and chills erupted across her skin.

"I was not the giver. I led you to believe I gave it to you."

"If you did not, who did? What aren't you telling me now, Sarah?"

"No one did. Unless you count your ancestors, that is." Sarah sighed and stepped back from Cessily to gain some needed space. "Cessily, the power you feel, struggle with, gain insight from—your ancestors are the source of it. You are a hunter . . . a witch hunter, to be precise."

"What? You did something, though. I could feel the power flow through me when you blessed me all those years ago," Cessily said, doubt flooding her words.

"Your power was dormant. All I did was awaken the power within you."

"No. I don't believe you. I felt something come alive from your power. Why would I never know about such a huge anomaly in my family? Why would no one ever tell me? My parents never said anything!" Cessily paced, her hands worrying themselves into a frenzy.

"Your grandparents asked my mother, the coven leader at the time, to inactivate their powers when they first arrived here from Europe and to never speak of it again. It took very strong magic. It is all written in this journal I brought for you. My mother had it hidden, but I recently found it amongst her things." From beneath her cloak, Sarah brought out a worn leather book, tied and bound with a long strip of red suede. She held it out for Cessily to take.

Cessily froze, all but her eyes as they took in the little book.

"Could it really belong to my family? Could it hold all the secrets you speak of?" she whispered, but doubt laced her tone. Moving slowly closer, she squinted and peered at the ancient tome. Cessily gasped. Her eyes widened in surprise. "I recognize this symbol on the spine."

Sarah turned it to see the spine, then handed it to Cessily, who examined it more thoroughly. "This cluster of stars on the spine is also on my shoulder and on each of the children except Rodney."

"Then it truly belongs to you," Sarah acknowledged.

"You knew all along then? Back when you offered me a gift of protection?" Cessily frowned, attempting to absorb all the information just thrown at her.

Sarah slowly nodded. "I did. What my nephew . . . what that man did to you, using black magic, was unforgivable. The anger you could have allowed into your soul would have awoken your hunter in an unpleasant way. You would have been overrun with the hunger and desire to hunt and kill all witches. I chose to awaken you in a way to be distinguished as a gift, instead of a reaction to hatred. It allowed you to control and learn your hunting powers more easily. That was my restitution to you, not the actual power."

Cessily gave a small smile. "I still am grateful for the sacrifice and offering you made to me and my family. I might not be here otherwise." She sighed and noted the bright morning sun streaking down through the tree branches, a glimmer of hope in a confusing time. "Do you know much else about my ancestors?"

"It is all in the book. Read it. I will be here if you still want to talk when you are finished."

Cessily nodded. She slanted her head slightly down and to the right, listening, pausing. Her eyebrows pinched, and she bit her lip in concern. "Thank you. I should go. I sense little ones of mine who should not be here."

"Blessed be, Cessily Blackstone."

"Blessed be, Sarah Stronghold." Cessily tucked the book protectively to her chest and headed back toward home.

As she passed the patch of full green shrubbery, she didn't stop and she didn't acknowledge the children except to say, "Best hurry along so your daddy doesn't catch you away from your chores for too long."

Cessily kept walking, enjoying everything around her. The flowers woke to greet the day, the sun warmed the path beneath her toes, and the birds and chipmunks greeted each other with friendly chatter. The bush behind her jostled, and the sounds of running feet thudded away from her. She knew her youngest children, Dante and Marie, would have plenty of questions for her when they next saw her. In fact, Cessily had questions of her own. Skirting by the small trickling creek near their home, she found a nice flat boulder in the sun to sit. So she did, and she opened her family's recorded history—the only one she was aware of—and read.

WITHIN THE WEEK, Cessily weakened in both body and mind. Her illness consumed her from the inside out. She had little time left. Her husband Henry Jackson Blackstone—known to his friends as Hank—was one of the most understanding and patient humans she had ever known. He came along her side and lovingly wrapped an arm around her waist, assisting her with his strength. His bright green eyes gazed down upon her face with love and sadness. Her face showed she was slipping away.

"Cess, you need to tell everything to the little ones—share the new information you have learned with them all. Soon," her husband encouraged. He walked with her through the fields behind their cottage with rows and rows of vegetables. Barefoot once more, and as she usually was, Cessily nodded her head in quiet response.

Her family had been excellent farmers before she had grown and married, but Hank had added his expertise of growing grapes to turn into wine. When Cessily married Hank, he understood all she was, including her "extra" abilities. When Sarah, the coven leader, had blessed her with her gifts—or awakened her hunting side, as she now understood—she had made Cessily promise to always keep the Blackstone name prominent in her family. Until now, Cessily hadn't understood those instructions were straight out of her ancestors' book; though she still wasn't sure why, she had kept up the tradition. Hank was so head over heels in love with his new bride, he didn't care what his name was.

"I will tell them tonight. I fear I will not be here much longer, Hank. I'm afraid to leave you and the children behind." Resting her head in the crook of his shoulder, she allowed the tears she had held at bay most of the week to flow.

Everything was happening too fast. She had just found out all about her heritage, and it gave such new meaning to who she was. Was it better to allow her children to believe their abilities were the result of a gift or something that has always been and always would be a part of their lives? It now made sense why her "gift" also functioned at times as a curse, an obstacle she needed to overcome or learn to control. The power, the abilities, the drive—they were all simply a part of her, her nature. If she was honest with herself, she wasn't sure if she would take that nature away from her children, even if she could. Would life be that much easier and better for them if they didn't have to handle being witch hunters? Probably, but it was their family's responsibility, their destiny. Would she change it? No. Would she make it easier if she could? Yes. It was the most challenging part of her nature. But she needed to prepare her children for what was to come.

CHAPTER 2

"Mama, you don't look so well," a young Marie Blackstone, at the ripe age of ten, commented as she stormed into her mother's room of their comfortable home, a moderate-sized log cabin in Virginia passed down from Cessily's parents. She had no other siblings to share it with —though she did have cousins nearby—so she and her family were blessed to live in it after her parents passed from this life.

"I have some things I need to share with you all. Go and get your brothers and sister, Marie. Hurry along, now." Cessily coughed as she pulled herself to a partial sitting position in order to see her children's faces. Marie paused at the door, watching her mother, concern written all over her. Little Marie's face paled next to her thin blond hair running down her back and tied with a ribbon. Marie ran.

Mere moments later, Marie came running back in after rounding up her siblings.

"Mama, here they come!" she shouted and bounced over to sit on the side of the bed where her daddy usually slept.

"Good girl, Marie."

"Should I get Daddy, too?" the little girl added.

"Not just yet. This is business I have special with just you kids."

Cessily stroked her hand weakly down Marie's face, and her daughter nuzzled in closer at the contact.

"Come in, Dante." Cessily beckoned him from the doorway, where he stood stiffly. His face paled, and his eyes were glued to his mother as they filled with naked fear. She patted the bed once more, but he only came to the foot of the bed and perched on the edge of it.

"LeAnna, Rodney, and Isaiah, fill in here as best you can and find somewhere to be comfortable for a few minutes. I have something to share with you all."

"What is it, Mama? Are you going to tell Dante and Marie about our gift?" LeAnna, the eldest child, asked with the air of one who felt she already knew what she needed to.

Dante's head swiveled toward his sister with a frown on his face. "What are you talking about, LeAnna?"

"We have a gift?" Marie perked up, her eyes wide with excited innocence. She then turned her inquisitive expression on her mother.

Cessily smiled fondly at her youngest. "Yes, Marie, we do. And I'm going to tell you all about it."

LeAnna moved toward the door, ushering the older brothers with her.

"No, stay, you three," Cessily said. "This will be new information to you as well. It seems I have been misled about the source of our power."

"Power?" Dante's eyebrow rose, his interest piqued. LeAnna, Rodney, and Isaiah paused inside the doorway to the bedroom, then trickled back in to find a place to sit or to lean against the back wall of logs.

"Yes, Dante, power. Our family has a special gift I want to tell you about. You are now old enough to know the truth, though I suspect you've been noticing strange occurrences already."

Dante nodded slowly, looking to each of his siblings. "I feel tingles sometimes at the base of my neck when most of you walk in from somewhere else. Though I don't feel it as much with Isaiah and not at all from Rodney. Why is that?"

Cessily nodded and took note of Rodney's face as his expression fell downcast. "None of that now, Rodney. You are not less than your brothers or sisters. You are a beautiful part of this family, just as your father is." A small smile lit Rodney's face as he accepted his mother's approval.

"I'll tell you a story. While you don't need all the details, it is the heart of the story I ask you to hear."

Marie folded her hands across her lap, her gaze filled with anticipation and intent upon her mother. The others leaned in, also expectant of what their mother was about to tell them.

"It began long ago in a country different from this one, taking place across the vast ocean in Europe. There was a family who had immense power—a strong and dangerous power. With power like that comes great responsibility to learn from it, to respect it, and to control it to use for good and protection. Unfortunately, as it has been chronicled throughout history, some of those with such power abused it, causing tremendous tragedy and pain. This story is not much different. But keep in mind that it can be." Cessily tapped Marie on the nose, then adjusted her position on the bed.

"What happened?" Dante asked, interest in his tone.

"Well, this particular family were called witch hunters," Cessily continued.

"Oh, this is rubbish, isn't it? It's just a tale for children," Dante huffed, disappointed with where the story was headed and crossing his arms in disapproval.

"No, dear one, this is not any tale I would tell my children unless absolutely necessary." Her eyes bored into her youngest son's, willing him to give her a chance.

"Let her finish, Dante," Marie scolded. "I want to hear the rest of the story!"

"Sorry, Mama, continue," Dante conceded.

"Thank you, son. Now where was I . . ."

"Witch hunters," Isaiah spoke up.

"Right. I don't believe they used this term back then, but perhaps they did. However, it was what they did—hunted witches, that is. It was a time in Europe when cries of witchcraft were becoming more prevalent, but not in any good ways, I'm afraid. The family took it upon themselves to seek out and sift through accusations of witches, deciding which were legitimate. You see, they could tell because of a particular sensation they could feel—a tingling that would travel up and down their arms."

Marie and Dante both held out their arms and looked down at their forearms simultaneously, stirring a chuckle and a snort from Rodney and Isaiah. Marie didn't care, but Dante shot them both a glare.

"Many of the witch hunters kept to themselves, not wanting to draw more attention to their oddities, but a select group of them took up the burden, feeling it was their duty and responsibility to shed light on any witches in the area. They figured they were given this ability, so they should use it for something."

"Makes sense," Dante said under his breath.

His mother gave him a reproachful look. "Except that they did not take into account the people they were accusing. People with families and children, people who didn't do anything harmful or against any laws of nature or men with their own gifts. Understand, there were witches who did terrible things with their magic and did go against nature—this was black magic, as we call it today."

"How could they tell the difference?" Marie asked wisely.

Cessily nodded, proud of her daughter. "When you feel black magic, you know it deep inside." Cessily placed a hand at her stomach and one at her chest. "It's an overwhelming sensation. You feel ill and want to vomit. It can be so strong, you lose awareness of your surroundings and can even black out. The trick is to learn to remain alert and remove yourself from the situation."

"Mama, what happened back in Europe?" LeAnna steered the conversation back to the story. Cessily smiled, grateful for the redirect.

"Most of the family went into hiding. However, those who didn't agree went into a madness of sorts as they continued to hunt down all witches—not only black magic users, but even those who used their magic for good. This incited some of the European witch hunts that led to hangings and burnings of many innocent people—both human and witches alike. You see, the hunters were so charismatic in their dealings, even humans joined in the hunts, and they had no discernment as to who were true witches and who were not. It was a terrible time in our history." Cessily paused for a moment, lost in thought.

"How does this relate to us, Mama?" Rodney asked, though his expression revealed he might already know the answer.

"Well, I'm glad you asked. Many of those original witch hunters—the ones who wanted nothing to do with the hunts, but to live in peace and leave all that behind them—migrated here to this new country when ships began transporting people to and from the New World. I'm still absorbing all this information, as it is new to me as well." Cessily smiled, her eyes softening as she took in each of her beautiful children. She pulled her long hair around her shoulders to the front. "I have come to understand, through this journal recently given to me, some of those who migrated here from the old lands are ancestors of ours—a direct line to me, actually. You each have the hunting gene, some more than others. I have discovered it has not affected you all the same."

LeAnna frowned, genuinely engaged in the story for the first time. "Mama, you said our powers came as a gift from a nearby witch coven. I don't understand. Are you saying it wasn't a gift?"

"Yes. I mean it is a gift, but one we were born with and not given."

"I don't understand. What happened? How did you not know?" Isaiah, mature for his age at fifteen, asked.

"Sarah, the coven leader, told me the story, and it is reiterated here in this journal. Apparently, some of those early settlers went to the coven and asked for a spell to suppress their powers, so they might live in peace with their neighbors. You see, during those first years, quite a few covens emerged in close proximity as they fled farther away from Salem, and it would have driven our ancestors crazy with the constant overwhelming sensations."

"No one ever told you about it?" LeAnna asked.

"They put their heritage behind them in favor of living as the humans did and made a pact to not speak of it . . . except for the one member who kept this journal—I'm guessing behind the others' backs. It is not understood how the journal came to be in the possession of the witches, except for the way the author speaks of them; it sounds as if they were trusted friends."

"With the witches?" Dante grumbled.

"I, too, have trusted friends amongst the neighboring covens, especially Sarah's coven. My son, do not take the witches for granted and do not project the assumptions of our ancestors upon them. Every being, every creature, everyone has a place in this great wide world, and it's only getting wider as people continue moving out west. Soon the covens will be thinner and more spread apart, just as the hunters will be. There is balance to life. Don't ever forget that." Cessily addressed Dante specifically, but all her children as well.

Suddenly, Cessily clutched her chest as her breathing hitched, and she coughed into her other arm. The sound was alarming, as if her lungs were about to rise up out of her chest. The children took turns glancing around at the others, concern etched on their faces. LeAnna moved to kneel right at the side of Cessily's bed.

"Are you all right? What do you need?" She reached for the wet rag placed inside the blue and white porcelain bowl on the nightstand. Dipping it in the cool water, she then wrung it out and dabbed at her mother's forehead, now beaded with sweat.

"Children," Cessily rasped, her voice scratchy from the cough. "I am ill. I have been for quite some time, but it is now coming to the end. My time on this earth is almost over."

"No!" they shouted simultaneously. Marie scooted up closer to her mother's side and tucked herself into her as close as she dared, tears streaming down her face.

"It is my time. This is no way for me to live. But I want you to know all about your heritage—know, understand, and learn to control your power. You are not bound by the assumptions of what and who a witch hunter is. Redefine the term and explore new purposes for your gifts. You may come across others who won't understand you. Always be kind and generous. Go to the witches if you need help learning, as I did. Sarah will instruct you as she did me.

After all, it was her mother and grandmother who helped our ancestors in the past."

"Can't they help you? Heal you?" Isaiah pleaded, tears in his eyes. Marie sniffled on the bed next to her mother.

"No, I'm afraid not. They do not interfere with the laws of nature when it is someone's time to go," Cessily said sadly.

"What? Didn't they wake up the hunter in you?" LeAnna asked, a frown creasing her brow.

"They have the power to heal you but refuse to? Maybe they did this to you? Did you think of that?" Dante asked, his arms crossed as he stood adamantly.

"No, they did no such thing. It is a long story, and I do not wish to spend my last moments with you sharing the how and why of my hunter side's awakening. When you are older, LeAnna can share it with you, but I have also added it to the end of this journal, so we will not forget who we are ever again. Learn who you are, but discover who you can be. Be reminded of the past, but write your own futures, each one of you." Cessily's voice grew weak, and her eyelids fluttered.

"Mama, don't go . . ." LeAnna's voice broke, and she laid her head on the quilts covering her mother's lap. Cessily loosely placed her hand on LeAnna's head and kissed the top of Marie's against her shoulder. Looking at each of her boys one by one in the eyes, she willed them to feel her heart.

"Be good. Help your father. He will need you. Grow strong and take care of each other. I love you always."

Cessily's eyes closed, and she did not reawaken.

CHAPTER 3

10 YEARS LATER

CENTRAL VIRGINIA ~ 1850

Twenty-year-old Marie sat cross-legged on a large boulder, enjoying the warm spring sun and noting the green sprouts of the newly planted crops emerging from their long winter's nap in the soil. Her grandparents, who had passed on when she was young, had built their beautiful log home set on acres and acres of land, on which they had made their money raising tobacco. Her father, Hank, had learned the trade of grape-growing from his side of the family, and he also grew a healthy stock of grapes for pressing into wine. Though Marie was of age, she and her siblings Rodney and Dante still lived at home with their father, while LeAnna and Isaiah had married and moved into smaller cabins on their property, to remain close.

Having taken her mother's role as ambassador to the neighboring witch coven, still led by her mother's old friend Sarah Stronghold, Marie would often take their excess vegetables to them as gifts of peace. None of it was required, but Marie felt compelled to do it. Additionally, Sarah's daughter, and successor as future coven leader, was Marie's best friend Rachael.

Rachael had trained with her mother for years, but still struggled to control her magic. Rachael's magic worked differently than her mom's—and most of the coven's, for that matter. She had a hard time doing things the way they had always been done in the name of tradition. Rachael had plenty of magic—Marie could feel her strength simply from the level of vibrations that would reverberate up her arms when Rachael would cast—it just wouldn't do what she wanted it to when she wanted it, such as at the command of her mother or during her training sessions, which were often.

Rachael and Marie had instantly hit it off when Marie brought a peace offering in the form of a large basket filled with vegetables and breads shortly after her mother, Cessily, had died. Young Marie felt it necessary to inform Sarah, since they had been friends, according to her mother. Marie had only seen the woman a couple times, though she didn't know she was a witch back then, not until her mama informed them all they were witch hunters. Marie and Rachael had been secretly inseparable ever since. Once LeAnna had let it slip in front of the boys who Marie's new friend was, they had given her a hard time, but none as hard as Dante. He couldn't believe her treachery of being friends with "those people who let Mama die," and he didn't let her forget it.

The winter—and ultimately year—after her mama's death had been the roughest that Marie and the rest of her family had ever faced. Especially her daddy. She had never seen him cry before that time. Her daddy was a big, strong man with broad shoulders, but he had a tender heart, and her mother's death had left a gaping hole—in not only his heart, but all of theirs.

Years later, Marie found herself reading once again the journal that enlightened and changed her and her siblings for the rest of their lives. The journal was ancient, but somehow still intact, even after all the years of reading material it had provided, for her especially. The others had moved on, but she read it over and over, sure there was more to their story, a deeper meaning and understanding of who they were as witch hunters. Her mother had talked about redefining and discovering who they could be anew, a dawning of a new era, and she was set on learning what that meant.

"I don't know if I'm expecting you to give me some kind of revelation or that the words of the pages and the heart behind whoever wrote in you will wear off on me, but I'm looking for some insight on how to keep control of my hunting drives without losing them completely," Marie said aloud to the book as she turned yet another page, then squinted up into the afternoon sun, allowing the warm rays to seep into her pores.

She just knew there had to be a way. So far, she had done pretty well, especially considering her best friend was a witch—nothing ruined a friendship like trying to kill your best friend. She had learned to limit her time with the entire coven; being around too many was near impossible at times. Marie found that knowing them as individuals and feeling the peaceful magic they performed helped. Sarah, the coven leader, would offer a temporary bandage of sorts when Marie planned to spend any length of time with the coven, to cushion the effects she experienced simply by being in their presence. As she grew older, however, the drive had gained in strength, and it was a constant battle to stay in control. Marie didn't even know what she would do if she did lose control, but that was a risk she definitely wasn't willing to allow. Too much was at stake.

A small white butterfly flitted across her peripheral vision, landing on an early flowering shrub and making Marie smile. The shape of the insect brought the cover of the book to mind. Marie closed the worn thick brown leather tome and ran her hand down the front. Inlaid within the leather was an intricately created design that reminded her of a butterfly or a cluster of small diamond-shaped stars, made out of latticed metalwork. It was the same symbol as the one etched on the spine, the same symbol marking every hunter's skin at birth—the hunter's mark. She ran her hand gingerly over the cool metal and what appeared to be some kind of locking mechanism.

"Why do you have a lock that doesn't appear to actually lock anything?" Marie wondered aloud, not for the first time. Opening it, she gently turned the first blank page to the next, and she began to read. The next hundred pages or so read like anyone's journal, recounting experiences and trials of the writer's time. In several places, the writing changed as the author changed—most likely, a descendant of the first. Each story, each obstacle they faced, described the pain they endured to control their hunting drives, mirroring her own struggle. Each author, at one point before their stories ended, spoke of finding the key or how the "key" showed itself to them in different ways than the last.

"But nobody explains what this key is or where to find it? That's not very instructional. How is this supposed to help me?"

"Talking to yourself again?" a male voice interrupted her. A tall and handsome man with broad, strong shoulders moved toward her with a lazy smile and a twinkle in his eye. The slight breeze picked up his blond hair and ruffled it the way Marie longed to do, sliding her fingertips through each wavy lock.

"I didn't think I was going to get to see you today, Judson!" Marie bounded off the rock, ran to him, and threw her arms around his neck just as he opened his arms wide enough to catch her with a twirl. She giggled as she always did upon seeing Judson after they had been apart. "I missed you."

"Ah, Marie, I missed you, too! I couldn't stand to not see you today. Are your brothers around?" Judson's gaze cautiously slid past her to the fields.

"No. I've been out here reading the journal Sarah gave my mother before she died."

Judson relaxed at the prospect of them having a few minutes alone. The Blackstone boys did not like Judson hanging around Marie. They had made their point very clear years ago when Isaiah and Dante forbade her from seeing him or going near that "condemned hellhole of heathens," as they referred to the neighboring coven.

"Did you find out anything you hadn't seen the other hundred times you've read it?" Judson asked, his lip ticking up at the side in a teasing fashion.

Marie pulled at one of his suspender straps and let it go, snapping it back onto his chest.

"Hey! That hurts!" he whimpered, rubbing the painful spot.

"Serves you right, teasing me," she said flirtatiously while she patted her hand against his chest. She then leaned up on her tiptoes and kissed the underside of his chin before she stepped back to allow some thinking space. "Actually, I did find something I haven't truly examined yet."

"What's that?"

Marie held out the journal for him to see as her fingers traced over the metalwork. "Look at this shape, Jud. I thought at first it was a strange butterfly, but I see the diamond-shaped stars of the hunter mark."

Judson peered closely at the cover, nodding with a studied frown.

"And I think something is supposed to fit in inside here, but I don't know what. Mother never said anything about a key or a lock. Except it doesn't seem to lock anything, as we have obviously opened and read through it. Doesn't that seem odd to you?"

"It is odd, and it's an oddly familiar shape, though I am not sure where I've seen it other than the marking on the back of your neck. I've seen this in metal work." Judson frowned, thinking. "I'll figure it out. I just need it to come to me."

"It's time to go," Marie said unexpectedly.

Jusdon's head snapped up. "Your brothers?"

"I feel them coming closer. I'll come to you later tonight. Meet at our spot?" she asked, suddenly shy and biting her bottom lip.

"I wouldn't miss it." He leaned forward and kissed that bottom lip until she opened for him and allowed him full access to her mouth, groaning as she did.

Marie pulled back. "Tonight then. Now go, quickly."

Judson turned and loped into the brush and trees beyond their property, disappearing out of sight just in time.

"Marie? Where have you been?" Rodney called. "You were due at the house some time ago."

Her brothers all headed in her direction. Rodney, the only one of them human like their father, with dark hair and brown eyes, was the only brother usually sympathetic to her quest for peace with the witches. Isaiah, the eldest brother, looked most like father, but with sandy brown hair and flat blue eyes void of any spark of excitement or joy. Next to them stood Dante, who was closest to her in age, but furthest from the desires of her heart. With their father's hair but their mother's face, Dante was a fair blend with dark hair but bright blue eyes always calculating, always watching. They all awaited her response.

"Sorry, I got caught up reading over Mother's old journal again," she responded truthfully.

"Why do you bother with that old thing, Marie? If there was any information that would be helpful, you would have found it by now." Isaiah bent down to secure one of his laces on his worn work boots.

"I think I found something new this time!" Marie said, excited to share what she had found on the cover of the book. "Have any of you seen this shape anywhere in the house? Did Mother ever say anything about a key that went to this journal? I was young. I don't remember everything before she died." Her voice grew quiet. She knew they didn't like it when she brought up their mother, but it was time they discussed everything.

The brothers each looked at the cover of the journal, frowned, then shook their heads in answer to her question.

"Why are you pushing this, Marie?" Dante began with a cool tone that spoke to the end of his patience on this matter. He looked beyond her and out into the trees bordering their lands.

"I'm not *pushing* anything, Dante! I just believe there is more to learn about our hunter side, more to know in order to control it better and to find peace with our neighbors. Don't you want to know if there is another way?" With hands on her hips in defiance, she looked to each of them. Rodney looked away from her, the fear of his brothers' retribution if he agreed with her resident in his eyes. She knew they were hardest on him especially, being human and not quite like them.

Isaiah scoffed. "I don't really care, no. I have everything perfectly under control, as you should, too. Or perhaps you're just weaker than the rest of us."

Marie glared at Isaiah. He was her least favorite.

"Enough, Isaiah," Dante interfered. Though younger, he was somehow the dominant brother. "Marie is and will be by far stronger than you. She just needs to get her perspective and priorities back to *this* family."

"That's got to be hard for her to do when all she thinks about is ways to be at peace with the witches," LeAnna, her only sister, interjected, heading their way with a snide look on her face.

Marie glared even harder at LeAnna. Out of her entire family, LeAnna and her father were the only ones who knew her secret—and LeAnna only knew because she happened upon her and Judson once, having followed Marie at a distance.

"Why do you care so much, Marie?" Isaiah blurted now with anger.

"Because I do! It's the right thing to do. It's what Mother believed, don't you remember that?"

Marie glanced at Dante, who simply watched the interaction with detached observation; however, a spark of knowledge flashed in his eyes.

"Why don't you just tell them and get it over with, Marie? They're going to find out one way or another." LeAnna hinted overtly that she would be the one to tell them otherwise.

"LeAnna! It is not your business to tell. You have ruined everything!" Marie shouted. Angry, fearful tears welled in her eyes.

LeAnna crossed her arms, bracing for what was to come, and raised an eyebrow. "No. You did, when you went off and married that heathen witch pretender!"

Shocked gasps reverberated throughout what felt like the entire world.

"You did what?" Dante seethed.

Marie crossed her own arms defiantly, staring her siblings down. "I married Judson Carter. In secret."

"Months ago," her sister supplied.

"Traitor," Marie shot back.

"No, Marie. You are the traitor," Dante whispered in a tone far worse than shouting, before he turned his back to her and left.

CHAPTER 4

*I*n the shed, Dante, Isaiah, and LeAnna gathered weapons while Dante spewed his hatred for the witches. "We act now. It's time those evil-doers knew where they truly belong."

"You know I'm with you, but I'm curious about the source of your hatred—other than being a witch hunter," Isaiah asked, cleaning off a blade on the leather of his work boots.

Dante hung his head for only a brief moment, breathing heavily as if grasping the frail tendril of his sanity. "They killed Mother. Is there any other reason necessary?"

His words were burdened with the pain of the young boy within him and bound to the deeds of the man he was now—a man ready to avenge the only real love he had ever felt, a woman the witches had called "friend." A woman *they* could've helped, but chose not to.

"They haven't bothered us in some time, Dante. Maybe it's okay to simply ignore their existence for now," LeAnna said, as if she wasn't truly sure she believed what she said, but spoke more for the sake of saying it. Shrugging her shoulders, she went back to picking at her nails, unwilling to look Dante in the eye.

"We have suffered those witches too long, LeAnna. You are either with us on this or against us, like your sister you so easily outed."

Dante's stare was fierce and unrelenting, and his determination pressed upon her until she nodded her head.

"I'm with you," she whispered, almost regretfully, and reached for a dagger on the wall before her. She spun away, toward the cracked open door, and walked out. "I'll be there. I need something from my cottage."

"We go at nightfall," Dante instructed, eyeing her as she left.

LeAnna stopped in the doorframe, half turned her head to acknowledge him, and nodded.

"GOING SOMEWHERE?" a voice uttered from the side of the shed, hidden in the shadows from the fading sun.

LeAnna jumped, hand held over her heart. She caught her breath.

"Oh, Marie, you startled me!" she whispered, grabbing Marie's arm and tugging her to follow behind her.

Marie jerked her arm away, but continued to follow her sister. "I heard Dante. He can't do this."

"I don't like the witches and don't think we should assimilate with them, but I don't think they all deserve to die." LeAnna's eyes saddened, then frantic fear quickly took over, bubbling up in her eyes. She looked over her shoulder. In a hushed but hurried tone, she added, "You have to go. You have to warn them."

"Oh, I plan to. But why, LeAnna? Why did you tell them? You knew how they would react."

"I . . . I didn't think he would go this far. I'm truly sorry, Marie. I was jealous of your control and your devotion to living your own way." LeAnna lowered her head, ashamed and genuine.

Marie gently pulled her sister forward. She leaned in and kissed the top of her sister's head. "I forgive you, but this is going to get bad. I have the feeling our family will never be the same after this night, and I want you to know forgiveness when you might not be able to offer it to yourself."

Marie turned and ran with all she had through their fields and into the forest, following the path to the secret place she and Judson had planned to meet, like they had multiple nights before this one.

~

"Marie, what's wrong?" Judson asked, his voice laced with panic at Marie's sudden and disheveled appearance.

She flung herself at him, wrapping her arms tightly around his neck, and held on as if her life depended on it. Sobbing uncontrollably, her words were incoherent as she tried to explain what had happened.

"Slow down. I can't understand you." Judson spoke calmly, as if to a frightened animal. Marie nodded quickly and inhaled several slow, deep breaths.

"We don't have time for this," she spoke between her breaths. "He's coming . . ."

"Who is coming? Where?"

"Dante . . . knows about us . . . not happy," she panted, still bringing her breathing under control.

Closing her eyes, she borrowed time she didn't have to collect her words. Marie gripped Judson's biceps as he held her steady, each arm bracing her shoulders. Her gaze found his, and she could see the resonance of their greatest fear coming to the forefront.

"Dante found out about us. He's beyond reasoning and planning to attack the coven tonight, after nightfall," she finally got out.

"We knew this day could come, Marie. It was a risk we took." Judson embraced her quickly, then pulled her back to see her face. "The coven is strong. They can fight back, defend their homes, their lives."

His words were strong, but a current of uncertainty ran underneath.

"But do they want to? It could mean a lot of bloodshed, Judson. Dante has more than just his siblings. There are others—our mother's cousins, their children, and other hunters sympathetic to his argument against magic users, whether good or evil. I couldn't bear it if any of your family—my friends—got hurt or worse." Marie buried her face in her hands, her body racking with sobs once more.

"Shh . . . Marie, it will be okay . . . somehow." Judson tried to soothe her, but fell short.

"What do we do? We have to warn them!"

"Yes, we will warn them. I haven't had the chance to tell you yet . . . many of the coven have already left. We've heard of other covens heading west, seeking better lives—even talk of other supernaturals wanting to live in harmony together. I wanted to be able to approach you about it when there was time to really think if it was something you wanted or not. I mean, your family is all here, and I wouldn't ask you to leave them behind, but it might be an alternative . . ." Judson's face filled with uncertainty. He was unsure of her reaction.

"Judson . . ."

"If you don't want to leave, I'll stay behind. We'll find a way to be together. I know we can." The words fumbled out of his mouth before she was able to finish.

"Judson! I think that's brilliant. Get the witches all to leave, right away. I'll go home and pack. There's no way my family—well, Dante and Isaiah—would let me stay anyway. This might be our only chance to be together. It saddens me, but I feel in my heart it's the right thing to do. Make sure Rachael leaves and doesn't try to stay and be some martyr, please."

Judson answered by picking Marie up and twirling her around, as he favored doing. "I'll go right now and tell them. Go home and pack. It will be a long and arduous journey with many unknowns. Is it safe for you to go home?"

"I'll make sure of it. Dante wouldn't hurt me—at least I don't think he would. Please hurry. I'll meet you in one hour."

Judson pulled her close and took her mouth deeply, passionately, and desperately, as if he might not get another chance—for all they knew, he might not.

Marie pulled out of his embrace, knowing she would never leave his side if she didn't go now. Too much was at stake this night. She had to do what she could to make it right.

CHAPTER 5

"You really love him, don't you?" Rodney asked as he stormed into Marie's room after she had burst through the house, racing to her space. He watched Marie frantically stuff things into a thick cloth bag with handles.

"I do. And I'm leaving with him, Rodney. What Dante is about to do is beyond what it means to be a witch hunter. I know it here." She placed her hand over her heart. Marie then stuffed her bag with some blouses and skirts, a couple cotton dresses, a wool coat and hat, and even a pair of trousers with suspenders she had stolen from one of her brothers long ago. Trousers were much more practical for working outside, and she didn't understand why women weren't supposed to wear them. She topped it off with some undergarments, including wool pantaloons.

"I agree, but I can't stand up to Dante. He can be crueler than you have ever seen." Rodney hung his head in shame and shifted his gaze toward her window.

Marie stopped rushing about the room and stopped in front of her brother. Her eyes held understanding and concern. "I know, Rodney. Come with me," she whispered, suddenly excited with that thought. "You could! Come with me. You would be welcome."

A quick glimmer of something akin to hope flashed across Rodney's eyes, but he quickly shut it down. "I can't. What about Father? And the farm?"

"The others will still be here. Take what you can. Gather supplies . . . what kind, I have no idea . . . whatever you think. You're coming with me. You can start over, have any kind of life you want!" Marie's face lit up with the possibility for not only herself but for her brother, who would never hurt anyone purposefully.

Rodney's face broke with the slightest tip of a smile.

"Really? I could go?" he asked, as if the thought never occurred to him to leave the family and begin his own life—perhaps it hadn't. Their family had once been very close. Over the years, however, things had changed.

Marie nodded, then continued rushing about her room, gathering smaller items such as her brush, some family jewelry she had inherited from her mother, and of course, the family journal she was enraptured with.

"Okay. I'm going with you," Rodney announced more to himself and left her room swiftly, presumably to head toward his own room to pack.

"Hurry, Rodney. Less than one hour," she said, following him out of the room to make sure he heard. He waved, not even looking back at her.

Finally, she was packed with all she could think to take, including a few small family heirlooms, sewing and medicinal supplies, and some blankets. Running down to the kitchen, she opened the side door, then filled a small wooden cart with sacks of grains, flour, sugar, coffee, dried beans, rice, tea, and anything else she thought they would need. After all, she had no idea what their travels would be like. Marie felt giddy inside, like a young schoolgirl with her first crush. Her life was about to change forever, and she couldn't wait to start.

A loud crash came from outside, beyond one of the outbuildings. Shouts echoed to her ears, and her heart sank. Something was wrong. The sun was setting, and the fall of night was fast approaching. She didn't have time for whatever was happening. Marie raced toward the noise and practically smashed into Rodney, a bag strapped around his back. He, too, heard the shouting and dropped his bag next to her supplies. They took off together toward the angry cacophony of voices.

A sight she thought she would never see was laid out before her eyes. Isaiah, LeAnna, some of their cousins—from her mother's side, who only recently had the hunter awakened within them and barely held any control—and Dante all stood around, their father facing off with Dante in the middle. LeAnna looked torn, uncertain where her loyalties truly lay, but unfortunately, it appeared she leaned toward Dante.

"Oh no," Marie gasped with trepidation.

"Father," Rodney breathed in terror.

They both stopped at hearing the strong voice of their father. "Dante, this is wrong, son. You have to know that in your heart, if you still even have one. Your mother never wanted this for you or any of her children. She would turn over in her grave if she knew what you were considering."

Dante's eyes narrowed. He stood rigid and still, the calm before a storm. Without warning, without even an argument, Dante let the strength of his hunter surge to the surface as he hauled off and hit their father in the face, knocking him back into a pile of straw, which broke his fall as he landed on the ground. Stunned silence weighted the air around them all. Dante simply flexed his fist and turned from his father to finish whatever he had been interrupted doing in preparation for his attack. One thing Dante excelled at was planning and strategy. He never rushed into anything. Confidently, he must have felt he had time.

Dante's eyes darted to Marie, who caught his gaze as she ran toward their father. A glint of knowing sparked suspiciously in his eyes. Marie guessed he knew the distraction of helping their father would derail her from her immediate quest. Tears fell from her eyes, acknowledging the truth of what she didn't want to admit herself. She had lost Dante and most likely Isaiah as well. She was pretty sure she knew LeAnna would stay, but the separation still broke her heart. Growing up, they had always had differences and strong disagreements, but in the end, they were still siblings, still family, and they felt that connection. But no longer. Now she had to do what was right—what her mother would have wanted them to do.

"Father!" she cried as she and Rodney ran to him. Rodney helped their father up from the ground and led him back toward the main house. Hank cradled the shoulder he'd landed on. Marie placed her hand gently against his cheek, afraid she would hurt him. His left eye was already purple and so puffy, he could barely open it. Just below, his cheekbone was also blue and green, mottled with bumps—he looked as if he had the mumps. The sight tore at Marie's heart.

"I can't believe he went this far—to strike you, his own father!" Marie sobbed, leaning her head on his good shoulder.

"Let's get you in the house, Father," Rodney said as he took steps painfully slow.

Marie hesitated, just slightly, but enough that Rodney noticed. "You go, Marie. I'll tend to Father. Maybe I can meet you along the way," Rodney said, but they both knew the truth behind his words: if he didn't leave with her, he would never leave.

"Marie, you should go. It would be safer for you. I fear Dante will never stop. I will be fine," her father said through gritted teeth, his face barely able to function properly. "I will miss you, my daughter, and you, Rodney, my boy, but you both need to go."

"How did you know? I was coming to tell you," she asked, baffled by her father's easy acceptance.

"Your boy Judson is a good fella. He came to me awhile back and asked for my permission to ask for your hand, and between the two of us, we decided it should be kept secret. He also spoke of travelers going west, and the decision the witches had made to leave."

"I had no idea."

"Marie, you need to go now," Rodney urged as they slowly walked back to the house, passing their supplies and bags.

Marie's eyes lit with a sudden idea. "Father, you will come with us. After what happened, I don't trust your safety here anymore. The witches can offer something to heal you, I'm sure. Rodney, go pack him a bag quickly. Father, tell Rodney what to pack while I get a few more supplies. I will not take no for an answer."

Hank eyed his daughter and then his son with his good eye. He nodded tightly. "All right. I believe it would be what your mother would want. Although it tears me up to leave behind all our hard work and your family's legacy with this land and this house. We planted tobacco and then grapes, building a lucrative business, with our bare hands and sweat and labor. We've done a mighty fine job."

"Father, you can always rebuild, if you want. We'll find a new place to create a legacy that will hold strong and true to our beliefs for generations to come," Marie preached with passion. Hank gave her the tiniest smile and patted her arm.

"Let's go pack me a bag then, son, shall we? Marie, gather some of the planting seeds, my rifle, and gunpowder." Hank hobbled on his own, but moved slowly as Rodney stayed right at his side, arms out, prepared to steady him if needed.

She nodded and nervously wrung her hands together, knowing her time was growing too short, as darkness had fallen. "Perfect, then we will go."

"Go where?" Dante's voice came from the other end of the house. Marie froze.

"I don't want trouble, Dante. I'm leaving," she said calmly.

"I don't want you to leave. I want you to join me." Dante's voice was cool, almost too cool.

"I will not join you. It's not how I want to live."

"You would dishonor your heritage, the very essence of who you are, your power and all you could be, just to be with the pretend-witch who lives amongst them? To befriend those evil-doers over your own flesh and blood?" Dante stayed still as a statue, stoic in his stance and expression.

"I do not see it the same way, brother. I want to be free to live how I want, and I am not able to do that here." Marie remained calm, her voice steady and unprovoking.

"I see. Then I must follow what I believe and hope you will come to your senses and come back to us, to the rightful Blackstone family.

Do not try to save your witches. You will be in the way." He turned to go, but snapped his head back her way, his eyes fierce with a raging fire of hatred. "I will not allow anyone to get in my way."

Marie's shoulders fell, and she breathed a sigh of relief at his absence. His presence was stronger than it had ever been before. She realized he had been holding his power back until that moment. The knowledge of that was crippling with the understanding of what he had to do to gain that power and further his control. He had to kill witches.

CHAPTER 6

*M*oving fast was a high expectation with Hank injured and Rodney pushing the cart loaded down with supplies. They also gained a few extra tagalongs in the form of some of Marie's cousins who decided they didn't want to follow Dante and feared to stay. Marie finally reached the place she had intended to meet Judson. But Judson was nowhere to be found.

Screams rent the night air, and an urgency in the form of an electric jolt shot through Marie.

"Stay here and hide. I have to find Judson," Marie told Rodney and the rest with her.

"We can help. Let us come with you," the eldest of the teenagers who had joined them pleaded. He was tall and lanky with dark hair and fair skin. Most of her cousins did not have the hunter gene awakened, as they were not directly from her mother Cessily's line. However, if they committed an evil against the laws of nature, their hunter could awaken in a most unfriendly way—such as those who had bonded quickly with Dante and his quest against the witches.

"Fine, but stay together and watch out for Dante and the others. I don't know what we're walking into." Marie paused and looked at each of them closely, examining them. "There are only a couple of you with your hunter awakened, correct?" Caroline, one of her cousins, and the boy, Michael, who had offered to help, both nodded. "Caroline, you are in charge of Uncle Hank, and Michael, you are in charge of the cart. I think if you have a focus, you may be able to control your hunting urges better. We head straight to the smithy to find Judson. Stay to the outskirts of the town. No matter what, stay clear of Dante. Am I understood?"

They all nodded and followed her the rest of the way into the town the Stronghold coven called home.

Nothing looked familiar. Marie paused just at the edge of the town, surveying all before her. Trees and homes were on fire, people were running and screaming from one end, and destruction and devastation were everywhere they looked. This was not the town she had been in just the other day. This was hell.

"Go that way," she yelled to Rodney, pointing her arm in the direction of the blacksmith's forge and hopefully to some sign of Judson. Stumbling over fallen debris and wreckage and breathing through pieces of material covering their faces against the smoke, they finally found the place Judson called home—the blacksmith's forge.

"Judson? Judson!" Marie called, sliding open the large barn door, then running into what really wasn't much different than a small barn with vertical planks of siding and small window slats up high. Pausing inside just long enough to let her eyes adjust to the dim interior, she searched frantically for Judson.

"He's not here, Marie," Rodney said, stating the obvious. His hands gripped each of his suspenders in an awkward manner.

"He has to be!" she shouted back, tears beginning to leak out her eyes, leaving tracks through her smoke-stained face. Angrily, she swiped those incessant tears away from her face.

"Marie?" a male voice whispered, coming from behind a hidden wall they hadn't seen. "Is that you?"

"Judson!" Marie ran to him, and he held his arms open to her.

"I couldn't get away to get to you. I'm sorry. I've been helping others to escape your brother's wrath and sneaking them into the bunker beneath the smithy," Judson explained. Strapped at his side was one of the daggers he had been working on.

Marie sighed a huge breath of relief, elated he was safe. "I was so worried," she whispered in his ear.

"As was I," he returned the whisper and kissed the soft skin just behind her ear.

A throat cleared behind them.

"What do you want us to do now?" her father Hank asked, breaking up their not-so-private moment. Marie blushed and pushed the hair out of her face that had fallen free of her clip as she stepped away from Judson. However, Judson gripped her wrist, not letting her far from his side. To his surprise, Hank gave him a slight nod of approval.

Marie looked to Judson. "How can we help?"

Judson examined each of those with Marie. "There are more of you than I thought, but we should manage just fine. There are several wagons prepared for us, but we can't leave now."

As if on cue, more screams pierced the night, followed by an explosion.

"This way to the bunker. Take what you can in case the worst should happen," he instructed, pointing beyond the wall just behind him. The others quickly followed his direction, down a narrow dirt tunnel that led below the forge into a cavern-like opening filled with other people.

Caroline and Michael paused at the top, clearly hesitant about going below to a confined space filled with witches. Marie gripped them each by their shoulders and turned them to face her. "You can do this. I believe in you completely. Stick together and focus on something simple, like helping someone. One of the witches should be able to offer a spell to help you, as they have for me when I come to visit."

They both took deep breaths and nodded, renewed by Marie's faith in them. Mission in mind, they quickly followed the others down.

"Judson, where's Rachael? And Sarah? Have you seen them? Did they get away?" Marie's voice took on a hint of panic and concern for her best friend.

Judson shook his head. "I haven't seen them. Sarah was waiting for everyone to leave before she left . . ."

"Of course, what else would a leader do?" Marie replied exasperatedly. She understood, but in that moment, she wished they had been selfish and got away. "I have to find them."

Determined, Marie turned to the barn door.

"Wait," Judson stopped her. "Take a weapon." He walked over to a wall with a lock on the edge of it. Judson slid a long skeleton key, strapped to his wrist with a piece of leather, into the lock. It popped and whirred with the sound of some mechanism giving way. Marie's jaw dropped.

"How did I not know about this?" She watched as the false wall split in two and flipped over with the help of some sort of clockwork pieces and cogs working together. With a puff of steam, the new side of the wall came to a halt, revealing multiple pieces of weaponry. Each was beautiful in its own right, with perfect metalwork, shining blades, and sharp edges. She gasped, eyeing all the weapons, from swords to daggers to maces and other types she didn't even know what to call.

"Pick one quickly," Judson instructed with a small smile, obviously pleased with her reaction.

"I'm not surprised, but did you make these?" she asked with wonder.

"I did."

"They're beautiful, Judson, really. Pick one for me?"

Judson reached forward and selected a slim dagger with a blackened handle, leading up to a darkened silver hilt covered with an elaborate design made of intricate metalwork. Marie's eyes grew wide, and her mouth opened in awe, ticking up at the sides to reveal a pleased smile.

She clapped her hands together and nodded. "It's perfect!"

Judson smiled. "Let's go."

She placed her hand on his arm to stay his movement. "No, I'm going alone. It's not safe, especially for you. I can move faster with my hunter speed if I don't worry about you keeping up with me. Don't be offended, Judson. It's just the way it needs to be. You have a job to do here. Keep them safe." She pointed to the bunker behind the wall.

"I'm not offended. I've known all along who you are and what you are capable of. I believe in you and will keep your family and mine safe. Just hurry and be careful." He kissed her on the tip of her nose and moved away, allowing her to go and do what she needed to do, trusting she was capable to achieve it and come back to him.

Marie did not tarry, but gingerly tiptoed out into the dark night lit only by the fires still blazing in some structures. As the night burned on, the flames began to dwindle. Though she didn't need the light because of her excellent hunter's vision, the fires provided extra shadows, which helped to conceal her. She lunged from structure to tree and then from tree to alternate structures, using whatever was left standing to help shield her. Voices rang out in the distance, hoots and hollers that she could identify as some of her relatives—it broke her heart to think of what they could still be doing to any witch they found alive.

Finally arriving at the Stronghold house, Marie dashed in the back door, which was hanging askew, off its hinges. Glass was shattered on the wooden planked floor. At the least, a struggle had happened, but what else, she couldn't determine.

"Sarah?" she dared whisper when the house was otherwise silent. Marie tiptoed through each room. "Rachael?"

Marie stopped. The sound of a boot scuffing on wood caused her to pause. Straining, she listened for which direction to go. Again off to her right, from a small darkened closet, she heard stifled sobs.

"Sarah? Rachael?" she tried again.

"Marie?" a broken voice whispered back. The door slowly opened to reveal Rachael, her hair matted and disheveled, her eyes red and swollen from crying, and cradled on her lap was her mother's head.

"Oh, Rachael," Marie mourned for her. Sarah obviously was dead, with her neck at an odd angle and her eyes open but unseeing. Marie moved slowly forward and gripped Rachael's hand while she gently closed the lids of Sarah's eyes.

"It's time to go, Rachael. They could come back," Marie quietly prodded.

Rachael shook her head adamantly. "No, no, no, I can't leave her. She died protecting me and others. I can't leave her here." She broke and sobbed so violently, her shoulders shook.

"Rachael, don't let her sacrifice be in vain. She protected you so you could lead her people . . . your people, the Stronghold Coven. You have to come with me now." Marie pushed her friend more than she wanted to. She wanted nothing more than to let her grieve and bury her mother in the place of their home, but it couldn't happen. Tears silently flowed down Marie's face as she helped pull her best friend away from her mother, away from every happy moment of her childhood and her home into an unknown and uncertain future.

Sadly and quietly, they made their way back to the forge and into the hidden bunker unseen.

$\sim$

THE NEXT MORNING, just as dawn approached, Marie stirred everyone who had finally and safely fallen asleep. Judson returned to the bunker after having scoped out topside, accompanied by several other men who hadn't been with them the night before.

"It's safe to go, but we need to go now. The wagons are waiting for us just outside. We need to put some distance behind us before next nightfall," Judson urged as he helped others gather their items. "These men are drivers who will be traveling with us. They brought the wagons."

One by one, they emerged from the smithy and out into the rising sun. The sight that greeted them was one that would forever be etched in their hearts and memories. Homes destroyed. Smoke still rising from the dying coals. Bodies of those unfortunate to have not found safety in time. Pure devastation. Judson helped by ushering them along into the wagons, not to linger, not to stare. Everyone moved somberly, and quietly they loaded all they had left into the multiple covered wagons pulled by two horses each. One wagon was devoted simply to crates and sacks of supplies as well as personal belongings. Cries were heard, but no one spoke until the last was loaded.

Marie reached for Rachael's hand before they loaded and gave Rachael an encouraging nod to speak to her people.

"Say goodbye, for this is the last we will see of this place. We move forward into the unknown, into the light of a new dawn, untainted by the evil of our past, into a future with new possibilities for us. For we are the Stronghold witches traveling with friends, and we will be strong." Rachael offered Marie a small smile, looking every bit the leader her mother always knew she could be. Marie couldn't have been more proud of her friend, knowing the pain she experienced underneath it all. "Many could point fingers and hope to blame and seek revenge upon those who we call friends because of their relations' sins, but know this: as of this very moment, they are under coven protection and considered ours."

Rachael stared each and every one of her people in the eyes to ensure they understood her message—mess with Marie and they mess with her. Marie's heart warmed while at the same time it broke, knowing what happened to them was her family's fault.

"For what it is worth, I am not my siblings, and my heart breaks alongside yours. I am truly sorry for what has befallen you and yours." Marie bowed her head, hoping they heard the authenticity in her words. Judson came to her side and laced his fingers within hers and kissed her temple.

"Time to go!" Judson announced as he helped Marie up into their wagon right after Rachael. The drivers flicked their wrists, jostling the reins of the horses, and off they went, putting the darkness of the town and the rising light of the day behind them as they traveled west.

CHAPTER 7

ARKANSAS ~ SUMMER 1851

*D*ays on the wagon trail were monotonous at best; one, two, three days soon turned into weeks. Sometimes they stopped only for one night, but other stops turned into settling for several days —even weeks and months—at a time, enough to give their backsides as well as the horses a break. Each stop only stoked the desire within their souls to continue west.

"Judson?" Marie asked one night as they sat around the fire, cooking a rabbit stew. He looked up lovingly at her, and she felt heat crawl up her chest. The man had a way of turning her insides into mush with a single look. "How will we know when we reach the place to be our new home? It seems we have been traveling for so long already."

The wagons were circled up around them, creating a barricade from the wind, allowing their fire to thrive in its shelter, and protecting them all from the elements and other dangers. Around the fire, they had placed several old logs to use as benches. Sitting upon them were those traveling with Marie and Judson: her brother Rodney, her father Hank, Caroline and Michael, and some of the other tagalongs they had adopted, as well as a few of the witches, who huddled next to Rachael. The days were quite warm to travel, but the evenings were chilling with early autumn breezes. The rolling green hills were beautiful during the day, and at night, they set the backdrop for the night's glory to unfold above them.

Roasting a piece of rabbit on a stick, Judson methodically rotated it for an even cook as if it was second nature to him.

"We will follow our hearts and our intuition." Judson patted his heart then his head. Marie glanced at Rachael, who nodded at his statement.

"And what of the rest of the Stronghold coven who left before Dante struck?" Marie asked hesitantly.

"We have several items of theirs to help locate them on the journey. We will find them," Rachael answered confidently.

Marie looked behind them in the opposite direction from the wagons and took note of the specialized tents they were given by the witches. Each tent was equipped with metal rods, which unfolded in segments, connecting together to provide a structure similar to teepees, then surrounded by thick leather stitched together to create "walls." On the outsides, where each end of the leather met, a large clasp held them together; the mechanism reminded Marie of the inside of a clock. When one pulled the lever, it made a ticking sound and then a click, which released the hook on the opposite end of the leather, allowing one to enter the tent and then reconnect it on the inside, even lock it for the semblance of privacy.

In the distance, a coyote howled, and a shiver ran up Marie's spine.

"I wonder where Dante and the others are?" she whispered for only Judson's ears. "Do you think they are looking for us?"

"I pray they are not," was his only reply.

"Many times while we've been traveling or after we stop, sometimes I get the faintest feeling of another hunter or that we're being watched. We can't let our guard down where he is concerned."

"Tonight, let's have Rachael and a couple of the others do an extra protective spell around the campsites," Judson suggested.

Marie nodded her agreement. "I'll ask her after dinner."

~

JUST AS DINNER HAD ENDED, one of the drivers, Butch, pulled out a well-loved five-stringed guitar and began to softly strum. Several people gathered around him and the fire to listen to the melodic tune as it floated up to the glittering dark sky above. Some men carved shapes and designs into sticks and pieces of wood to pass the time, a few of the women worked on hand-stitching pieces of fabric together to create more blankets for the coming cold, and Judson tinkered on some delicate metalwork inside his tent. Marie reached for Rachael's hand and pulled her over near one of the wagons for a semi-private conversation.

"How are you doing since . . . ?" Marie asked cautiously, concerned for her friend. Rachael was usually full of life and joy, but since they'd left and her mother had died along with many others from her coven, she had grown sullen and quiet.

"I'm making do, Marie." She sighed and gave her friend a small sad smile. Marie squeezed her hand. "I know the coven needs me, so I'm trying to get my heart and my head figured out."

"Give yourself time, Rach. You've all been through a lot, and your coven is dealing with it all still, as well."

"I know." Rachael gazed back at the fire, toward the remainder of her coven who hadn't left before Dante struck, and sighed again, shifting her gaze to her shoes. "I don't think they are going to accept me like they did my mom. My magic has always been a little different. They humored me while Mother was training me, but now . . . I'm not so sure." Rachael shrugged dejectedly.

"That's not true. They will love you. Right now, they're watching you to see how you respond to this tragedy, to see if you're strong enough to lead them—which you are, you just don't know it yet."

Rachael let out a brief laugh of disbelief.

"You are going to lead them into their destiny, and they will respect you for it," Marie continued, unfazed by Rachael's sarcastic sound.

"I don't know about that, but thanks, Marie. I appreciate you trying." Rachael gave Marie a quick hug.

"Before you go back to the fire," Marie started, "I think I've felt hunters." She held up her hands in a placating gesture. "Before you panic, whoever it is is not close, and I felt it a ways back. But just in case, Judson and I thought it best to ask if you can add an extra layer of protection tonight when you work your spells."

With hands on her hips and her head cocked to the side, Rachael raised a brow in attitude. "First of all, I have never panicked on you. Secondly, I have always known being your friend came with risks and have accepted them wholeheartedly, just as you have accepted my coven."

"There's my Rachael back." Marie giggled.

"But yes, I will add to the spell tonight. I'm even going to bring in some of the other witches to help." She paused, uncertain her decision was right after what they had been through. "Yes, that's what I will do. I am not going to hide things from them. They knew traveling would have its risks, and if we are to be a strong team, we need to be honest and work together." Rachael nodded decisively.

"Good plan," Marie agreed. "Thank you."

"No problem." Rachael hesitated, then added, "What do you think of the new men who joined us at our last stop?"

Marie frowned, then remembered. "Do you mean the Ahusaka brothers, the native shifters?"

"Yes, I haven't been around many shifters before. Mother had a few contacts who were wolf shifters, but their magic felt different than the brothers' magic does. They keep pretty much to themselves. Do you think we can trust them?"

"I haven't had many dealings with them either, but there is kindness in their eyes. I think we can," Marie answered. "Plus they're easy on the eyes, don't you think?"

"I suppose so, though I haven't noticed much," Rachael said, pretending to be haughty. But Marie knew if it weren't so dark, she would see a blush creeping up her friend's neck.

"Well, I'm not looking, but if I were, I think they are quite nice to notice."

Rachael giggled under her breath, knowing what her friend was after. "Well, I'll let you know if I do—notice that is."

"Sounds like a plan. Let's get back to the evening festivities. I need to check on Judson."

"I saw him enter your tent. I bet he'd allow you to observe how nice he is to notice," Rachael said in a teasing manner.

Marie laughed. "You need to work on your suggestive phrases. That could have been so much better."

Rachael laughed in return, then looped her arm through Marie's as they walked back to the group, sauntering with lighter steps than they had started with.

MARIE WOKE in the morning to find the sleep sack next to her empty. She stretched her body and felt it pull deliciously in places that made her ache for Judson again and again. He was her match in every way, and she couldn't imagine her life without him in it, which made his absence even more of a disappointment this morning.

She rose to find him speaking with a small group of men from their camp—a mixture of witches, the Ahusaka brothers, her father Hank, and the drivers of their wagons.

"Now what is going on?" Marie said to herself as she fastened their tent entrance back up, then headed to the group.

Smoke still drifted from the mostly burnt logs left over from the fire the night before, lifting into the rising dawn of the chilled morning. She could hear others stirring in their tents, preparing to come out to begin chores for breakfast. They had discovered the easiest way to work with everyone was to split chores and rotate them, so everyone pitched in and no one felt burdened with the bulk of responsibilities.

"Morning, everyone," Marie chirped, joining the group just as Rachael joined from the opposite side. The sun was just barely peeking above the plateau and the sounds of the nearby gurgling creek set the stage for a lovely day. Unfortunately, she had a feeling their meeting was anything but lovely. "What's going on? We haven't even had coffee yet."

Judson reached for her and pulled her to his side, tenderly kissing her temple. "Morning," he whispered in her ear, causing her to giggle before remembering they had an audience, and then she blushed.

"Do not be ashamed of your love," the older of the Ahusaka brothers, Alo, admonished. "It is always a joy to find love. It brings hope to all here." He gestured out toward the cluster of tents.

"Thank you." Judson acknowledged him with a nod.

"You are welcome, Atsidi," he returned with a slight incline of his head. Atsidi, Judson and Marie had learned, was their word for a blacksmith, and he recognized Judson as such.

"One of the brothers spotted a group traveling north of us," one of the drivers said, changing the subject.

"Is it the group we are hoping to meet up with? The other Stronghold witches?" Rachael asked, jumping in the conversation. They all turned to her as if just noticing she had joined them. Ahote, the youngest of the brothers, kept his gaze on her longer than the rest of the group as the driver answered her question.

"No, we do not believe it is."

Cetanwakuwa, the middle brother, confirmed his belief. "Alo felt darkness around them."

The Ahusaka brothers had explained when they first arrived that they were bird shifters—hawks to be precise. Each had additional gifts in addition to the shifting ability. Alo was the spiritual guide, a shaman to some. Ahote was a wanderer, but would argue it was his nature and not a gift at all. Cetanwakuwa was a fighter, and they called him the "attacking hawk" when speaking of him.

"Are we threatened by this group? Do we need to move on?" Marie asked.

"That's what we were discussing, whether it was time to move or if we should hold still and wait for them to pass farther away from our route," Judson explained.

"Could it be Dante? I don't think I could feel him that far away."

Judson and Marie had explained the situation, to those not aware, of Dante and the rogue hunters. Alo shook his head, his long black hair falling in front of his face as he did so.

"It does not feel like you." He turned his head toward Rachael. "It feels like you—magic users—but it is dark and harmful," he elaborated.

"Okay, so we've got some black magic users, dark witches, on our trail . . . literally. The question is, do they know we are here?" Marie shuddered at the thought.

CHAPTER 8

*a*fter much debate, the group decided to stay for a little longer. The motion of the caravans and the dust they kicked up during the day ultimately could have been more of a beacon announcing "come to us, we're over here" than they wanted. Lying low potentially could provide more protection as long as the dark witches kept on their current traveling path. After breakfast, they doused the fires, hoping to rid the sky of the smoke announcing their presence, and no one was allowed to make loud noises or play music. Perhaps they were overreacting, but they didn't want to take any chances of stirring up trouble.

"This is not ideal," Rachael complained as she and Marie took buckets down to the stream. They wandered a short walk through a forested area that brought Marie a smile; the air was invigorating. She hoped where they ended up settling would have beautiful scenery and flowing water even better than this place.

"No, it's not. But they were right—we're not ready for any kind of attack," Marie said with frustration. "We have witches and hunters and hawks . . . we should be prepared to face anything that might come our way. We should not cower in fear and hide, but at the same time, I understand. We have young ones with us too, and we don't need the trouble right now."

Dipping the buckets into the cool, shallow stream, they filled them.

"Why don't you train them then? Get them ready?" Rachael asked innocently.

"Me? What about you? You can work with the witches to come up with defensive and offensive spells, if necessary."

Rachael backed off. "Touché. They won't listen to me yet. I can feel they're not ready."

"Maybe you need to tell them that they're ready. Did you think of that? You can't coddle them. This is not the time or place for that. They will have time to nurse their scars when we settle, but not now."

Rachael sighed. "You're probably right. I'll come up with a list of spells and see how that goes over."

"Good girl!" Marie flicked a small splash of water at her friend. Rachael sucked in a deep, harsh breath.

"That is so cold!" Rachael retaliated with a slightly larger splash at Marie, who giggled and grabbed her bucket and ran back to camp, away from her friend who followed behind.

AFTER NIGHTFALL, the camp was quiet as everyone retired to their tents. Marie tossed fitfully and turned in her sleep sack while Judson slept soundly beside her. Something pulled at her subconscious, an itching . . . an unpleasant feeling deep in the pit of her stomach she hadn't felt before, but had wondered about ever since she first read her ancestors' journal. Quietly, Marie slipped her traveling dress and her boots on, but left them unlaced, grabbed her shawl, and slipped out of their tent. Just enough chill in the night air had her wrapping herself with the wool shawl she was now grateful to have grabbed.

Marie tiptoed her way through the camp and around the wagons until she was able to peer into the dark night and the vast expanse of dirt laid out around them. Not much could be seen except the amazing array of twinkling stars against the black backdrop of the night sky and the occasional firefly still buzzing about before it retired for the night. The sight took her breath away each and every time she had the privilege of seeing it. Marie inhaled deeply and slowly, calming her nerves. Her intent wasn't even clear to her, but she knew the sick feeling in her stomach had something to do with the band of witches traveling parallel to them. She just needed to know what they were up to.

Stepping beyond the shelter of their campsite, heading toward an outcropping of tall boulders, she stopped dead in her tracks when a tall shadow emerged from the tree line not far from her.

"Going somewhere in the night, miss?" a deep male voice asked with somewhat broken-sounding English. "It is dangerous out there. Wild animals and more."

Marie's breath caught in her throat, and her heart pounded so hard it was about to burst from her rib cage. Not until the man stepped away from the shelter of the trees and into the glow of the moonlight was she able to recognize which of the Ahusaka brothers he was.

"Oh, Alo, you frightened me," Marie breathed heavily, placing her hand upon her heart as she attempted to catch her breath.

"Apologies, ma'am." Alo tipped his head toward her, but didn't move any closer. An awkward silence descended between them. He didn't press her any further, but she felt she owed him an explanation to answer his first question. Knowing Alo the little she did, he probably already had an idea of where she was off to. He had a way about him that suggested he knew much more than he let on about everyone and everything. It was slightly unnerving, but he had never done anything to suggest he was a danger to their group; quite the contrary, in fact.

"I have a strange feeling. I believe it's related to the other travelers you spotted earlier," she admitted freely.

Alo nodded thoughtfully. "With your gifts, I can understand. You cannot go out there on your own. I gave my word to your Atsidi to watch over this camp and you. I will not allow it on my watch."

Slightly deflated and slightly relieved at not having to sneak around, Marie nodded with understanding.

"I won't get you in trouble, Alo. It just bothers me I don't understand what it is I'm feeling yet." Marie rubbed one forearm, then the other.

"Trust your instincts, and they will guide you," Alo directed in a voice full of wisdom. His brothers had referred to him as a shaman or a spiritual guide, so she took his instruction to heart.

"Thank you. Good night," Marie said as she turned and went back to her tent. She couldn't shake the feeling that something bad was happening, but somehow believing in herself allowed it to move to the background of her mind for the rest of the night.

CHAPTER 9

Days had passed with much the same routine as the ones before, and no trouble had arisen from the band of witches who traveled parallel to where they were camped. Rachael practiced her magic at the edge of their campsite, between large boulders and the stream to shield her and give her privacy. However, Marie couldn't help notice a certain Ahusaka brother who watched from higher up on the cliff of one of the plateaus, overlooking where she practiced unaware. Ahote seemed to study Rachael, and perhaps he was simply curious in a witch's magic, but Marie saw something much deeper in his eyes.

"Judson?"

"Hmm?" Judson didn't look up from the work table he had crafted out of two barrels and a fallen log he had split on both sides to make flat for his use. Marie moved closer to him to inspect what he worked on.

"Have you noticed how Ahote watches Rachael? I think he might have feelings for her." Marie tested her theory on him. Judson glanced up at Marie, and she nodded to where Ahote sat curiously on the cliff. Judson's gaze followed hers.

"Perhaps he does. Do you have thoughts against that?" he asked.

"No, just wondered what you think. If she likes him in return, I see no harm. I just care for her and her well-being."

"I know you do, as do I." Judson turned back to his project, unconcerned.

"What are you working on so intently?" Marie crossed her arms and bent forward to look closer.

Judson's face turned toward Marie. He was lit up like a star, his smile reaching his eyes—the excitement he showed couldn't be contained. "It's for you! Well, I actually already gave it to you, but I've refinished it."

"What is it?" Her own excitement mirrored his as she bounced on her toes and clapped her hands.

Reverently, Judson held out his flattened palms, where his pet project these last days rested—a small dagger, the edges blackened within the blacksmith's fire. The shiny blade held an inscription in Latin, and intricate metalwork decorated the front of the hilt. Marie gasped.

"It's the dagger you gave me before we left. You fixed the mangled metalwork. Oh! It's the same design from my family journal! How did you replicate it?" Marie asked in shock and a bit of awe.

Judson's face held a sheepish expression he rarely showed, and he hesitated.

"What? What is it, Jud?"

"I wanted to tell you earlier, but I wanted to see if I could remake it first. My mother gave it to me before she left for the northern coven where her relatives lived. She said it had come to her from Sarah's mother, who had asked her to keep it safe and hidden. My mother told me it had belonged to hunters who had given it to her as a symbol of their vow to protect and not hunt the coven."

Marie's eyes grew wide as she listened to Judson's tale, even though they refused to leave the dagger he had placed into her own hands.

"I hadn't thought much more about it, other than it being an interesting dagger I was drawn to, but when I saw the design on your journal, I knew they were connected—items in partnership. It was in rough shape—some of the metal pieces were bent out of shape or broken, the blade had dulled over time, and it needed care and attention. I gave it some," he said proudly and puffed out his chest.

"Indeed you did. It's beautiful. This colorless stone in the center is amazing and truly unique. What does the phrasing mean?" She pointed to the words inscribed horizontally on the blade from tip to hilt.

"*Elige tibi*. It means 'Choose yourself,'" he translated.

"That's amazing. Thank you!" Marie reached up and pulled him closer to her by placing her hand behind his neck. She leaned her forehead against his and simply rested against him, sharing the air between them. "I love it, and I love you."

Then she kissed him softly and tenderly on the lips, but before he could take the kiss deeper, the sound of a hawk's cry pierced the sky, and they startled apart.

"It's Cetanwakuwa. That's a warning someone is approaching our camp," Judson explained as he grabbed Marie's hand and pulled her after him. "Hold onto your dagger, Marie. We don't know what kind of danger approaches."

Judson and Marie reached the edge of the wagon circle. Men stood around, hoping for a nonchalant appearance, but each one held a rifle or another weapon—some more inconspicuous than others—from Judson's weapons cache that he had brought with them. Marie's brother Rodney and her father Hank were among them, looking just as fierce, comfortably holding their rifles as any with metal weapons.

"What's the trouble?" Judson asked the men out front.

"Wagon headed this way," Marie's cousin, Michael, stated, signaling off in the distance just beyond the gathering of rocks standing as pillars.

A cloud of dust kicked up, announcing the visitor before the wagon even came into view. It didn't move fast, but clipped along at a steady pace, allowing them a few minutes to breathe and prepare before their guest arrived. Several of the witches strategically arranged themselves behind the wagons and sent the younger ones into one of the tents with an extra protection spell. The male witches were less common than the women from the Stronghold coven, but the ones who were skilled in their magic hid in a few of the covered wagons, watching carefully. Presenting a fairly large welcome party, Marie stood just behind a large wagon wheel, waiting to get a read on who approached them. She didn't have offensive powers like the witches, but what she did have she would use if the time came.

"It comes," Ahote said from where he leaned against one of the large wagon wheels off to the side from everyone else. He crossed his legs at his ankles and folded his arms, but kept his head up and his eyes trained on the approaching wagon.

Marie shook her arm with the familiar tingling she would get when visiting the coven.

"Witch," she whispered.

The wagon slowed to a stop not far from where they all stood. The wagon itself—pulled by only one horse—was smaller than one of their traveling ones and shaped more like a rectangle with cut outs for windows and a railing on the back of a platform from which stairs could be pulled down. On the side of the box were words in a fancy script, advertising tonics, potions, lotions, and spells. It appeared they were dealing with a traveling salesman looking for his next pitch.

However, the man in the driver's seat looked like anything but a salesman. Slumped over, he barely held the reins for the horses. His hair was disheveled and matted. The clothing he wore was tattered and singed. As Alo approached, the horse reared back, a hint of madness in his eyes and foaming at the mouth.

"Whoa!" Alo called to the beast. He then spoke in a soothing tone in his own language, and the horse slowly calmed down. Alo grabbed the reins and pulled the horse to a stop.

Judson and Rodney were the first to reach the wagon while others raised their rifles, ready for anything.

"Is he okay?" Marie shouted.

Most couldn't hear what the men were saying, but Marie heard them trying to get information from the man, who appeared to be barely conscious. What she did hear from his garbled words was that his camp had been attacked in the night. He barely got away and didn't know if any of his people were alive. He came looking for help. Marie ran up to the wagon next to Judson.

"Who attacked you? Do you know?" she asked with a slight panic in her tone. Fear gripped her heart.

The man raised his head and looked at Marie. His eyes widened and his face flinched.

"You. His eyes looked like yours do," the man said with fear in his voice. He pointed a shaking finger in her face. "You're one of them, aren't you? You're a witch hunter!"

Marie gasped and stumbled back to the ground, away from the man and the wagon. Her fear was realized: Dante. Dante had attacked them. Guilt gripped her heart. She wondered, if she had been able to follow her gut feeling the other night, whether she could have warned those witches.

"You're safe now." Rodney tried to soothe the man.

"Not safe. You have a hunter in your camp," the man said with a sudden renewed energy as he sat up and gripped the reins out of Rodney's hands. "I will save myself."

The hawk overhead screeched once more and dove from high in the sky down toward the wagon, now pulling out from their camp. The man shouted at the top of his lungs, "They will come for you, hunter! And take out everyone with you, you and all your abominations! We won't let more of our people fall to your kind again."

The hawk dive-bombed the driver, attacking as he chased him away from the camp.

"Come back, Cetan," Alo whispered to his brother as if he could hear him all the way up in the sky. Maybe he could, because the hawk stopped attacking and circled back toward the camp.

Marie and the entire camp stood in stunned silence. Her brother most likely killed that other band of witches—good or bad witches, she didn't wish her brother's wrath upon anyone.

CHAPTER 10

"I think it might be time to discuss moving on to a new location," Rachael brought up later that day when they were gathered around the fire, preparing the evening meal.

Marie knew she needed to be grateful for fresh food while they were able to find it, but she was tired of the fish from the stream, the rabbit she had to pick out buckshot from, for fear of cracking her teeth, and the random bits of fur clinging to the occasional elk. Once they were back on the trail, they would only have available the breads they had been making while camped and the beans, rice, and jerked meats that wouldn't spoil along the way.

"I think you might be right," Marie responded reluctantly.

"We were going to wait a few days longer, but it won't make much difference." Judson shrugged.

"I'm not excited about getting back in the wagons, but I feel something bad might happen if we don't," Michael said, fidgeting uncharacteristically with his hands.

"I agree," Marie said with certainty. "That man in the wagon said they would come for us, but he also said he wouldn't allow for more of their people to fall to my kind—the hunters. Dante. He had to have been speaking of my brother, Dante. Which means he's out there somewhere and perhaps not far from us. I don't want to risk any of you by staying in one place too long."

Judson reached for her hand and laced his fingers with hers. She squeezed his in return.

"I think we all echo that sentiment. Sounds like it's time to pack up," Hank said with a discouraged tone that caused them all to glance his way. He nodded decidedly despite his tone, but added a small smile. Marie knew anytime Dante was brought up, her father felt like he had failed somehow. She went over and leaned against her father's healed shoulder and allowed him to wrap his arm around her own.

"He made his choices, Father."

"I know, but it doesn't make it any easier for a parent," he said softly.

"Then it's settled," said Butch, one of the drivers of the lead wagon, to all present. He was a no-nonsense man in his late sixties with skin leathered by time and the great outdoors. Butch had traveled with the wagons on several different occasions and knew the route better than anyone with them, so he called the shots when it came to traveling. His plan was to get them west to their destination, then head back east to start another wagon train all over again. His life was the trails. Butch wasn't bothered by the witches and other supernaturals who traveled with them. He himself was a bit of a mystery, but was indeed not wholly human. Then, in a much louder voice perfect for herding cattle, he yelled, "Round 'em up! We leave at daybreak!"

ROLLING hills of green dotted with hints of gold, separated by rivers and lakes, was a landscape worthy of traveling through. After being on the trail for a couple days with only brief stops, trying to gain as much ground as the caravan could, they had reached the Ozark Mountains, where they needed to turn north to reach Independence, Missouri.

"Judson, how far out are we from Independence?" Marie asked as their wagon bumped along a rugged section of the trail. She and Judson had opted to drive one of the wagons for the day, which allowed them some time to themselves, at least until someone came up and joined them from the back.

"A couple days still, I believe. My navigation skills with the landmarks and stars is not near what Butch's ability is. I think he has some kind of magic for it, if you ask me."

"How long will we stay in Independence?"

"It will depend on whether the others from the coven are there or we have to wait on them. It was their plan to reach that far. It will also depend on our route and where we want to spend the winter. It could be quite dangerous to travel near the Rocky Mountains during the peak of winter. Plus, there are supplies in Independence, so we will take some time and make sure we have enough gunpowder, food, and supplies, and most likely trade some of the mules and horses in for oxen."

Marie's forehead scrunched as she thought through his words. "Why would we want oxen instead of horses? Aren't they slower?"

"Yes, but there have been rumors of the Comanches and Apaches attacking those traveling through parts of those areas. The trail has been protected by the government, but we don't want to risk it either. I don't know if the addition of our Ahusaka brothers would be an asset or an obstacle if we came across any intent on attacking us."

"But why the oxen?"

"Oh, right." Judson trailed off as he adjusted the reins in his hand, steering the horses back to the center of the trail. "It's said they are attacking for the horses and mules. And those with oxen seem to get left alone." He shrugged, uncertain of the truth of it.

Marie scooted closer to him and placed her hand on his thigh, laying her head on his shoulder. She sighed contently just to be with her man on such an epic adventure. Judson turned his head and placed a simple but tender kiss on the top of her head. Marie bumped and jostled with every rock they hit and every hole they rolled into. She giggled, unable to keep her head still, so she lifted it.

"I hope when we arrive wherever it is we're going, we can build a home where we can grow old together and raise a family in the safety and peace of our new life together," Marie said dreamily, gazing up at the beautiful blue sky that was so vast, it reached from one side of the horizon to the other, not a cloud to be seen.

"Mmm, as do I. It is what keeps me going day to day out here in the wild lands—well, that and seeing you and touching you every day, not having to hide my love for you any longer." They sat in companionable silence for a while after that, simply enjoying the time together and seeing parts of their country they had never dreamed of seeing before.

"Oh no! Look! What is that?" Marie leaned forward, pointing off in the distance. Smoke rose into the sky, too far off to see where it came from and too much smoke to have come from a simple fire.

"That's a large fire. I didn't think there were any towns on this route for a day or two yet. I'd better alert the others." Judson let out a high-pitched whistle between his thumb and finger. Then he flicked the reins and shouted a command to order the horse to pick up speed. He directed the horses out of the line of the other wagons to pass along the outside, and made his way to the lead wagon driven by Butch and a younger boy named Dillon, whom they had picked up at one of their stops.

"Butch! See that fire yonder? Think we should check it out?" Judson called from his wagon.

Butch and Dillon both peered over at the pillar of smoke growing steadily larger as they drew closer.

"What was there is probably gone now," Butch said. "But let's make sure no one needs our help."

Judson pulled the reins, slowing the horses down so they could move back into the caravan line where the trail was smoother. As they approached, they could see more of what burned.

"Oh, Judson, it's another traveling caravan like ours," Marie said sadly, looking at the wreckage of what was once probably fifteen or so wagons in a circle with tents scattered around inside it. Marie sucked in a gasp as she gripped her forearms. "Witches, Judson. There were witches here . . . bad ones, if my stomach is any indication."

Marie held her arms across her stomach at the dull residue of whatever black magic had been practiced there. Judson frowned, and his eyes went on sudden alert.

"Do you feel anyone else about?" he asked, his voice low for just her ears.

Marie knew he was referring to Dante and the other witch hunters.

"Do you think this is the camp that man was from?" she whispered to herself, not expecting an answer. But then her question was answered. A tingling erupted behind her neck at the base of her skull, the recognition of another of her kind.

"There's a hunter here," she whispered to Judson. "Turn around. Get the wagons to turn around, now!" she almost shouted, but it was too late.

They were almost upon the still burning circle. Smells of gunpowder, burning flesh, and fear permeated the air enough to make even one with the strongest constitution revolt. Marie kicked herself that she didn't notice the signs sooner. She could have prevented them from being seen. It was possible another hunter could be in the area, but somehow she just knew it was Dante and his group. But why did they wait around?

Judson had given the secret warning signal by way of whistle, and the wagons all took off, away from the campsite and back on their trail, moving faster than advisable, but it was worth the risk to get away fast. Marie's foot bounced nervously, and her hands gripped the edges of the bench seat she shared with Judson until her knuckles turned white. She kept looking back, ensuring herself no one was following them. Marie hadn't seen anyone, but she felt them watching. She knew they were there, but why did they hide? Were they simply sending a message—an abhorrent and heinous message—or were they in the wrong place at the wrong time? Knowing her brother, she was sure it was a message sent directly to her.

Right as Marie was spiraling into guilt that she hadn't stopped Dante already, Alo peeked his head through the wagon tarps separating their seats from the back. "Darkness is in this place. A trap was set to follow you. We must be on alert. Cetan flies above."

Then he slipped back into the back without another word.

"Well, that was ominous," Judson said with a slight nervous chuckle.

Cetanwakuwa would serve as their eyes behind them as they traveled, at least until he needed to come down for a break.

"He's right. I can feel it. This is my fault," Marie said as tears now streamed down her face.

"No, this is Dante's fault. He chose. He could have chosen to live differently just as you did, but he didn't. This is his fault alone, Marie Marcella Blackstone," Judson said with such passion, Marie couldn't help but feel the love in her heart for him swell. She reached for his neck and tugged him to her lips, kissing him with such intimacy, she would have blushed if the others could see her brazenness in public. But right then, she didn't care.

When she pulled away, his eyes were filled with a starry gaze, but he quickly recovered, regaining his focus on driving the wagon. He checked his surroundings and the leads on the horses. He chuckled, then looked over at his wife. "I am proud to be your husband and proud to take on your name, Marie. Don't ever forget it."

She leaned over and pecked his cheek, then allowed him to continue steering.

A hawk circled above and cried out with an eerie call. Cetan. Marie felt a cold chill sweep down her spine and turned one last time to look at the smoke, now lessening the farther they got away. She could still see the outlines of the wagons—or what remained. It was a scene that would forever be etched upon her memory. But the sight of her brothers Dante and Isaiah, stepping out from behind one of the wagons and staring directly at her with hatred, was something else entirely; the sight was something of a nightmare. She gasped and held her heart. The thumping staccato beats were out of control. Fear gripped her as she watched Dante, not for herself but for all those she had grown to love who traveled with her. The promise in Dante's eyes told her this was just the beginning. Not only was he following them, but he was now hunting them.

CHAPTER 11

MISSOURI ~ AUTUMN 1851

*A*rriving at Independence, Missouri, without further incident was a huge relief for Marie. Though she often felt eyes on her, she never saw or felt anyone from Dante's group. Coming into a town after traveling the open trails for so long was refreshing. Marie soaked up seeing people milling about or on their way with purpose. Women strolled by in proper dresses, some with bustles and some with high collars buttoned up to their chins—a far cry from the traveling clothes she had become accustomed to seeing. The men wore top hats and suit jackets covering clean shirts with suspenders attached to proper trousers. Their group had been traveling for so long, they looked a little worse for the wear. Marie couldn't wait to get settled like the folks in this town were and wear clean and proper clothes.

Building after building lined each side of the main dirt road they traveled in on. Businesses such as the mercantile, the bank, a dress shop, a feed store, and many others boasted new goods, welcoming patrons to come and shop. Signs pointed toward the end of the road, toward the forge where they could find gunpowder, ammunition, and the blacksmith. Another sign pointed wagon trains to a large field area, where other wagons were parked. Judson followed the wagon in front of him in that direction.

Days went by, and Marie and her group rested themselves and their livestock. To their happy surprise, the other band of Stronghold witches were already there when they arrived. It was a joyful reunion for families and friends to reconnect and trade stories of their adventures on the trail. Rachael was happiest to have her coven back together.

The men had gone into the town and purchased new goods such as flour, rice, lentils, and beans. They also traded some of the goods they had brought with them from Virginia. The tobacco, homemade wines, and seeds from their garden were favorites. After the horses and mules had time to rest and feed, Judson, Hank, and Butch found ranchers who were looking to trade their oxen. They were almost ready to go.

"It's been so nice to be here, Judson," Marie commented one day, bringing down the clothes from the line. They had been there not much more than a couple months. "But I feel a restlessness in my spirit, a pull to keep going, to find where we belong."

Judson came up behind her, wrapped her in his arms, and held her tight. She giggled and dropped the linens she was folding and leaned back into him. Judson nuzzled her neck. "You smell good, woman."

"I hope so. I got some new lemon soap from a shop in town."

"I like it." He kissed the sensitive crook between her shoulder and neck. His mouth moved slowly and deliciously over her skin. She tipped her head back, baring her neck for him to continue. "I can't wait to find our home, but I know I belong with you no matter where we are."

She turned in his embrace and placed her hands around his neck. Gazing into his beautiful warm brown eyes, she smiled, then stood up on her toes and tenderly brushed her lips across his, teasing him. He groaned.

"We don't get enough time to be alone," Judson lamented.

"And it looks like we don't get that time now either," Marie complained, nodding out toward the road where another train of wagons was entering the town of Independence. She stole one more moment and kissed him fully on the lips, a promise for another time in the future.

"It's a good thing Independence has a vast field for wagons. We seem to be quickly filling it up."

"I sense witches! I had no idea we would find more of them on our journey, not to mention the one group we had already came across. I'll go gather the others," Marie said excitedly and took off to find them.

FOR THE NEXT SEVERAL DAYS, the group became acquainted with the newest band of travelers, which included a coven of witches called the Luna Coven. Marie was excited to get to know all the new faces and to find others with such similar goals. She and Rachael had gone around and introduced themselves to the others. They had met a witch named Anne-Marie Beaumont—and her baby Saundra—who seemed like someone they would both get along with, but possibly might be someone Rachael could really learn from as a witch. Several witch families made up the new caravan, including the Beaumonts, the Bishops, and the Augustines—Raffaele and Priscilla. They were accompanied by a couple of vampire families by the surnames of Petran and Roca, and a few other families Marie could only assume were humans without boldly asking them: the Mills, the Alversons, the Fairchilds, the McFeenys, and the Stuarts. Marie found it overwhelming at first to remember who belonged to whom, as her gifts didn't identify more than witches and witch hunters, but over time she started to figure it out.

"Rachael!" Marie called, spotting her friend heading into the town.

"Marie, there you are! I was hoping I'd find you," she replied. "Come with me into town. I need to procure a few ingredients for a couple spells Anne-Marie and a few of the other Luna Coven witches are going to show me."

"I'm so happy you have someone else to trade spells with." Marie looped her arm inside Rachael's and walked with her.

"Where have you been?"

"I was speaking with the elders of their caravan," Marie answered, but her tone was hesitant and distracted. Of course, Rachael didn't miss anything.

"What's wrong, Marie?" Rachael stopped, twirling Marie around to face her, and pushed her over to a bench under a shop canopy, where they sat.

Marie blanched, and her gaze focused on a horse tied to a post across the road.

"We've discussed joining with the other caravan, but they are hesitant about traveling with us—with me specifically." She sighed, disappointment escaping in the form of a tear she had refused to shed until now.

"*What?*" Rachael asked in outrage. "Are they serious? What reason did they give?"

"I'm a hunter. In their travels, they've heard the Blackstone name, met others who had heard of Dante's destruction," she grumbled. "Much of their band are witches, and I'm a hunter. They have to think of the safety of all their people. I understand that."

"What are we? Buffalo? Shouldn't our history speak for your character? We wouldn't be here if you couldn't be trusted." Rachael crossed her arms in front of her chest in a pout.

"Of course you're not a buffalo, Rach, but they don't know me, and I can understand that," Marie said sadly.

"Well, then we will just need to prove it to them. We have a little more time. I think we may search for a more secluded place to make camp for the winter."

Marie twisted her face in thought. Rachael gripped Marie's hand and squeezed.

"We'll figure this out together. We're a team, you and I. If they can't see the value you bring, then I say we go on without them. We've come this far, and we can find our own place to settle."

Marie turned and fiercely hugged her friend. "Thank you, Rach.

We are a team, but I have a dream of the home I might get to have in a place just like the one they're searching for. I'll build my own if I have to, but I'd rather build it with everyone here I've come to know."

"We'll figure it out. Oh! I wanted to tell you. I met the Augustines just now and Mr. Augustine—Raffaele—has the most beautiful ring he wears on his hand. I didn't dare ask, but I can practically feel magic coming from it. It's an elaborate silver setting holding a gorgeous moonstone in the center. Moonstone has tremendous psychic properties!" Rachael practically bounced. She loved jewelry, especially magical pieces.

"I'll have to see it. Come on, let's go get your ingredients. Maybe I can be your spell assistant," Marie said with a small smile and a wink as she tugged Rachael up from the bench.

BACK AT THE CAMPSITE, the women prepared several pots and kettles over three different fire pits, while Ahote and Dillon, the young orphaned witch, built the fires to light underneath them. Marie was concerned the Luna Coven group might not take to the Ahusaka brothers as her group had, but the only ones they seemed suspicious of were Marie and her family.

One of the elders of the other group was a man named Elsmed—a fae—whose appearance was very intimidating. He seemed to watch Marie, peering into the depths of her soul, and maybe he could. Maybe he could decipher if she would fail in her pursuit for a peaceful existence as a hunter. She couldn't live with herself if that was the case. She couldn't fail.

Marie couldn't help but notice a few figures off in the shadows in what seemed to be a heated debate. Bishop. That was their name. She couldn't remember their first names, but she thought they were brothers; or two of them were brothers and one was a father. Though they were a part of the Luna Coven, she couldn't help but feel something dark in them, or in at least one of them. All three whipped their heads in her direction, as if they had been talking about her. Marie couldn't fathom why they would be discussing her unless they were plotting her demise—or she could just be paranoid at this point.

Suddenly, the campsite was stuffy and confining, and Marie felt a panic rise in her chest. She needed to be by herself. She needed to get away from all that was the traveling caravan and people speculating about her when they didn't even know her. Marie clutched her chest and turned back around toward the town. Evening was falling, and she really should have let Judson or Rachael know where she was going, but she had to get out right then.

She ran, not knowing or caring where she was going. Heading behind the businesses, she ran full out until her chest heaved and her breath was cut short. Back home, she used to run like that when she was frustrated, or even just for fun. She hadn't been able to escape like that since home—the home she would never return to.

Her heart hurt a little at that thought. It had been her family home for as long as she had known, and even before then. But home was where you made it and where you let your heart grow. She would find her home and make it something new; she was determined to do so.

Once she caught her breath, she slowly walked a little bit farther toward a barn set apart from the town. The moon rising above it was striking, and Marie moved closer to see the view behind the barn. She hesitated just before reaching it. Was it a good idea to go behind a barn by herself as it was growing dark? No, probably not, but Marie touched the dagger Judson had given her, now strapped at her side, and it gave her a small sense of security. With that in her mind, she slid stealthily around the barn, listening the entire way. At one point, she almost giggled at how absurd she was being. Most likely, there was nothing around the corner but the back of the barn and maybe a wild animal, but she could handle that. However, she wasn't expecting to find what she did.

Behind the barn, between the back wall and a large boulder, stood three figures. Two she couldn't quite make out from her vantage, but one she could. Dillon. The young witch who had joined their caravan months back. Marie's chest hitched. She didn't want to leap to conclusions before she had any facts, but the situation did not present itself well for him.

Marie held her breath and flattened herself against the side of the barn as best she could. She couldn't detect who the others were with him, but that didn't mean they weren't up to trouble. She listened, using her hunter hearing, which was much stronger than her human hearing; she had learned the ability to use each separately to save her sanity from sensitive hearing.

"Where is Dante? Is he here?" she heard Dillon ask in a whisper.

"No, he's waiting at our hiding place. Didn't want to be sensed too soon," another voice, a female, responded to him.

"What's the plan? What should I do?" Again Dillon.

"Do nothing. Keep your nose down. Well into the night in two days' time will be when the witches are at their weakest, and Dante will make his move. The witches' powers will be strained and so will their wards, due to it being the furthest night from both the new moon and the full moon." The second voice, a male, was more commanding.

"Thanks to your information about the wagon train not leaving soon, he will be able to make his move before they can escape him again," the female voice said.

"I get away with a clean start, right? That was the promise." Dillon's voice suddenly took on a tone of doubt. Marie didn't blame him. She wouldn't trust them.

"Don't be there that night. Dante is there to wipe out the witches and take back his family, but anyone who gets in the way will be collateral damage. Do you understand?"

"Understood," Dillon said, his voice weakened.

Marie hoped his decision weighed heavily upon him. She hated that he betrayed them after they had accepted him, the orphan of the group. Her cousin Caroline had taken a liking to him, and that he could betray her like that made Marie even more livid. She waited a few more beats, then turned to leave and sneak back until she was able to run without being heard.

She had to get back to tell the Luna Coven as well as her own people. Whether they trusted her or not, she would warn them, and they would believe her. They had to.

CHAPTER 12

"It could be a trap," the oldest Bishop said in a tone laced with casual indifference, yet with an underlying disgust that Marie would waste their time.

Marie had called a meeting with Anne-Marie Beaumont and asked her to gather the others, and she brought her group's leaders, consisting of Rachael, Judson, her father, Butch, and Alo. From the other caravan, Lawrence Mills, who Marie discovered was a frost dragon shifter, stood with his arms crossed and a tight look on his face as he grumbled something about just trying to get attention.

"It *is* a trap . . . for us!" Marie reiterated to him.

The Bishop—Rodavan she thought his name was—leaned down to her face. "It could be a trap set *by* you."

Marie threw her hands on her hips, ready to battle anyone who not only called her a liar, but also insinuated that she would put her people, her *family* in danger. Judson stood behind her and placed his large hands on her shoulders, steadying her—making sure she didn't throw a punch or two.

"It could," Anne-Marie said, nodding slowly. She was regal—power exuded from her—and she was friendly, but not overly warm, yet there was something about her Marie trusted. "It could, but why would she endanger her own people with whom she has traveled for this long? What is her gain?"

The group was silent for a moment.

"I know I'm biased toward Marie," Judson interjected. "But I also know her brother. He will stop at nothing to accomplish his goal, no matter how insane or absurd it may sound. There is no reasoning and no rationality at this point. I'm afraid his humanity is hanging on by a thread, if at all," Judson said with sensitivity, having Dante's family right next to him.

Butch and Alo went on to explain what they had seen on their travels to Independence, with the black-magic-using witches they had passed and the wreckage and devastation done by Dante.

The conversation went around for many more minutes, and finally Marie was finished. "Look, I know you don't know me, and you don't have any reason to trust me. But trust that I want the home you are looking for just as much as you do, and I will take my people and go out searching for it without you, if that's what you want. If you can't handle my presence—even though *I'm* the one fighting the feelings I get from your power every minute of every day—I understand. You should know the Stronghold coven has gifted us with spells that help control and subdue our hunter drives, but I still make the choice every day to rise above it. Even if we go our separate ways, promise me you will leave this place right away. I couldn't handle having your deaths on my conscience too. There have been too many deaths already."

Marie sighed. Everyone remained silent, contemplating her future or simply listening, so she continued.

"I want Judson and me to have a life, a family, one in which we can live peacefully with all different supernaturals. I want a home where generations of Blackstone witch hunters come after me, and I can leave the legacy of what it can mean to be a hunter without the actual hunting. So that's me. And we will be leaving in the morning. I hope you all will join us. I have enjoyed getting to know you and would never forgive myself if anything happened to you."

Marie stepped back and gripped Judson's hand, turning them both to leave.

"Wait," Anne-Marie called to her. Though her face was serious, a slight twitch of her mouth gave Marie the feeling she was impressed. "The Luna Coven and those joining us will discuss everything you have told us and come to our decision in the morning. Thank you for coming forward. I trust your people have the ability to deal with the traitor in your midst?"

Marie's throat bobbed as she gulped, but she nodded nonetheless. They had ways of dealing with traitors; she had just hoped to never need them.

"It will be taken care of," Butch announced, but the sadness in his eyes told Marie he had grown fond of the kid and was feeling the sting of betrayal heavier than most.

Marie and those with her left the meeting and went to pack up what they could in the dark. The rest would wait until morning. However, Dillon couldn't wait. They didn't want him to tip off Dante before they had the chance to leave.

Butch, Judson, Michael, Cetan, and a few others from the Stronghold coven went to restrain Dillon. Marie didn't have the heart or the stomach to "deal" with him, so they agreed to tie him up and leave one of the tents. Rachael came up with a spell and had one of her witches place it upon him so he couldn't yell for help. He would sit there and wait for Dante to show up, leaving him a message of their own.

MARIE, Judson, and everyone available packed up their camp and gathered all their supplies as dawn quickly approached. All except the Stronghold Coven who had been in the other caravan. Rachael came to Judson and Marie with tears in her eyes.

"The coven has decided to overthrow me. Well, they gave me a choice. I could remain with them or not, but they decided to stay and settle in the nearby region. They are finished traveling."

"Oh, Rachael. I'm so sorry," Marie said, gathering her friend in her arms. "What will you do? I couldn't bear to be without you, but I would understand your choice."

"There is no choice. You are my only family left. I go with you. I've already discussed it with Anne-Marie, and she will allow the Stronghold members who choose to go with us to join their coven," Rachael explained.

Marie held her friend out so she could see her eyes.

"Then it is settled. You will become an honorary Blackstone." Rachael giggled, which Marie was aiming for. "Come, we have much to do still."

Anne-Marie Beaumont and a couple Marie had recently met named Mihail Petran and his wife Irina—who Marie learned were a type of vampire called moroi—approached them.

"We will be leaving with you this morning. It is earlier than we had planned for, but the threat to all parties involved is more than we want to risk. We may need to stop for extended stays, depending how fierce the winter is as we head toward the mountains," Anne-Marie informed them.

Irina Petran added in her thick Romanian accent, "Though others may have speculations regarding you, we are willing to give you and yours a chance. However, some in particular—" She paused and cleared her throat. "Some have asked this be on a trial basis. I'm sorry, but it was the best we could do."

"So I just have to prove myself to secure the future we're all dreaming of?" Marie asked. "I could be offended, but it could be worse. I'll take it. I've proven myself most of my life that I could be who I wanted to be—and not who it was dictated to me to be."

Anne-Marie and Irina breathed a sigh of relief.

"Did you expect me to throw a fit?" Marie asked with humor.

"Well, we've seen all types, dear. You never know." Irina chuckled.

"Then let's pack up and depart Independence, Missouri. We have a destiny to find," Marie announced with joy.

~

MARIE HAD DEVELOPED a love for being on the dusty trail as they headed west toward the Rocky Mountains. There was a familiar lulling to the hypnotic rhythm of the wagons—that combined with the hope of a new day dawning gave Marie a feeling of positivity she hadn't known for a while. Things were looking up for her and her family. They would get their new start, and they'd have new friends to accomplish that with. The weather had grown chillier as the fall progressed into winter in the year 1851, and the wagon leaders from both caravans decided to go a little south on the Santa Fe Trail in hopes of a slightly warmer climate, giving themselves more time before they went into the harsh Rocky Mountains. They couldn't get past the feeling drawing them, pulling them, in the direction of the mountains. There was something there—they just weren't sure what it was yet. This trip was about faith, instincts, and a little bit of magic.

Marie had discovered upon dropping in on one of the meetings discussing direction that the witches had a strange little device that looked like a compass, but was bigger and had clock parts that made a ticking sound. She watched in awe as one of the witches performed a spell similar to a scrying spell she had heard Rachael do, and the little device whirred and lit up, pointing in a direction only they could see. It was part of what guided them on their way, and she loved all of it.

This part of the trip was much slower-moving than before—the big oxen simply moved slower than the horses and mules, but a strong sturdiness was apparent in every step they took.

"Oh look at that, Judson," Marie said and pointed out the vast grasslands of the prairie before them.

"It's beautiful," he agreed.

DAYS WENT BY, and finally by late 1851, they found a rare place of shelter amidst the prairie made of a cluster of tall rock monuments made of chalk to circle the wagons and set up camp, just far enough off the Santa Fe Trail to be safe, but still close enough to get back on the trail when weather allowed. Marie was pleased to see the few Stronghold witches who remained mingling with those of the Luna Coven. Rachael seemed happy having other leaders around whom she could share ideas with. Since her mother's passing, she hadn't felt comfortable showing her weaknesses in front of her own coven, though Marie knew them to be an understanding group. After all, they had taken her into their midst and made her feel like family.

"Marie!" Rachael bounded over to where Marie sat on a clay-like boulder. She stretched out on top of a blanket, having experienced the red dust staining her clothing earlier. "What are you doing?"

"I was looking over my family journal again. I can't help but feel like there's more to it. I keep coming across passages mentioning the awakening of the two pieces and wielding the weapon. I thought at first it was referring to uniting my human part with my hunter part—but I don't think it's quite that simple."

Rachael frowned.

"That sounds crazy doesn't it? Maybe I'm just looking for something because I desperately want there to be more to it, more for me to hold on to."

Rachael sat next to her friend and lightly ran her fingers over the leather book cover. "It hums a bit. I can feel an energy pulsing just under the cover. I think you're right," she confirmed with an excited smile.

"Do you know a spell that can unlock it?" Marie sat up straight with renewed anticipation.

Rachael twisted her lips in concentration. She then shook her head. "No, I can't think of anything at the moment, but let me think on it."

"Why can't I feel it?"

"I think because it's infused partially with witch magic. It's not dark, so you wouldn't feel it, right?"

"No, I guess not," Marie conceded.

A scream rang out of nowhere. The thought that Dante and his group had found them shot fear straight through Marie. She and Rachael jumped up and took off toward the sound. People gathered, and some rushed in to get closer, but then the line stopped abruptly. No one moved past it.

"What's going on?" Marie asked Caroline. The girl looked up at her with eyes reminding Marie of her sister LeAnna, and it struck a pain in Marie's heart to know that she may never see LeAnna again.

"Rattlesnake," Caroline said shakily, her eyes wide with fear. "Got one of the cows, I think."

"Everyone clear out. We got a rattler. No one goes near it until it's dealt with," Butch announced in his rough, loud voice.

"I hate snakes," Rachael said with a shudder.

Not a minute later, Ahote brushed up against her arm as he walked by and straight through the crowd to stand directly in front of the snake. Marie noted the chills that erupted on her friend's arm, and she nudged her playfully with a wink.

"He's being your hero," Marie whispered excitedly.

"Shh, I don't know what you're talking about," Rachael replied, before her attention was drawn raptly toward the tall Ahusaka brother with straight black shoulder-length hair he had tied back in a strip of leather. Ahote, which he had explained meant "restless one," was showing his bravery as he faced off with the desert snake. "He's so brave. I hope he doesn't get bitten."

"I'm sure he knows what he's doing." Marie thought he might in more ways than just with the snake. Her friend was slowly being wooed, and she didn't even know it.

The next thing they knew, Ahote was doing some kind of hypnotizing movements with his hands and the snake was in his thrall, as was almost everyone else. Out of nowhere, the hawk—his brother, Cetan—swooped down without a sound and dove for the snake's neck, severing the head cleanly off. The crowd gasped, also unaware of the stealthy move. Just when they felt they could breathe again, a loud bang shot off, echoing off the surrounding monuments of clay and dirt.

"It's all right, everyone. The boys took care of the snake. It's all clear," Butch announced.

"What was the shot for?" someone asked.

"Had to put the cow down," Hank added, now standing with his musket over his shoulder, next to Butch. "There's no coming back from that venom."

After the excitement, the crowd dispersed back to their daily chores or whatever they had been doing to prepare for the coming night. Marie watched Rachael cautiously approach Ahote and begin talking. It made Marie smile, another new dawning to add to her future hope.

AFTER WINTERING in the shelter of the chalk-like rock monuments, the band of travelers returned to the Santa Fe trail in the spring of 1852. Through the remainder of that year, they made their way slowly toward Santa Fe. After passing through what had recently become the Republic of New Mexico from the Republic of Texas—now the state of Texas—the land grew in height with the presence of high steppe-like plains, and to the north, snow-capped mountains loomed with the threat of the coming winter. The farther they traveled, the more the land dipped and rose. Large monuments of rock grew out of the ground, with intense reds lightening to oranges and then to lighter tans as they reached the sky. They decided to remain there until the paths through the mountains would be less treacherous. The party grew restless, but ultimately found ways to keep busy and find work through the winter, saving up for the new supplies they would need in the coming months. Santa Fe had become a real trade route for furs especially, and they were definitely going to need those up in the mountains. Only time would tell if the pull toward whatever it was in those mountains they sought would grow strong again, or if Santa Fe was to be their new home. After much discussion, most still felt a restlessness in their spirits to continue toward the mountains, but for now they would remain.

CHAPTER 13

*E*arly summer in the year 1853, Marie and others had been working for a local farmer, when one day, she heard Rachael run through the field, yelling her name. "Marie!"

Marie and Judson both dropped their tools and looked up to see what the urgency was.

"What is it?" Marie shouted and ran to her friend, concern all over her face.

"It's time! The Luna Coven says it's time to go!" She jumped up and down excitedly. It was the moment they had been waiting for—the signal it was time to head into the mountains.

"When do we leave? We have to finish our work here." Judson spread his arm wide, indicating the jobs they had all taken on.

"End of this week. We have time to end our employment and obtain the supplies we need," Rachael informed them.

"It's time. We're heading home," Marie said with a large smile on her face, and Judson couldn't help but lean over and kiss her.

THE SUMMER in Santa Fe had been lovely, with desert blooms, warm days, and cool nights. Marie would miss it, but she kept her eyes on the horizon as they drove the oxen and the wagons north with all their newly acquired supplies. The mountains were calling them home.

Alo had explained earlier how there were what he called "dead zones" in these valleys. When Marie didn't fully understand, he went on to share how some of the local tribes had joined up with witches and put spells on some areas, as traps of a sort, to nullify the magic of those passing through. Witches wouldn't be able to cast spells, and shifters wouldn't be able to shift, but Marie wasn't sure what would happen to her, since she didn't have active magic. He explained it was to give the tribe whose territory it was the advantage and time to prepare. He reiterated how dangerous dead zones could be as they were getting close to an area where he thought one was.

An eerie feeling of foreboding settled in Marie's stomach. Something wasn't right, or perhaps it was just the way a "dead zone" felt. She couldn't shake it, though.

"Judson, can you give the whistle signal for everyone to stop? I need to speak with each wagon before we go any farther."

He nodded and gave the loud and shrill signal that hurt her ears every time. Marie jumped down from her wagon and ran to the lead wagon.

"What is it?" Anne-Marie asked from the front of her wagon.

"I'm not exactly sure, but something is wrong here. I needed to warn you to be prepared. I feel tingly all over, so I don't know if it's other hunters or just the dead zone, but we might need to be prepared. Have your weapons and spells ready as soon as we pass through the area."

"All right, we'll be ready. Inform the other wagons," she directed, and Marie did so, grateful to be taken seriously.

Marie knew each wagon was equipped with rifles, swords, knives, bows and arrows, and an assortment of other weapons, many laced with magic, and many creations of Judson's. Once she was satisfied all had been warned and would prepare, she climbed back in her wagon, and Judson gave the whistle again to indicate forward movement.

It took longer than Marie thought it would to travel through the dead zone. An eerie silence permeated the arid air, nobody spoke, and all that could be heard were the sounds of the wheels tumbling over rocks and the clopping of the oxen. Just as they felt the dead zone coming to an end with an almost audible buzzing, Cetan jumped out of the wagon. He ran ahead to breach the boundary, transformed into the hawk, and flew to the sky to serve as their overhead eyes. Only moments later did the hawk screech a warning. Everyone drew their weapons as they came out of a narrow, open-air tunnel made of large sand cliffs on either side. The path opened into a wide plains area, where a line of wagons attempted to block the path.

Marie gasped and scratched at her neck at the same time. "Dante."

Her brother leaned casually against a wagon while those on either side of him had weapons drawn. Their faces were hard, and their stances ready to fight. They simply waited. She couldn't help but be saddened at the sight of her two brothers, Dante and Isaiah, her sister LeAnna, and other family members, some not even hunters, ready to fight them. And for what?

"Marie!" Dante called out. "I've been waiting for you. But it seems you are not nearly as surprised to see us standing here. I must have taken your ability to adapt for granted. I won't again. Father, Rodney, Michael, and Caroline, it's so nice to see you again. I'm ready to take you home, where you belong. It's time for you to end your foolishness now, Marie, and join me in the family . . . business, as it were." He sneered, the only indication of the madness taking over him.

"I've made my choice, Dante. You need to leave and let us move on," Marie returned.

"But your choice is wrong, dear sister, and I am here to right your wrong."

Marie could feel the unease trickle through the wagon train. They had tried to spread themselves out as wide as they could so they had a better chance. Weapons were drawn on both sides. She feared it would not end well.

"Dante, what you're doing is wrong. These people have done nothing to you. Let them pass unharmed."

A spark flared in his eyes. She had called him "wrong."

"Their existence is their sin, and they need to be punished for it. Don't you understand this is our purpose? This is who we are meant to be—the Blackstone witch hunters! We are to hunt the witches!" He was yelling now, losing his grasp on the thin thread of his sanity he held onto.

Instead of battling him, she needed to find a way to get everyone past him. Or at the least, she needed to convince him to leave, but she could only think of one idea to do that.

"Young man, many of us are not witches, and by your reasoning, we are innocent. Let us go through unharmed, then you may take your turn with the witches," Mihail Petran announced to the shock of many. True, he was a vampire, but perhaps this was his way of getting some of the wagons to the other side.

"Nice try." Dante lifted a brow. "You travel with them, you die with them."

He pulled out a blade from his hip holster, apparently a silent signal, as many of the others extended their weapons as well.

"Are we almost through here?" the elder Bishop droned as if the whole situation was a bore to him.

Marie's mouth dropped, but the fire she saw in Dante's eyes at being disrespected by a witch must have been what Rodavan was after, because Marie could see the slight lift of his lip—he was itching for a fight, apparently.

"We are done when you are all dead," Dante countered, pointing his blade at Rodavan.

"No! Dante, this doesn't have to be this way. Let them go," Marie pleaded as she jumped down from the seat of her wagon.

"Marie, no!" Judson shouted, but didn't grab her in time. He jumped down on the opposite side and ran over to her.

"Let them go, and I will go home with you," Marie announced with a hitch in her voice.

"No," she heard Judson and several others add in shocked whispers.

Others now joined them on what would seem to be the front line of their side, coming down from their seats and out from the backs of the wagons. Marie could still see Cetan circling above, and out of the corner of her eye, Alo and Ahote moving stealthily up to higher ground, blending in with the landscape. She hoped they had a plan.

Marie calmly took steps forward, one at a time. With one last look to Judson, she gave him a smile—one that encapsulated all the love she had for him, the promise of their future, and that she would be all right. "This is my choice. I will find my way to you in the end."

Tears welled up in his eyes, but he knew it was her choice to save all of them. He would get her back one way or another, even if he had to run across the country. There was no home without Marie for him.

Dante watched carefully, waiting for her to spring an attack on him, but she didn't. Standing only feet in front of Dante, Marie stopped. "Do we have a deal?"

"Oh, Marie, we have no intention of making a deal," Dante said snidely. He grabbed her and spun her around to face the rest of them. He held her tightly against his chest with his knife at her neck.

A clap echoed around them.

"Dante, no," Marie struggled to say, a single tear falling from her eye.

"Shh, sister, you will be set right soon enough," he crooned madly. To those on his side, he said, "Do it."

Everyone simultaneously advanced, weapons ready to take out the witches. Except when they moved forward, they were blocked by an invisible barrier.

"You see, we are not naive and will not let you simply slaughter us. Be warned that we will fight back, and we will not have mercy," Anne-Marie declared, standing regal and powerful with her hands outstretched, ready to use whatever magic was necessary to defend herself and her people.

Everyone standing with her joined her at the line. Vampires held weapons, and shifters shifted. Even Lawrence Mills had transformed into a mighty creature—a sight never before seen in the desert.

He grew to about fifty feet tall and twice as wide, Marie gauged, eyeing the tip of his enormous tail. She had only heard of dragons in stories she was told as a child. But he was unlike anything she'd imagined. The top of his head was circled with a crown of thorns, and his already pale green eyes shone with a vivid brilliance. His skin had become grayish-white scales covering him head to tail. From his back extended a large expanse of wings. Lawrence was quite the contrast to the tans, reds, and oranges of the desert. Instead of smoke and fire emitting from his mouth, mist and frost spewed forth in a great demonstration.

Eyes from everyone on the opposite side widened in surprise and a little fear—apparently it was a sight they had not yet seen either. Several faltered in their stances.

"What madness is this?" Dante said with slight alarm. He took several steps back, pulling Marie with him toward what appeared to be a getaway wagon.

"They have the upper hand, Dante. Leave while you can," Marie pushed. "Your people . . . our family could be hurt."

Dante growled, obviously frustrated they had foiled his plans. "No, you will still come with me."

"Ready, witches?" Anne-Marie shouted.

"Let us be done with this already," another one of the Bishops—Dragan—interjected, his voice impassive and bored, but the light in his eyes the opposite, as they gleamed with a spark of dark desire and an intensity in focus.

Marie groaned in pain as her eyes found Dragan's. Why was his magic different? Could he be infusing it with dark magic? But just then, Dante grunted also and poked the skin at her neck, causing her to jerk back.

"Looks like one of your witches you associate with might have some secrets of his own. Naughty, naughty," he taunted.

"Shields down!" Raffaele Augustine yelled in a deep baritone.

Another clap echoed through the mountains, and Dante's people moved forward as if their suspension had lifted. The witches began firing off spells, and those with rifles kept them trained, ready to defend, but only if Dante's rogues broke through their lines. Ahote and Alo made high-pitched sounds as they came jumping down from their places on the hillside and began fighting with knives. Metal upon metal clanked. Spells were uttered into the wind.

Dante pulled Marie with him quickly to the wagon and pushed her around to the front. "Time to go, sister."

"I don't think so." Rachael's voice came from the side of the wagon. Somehow she had slipped through the lines of fighting and awaited them there.

"And you are going to stop me, witch?" Dante laughed in her face. She flinched but straightened her shoulders.

"Yes, I am."

"Get in, Marie. We're leaving." Dante ignored Rachael and pushed Marie up into the seat. She struggled to make it tough on him.

"You would just leave your people to fight and most likely die while you escape? You are a coward, Dante." Marie couldn't believe it took her so long to see his true fear.

Rachael began uttering words Marie could barely hear until they grew louder in cadence and the strength in her voice sounded confident, then she spoke them loud and proud. Her intent and her words carried strongly with power.

"I curse you, Dante Blackstone. Marie will disappear to you. You will lose connection with her and be unable to find her for all the days of your life. Your hunter will be hidden from you, and you will regain your humanity. I curse you, Dante Blackstone. Hear me, goddesses of sky, earth, water, and fire. Hear my cry and bid my words flight."

Rachael took out a ritualistic athame she kept under her cloak and sliced the blade across her palm, drawing her own blood, then flung the dagger end over end until it landed in Dante's stomach. It wasn't a fatal wound, but it would definitely slow him down.

Dante pulled the dagger out and flung it away from him. Doubling over, he fell to his knees as he tried to staunch the bleeding.

Marie took advantage of the distraction and jumped down from his wagon. She ran over to Rachael, grabbing her arm and running back toward their wagons. Several people Marie didn't know from Dante's side lay on the ground, hurt, bleeding, or worse. A few wounds could be seen on the witches' side, but overall, they were in total control and had the upper hand, especially when the dragon kept freezing those who came too close to the wagons and the young ones hidden within them.

Marie's other brother Isaiah saw her fleeing and was about to give chase, but noticed Dante on the ground and rushed to his aid.

"Retreat!" Isaiah shouted, and he loaded Dante into the back of the wagon just before he jumped in the driver's seat and took off. The other wagons in their group followed, leaving a trail of dust in their wake.

Marie ran to Judson and threw herself into his arms, where he caught her and spun her around just like he used to before they left Virginia. He held her so tightly, she couldn't breathe. "I thought I was going to lose you."

"You could never lose me. You are my home, and I would always come back to you," Marie whispered into his ear, before he took her mouth and kissed her with a fierce desperation.

"Is anyone hurt?" Marie shouted, once she could breathe again.

Cetan and Ahote approached. In Cetan's arms lay a limp Alo. Marie rushed to him.

"Hurry! Can anyone help him?" she pleaded with the witches, but no one moved.

Ahote placed his hand upon her arm. "He would not want that. He is at peace. We will let him go."

Though his words were strong and brave, his eyes held immense sadness. Tears streamed down Marie's face for their loss.

"May we take a moment to bury him in the hills he loved so much?" Cetan asked quietly.

Marie glanced at Anne-Marie, who gave her a slight nod. "Of course you can. Take your time. And we are so sorry."

"It was his choice to come and his choice to fight. He died protecting something he believed in," Ahote added. The two brothers took their fallen up the side of the nearest hill, where the sun would set upon him, and buried Alo. Once they were finished, the others joined them at their sides and took a moment of silence in respect, then headed back to the wagons.

"Load up!" Butch shouted, getting everyone back on track. They had miles to make up for today yet. Judson refused to let Marie go as he tugged her toward their wagon, Rachael following behind them. Marie reached back for her hand and brought her close. She could feel Rachael shaking.

"What you did back there . . ." Marie started.

"It needed to be done. For the first time, my magic worked just as I intended it to. I could feel it well up from deep within. He should leave you alone now." Rachael smiled, but it was weak and uncertain.

"I believe your magic is strong enough to do just that . . . but, Rach, by cursing him, you tied the curse to you. So you're never allowed to die, or the curse will be broken and he'll come for us again."

"I know." Rachael gulped, the residue from her spell still lingering on her. She was spent and looked like she was about to faint when Ahote came up behind her and caught her just before she fell. Without words, he scooped her up and carried her to the wagon, where Marie knew he would care for her friend. Ahote caught Marie's eyes. She nodded her thanks.

"Marie," Anne-Marie called out. "What you did was foolish and reckless, but you put your life on the line for all of ours. You have our trust, and we welcome you and yours to stay with us."

She angled her head slightly, giving Marie a show of respect. When Marie looked up, she noticed all those with Anne-Marie standing with her, even the Bishops, who were skeptics from the beginning, each nodding their agreement—some more enthusiastically than others. She hoped one day to get to know them all more, but now they had a trail to blaze.

"Thank you all. Your support means more to me than you could know. Let's go home." Marie smiled when others cheered and agreed. They loaded up and hit the trail, a looming chain of mountains ahead of them.

EPILOGUE

*I*t took the caravan the rest of the year and into the beginning of 1854 to make it through the mountains. The journey was slow and arduous. Some of the humans had the roughest time with sicknesses that didn't affect the supernaturals in the same way. They even lost a couple who weren't affected by any of the healing spells and tonics. Blizzards hit them, causing them to camp in caves at the bases of the mountains for long periods of time, waiting for the snow to lift. Even though they used magic to assist in the traveling, sometimes Mother Nature won out.

The pull up the mountain grew stronger and stronger the closer they drew to the summit. No one knew exactly what it was that had been pulling them, but no one could deny the powerful force either. Evergreens and pines stood tall and thick before they thinned out again near the top. The path was often overrun with snow and ice. It grew dark early, and the sun took too long to rise in the mornings. Marie thought they would never make it. Until one day, the sun rose warm and strong in the sky. Snow began to melt, and tiny green foliage peeked its crowns through the cold ground. Spring had finally arrived, and they had almost reached the top.

It was spring, March 1854, when the caravan reached a box

canyon nestled between several mountain peaks. They all breathed a sigh of relief.

Home.

The canyon provided everything they had been searching for—seclusion, space for shifters to roam, land for their homes and crops, all the resources they needed, and the perfect conditions for protection wards. Overwhelmed, they slowly moved into the area, eyes wide with wonder, excitement, and shock. It was real. Their dream of a place to call home was real, and they had finally made it.

MARIE COULDN'T BELIEVE they had actually arrived. They had set up the wagons and tents right in the center of what would be their new home. The air was cool and fresh, and the mountains held something magical. With snow-capped mountain peaks in all four directions, privacy and seclusion was all theirs. Building the town of homes and businesses would take time, but she was excited about the prospects.

Upon arriving, they had been compelled to the northwest corner, where the magical pull was the strongest. A waterfall nearly three hundred feet high roared with the melting snow from the mountain it was cozy with. The falls poured into a pond surrounded by forest and large boulders; it was the most serene setting Marie had ever seen. A magical energy emanated from the falls itself and wafted into the town. Rachael had speculated that that energy was what pulled them from the very beginning.

With Marie and Judson's experience working the land and growing strong tobacco crops and vineyards back in Virginia, they had been granted land at the lower edge of one of the mountains, where the base met the plateau of the town, to grow a new vineyard and other large crops. It took time and magic, but Judson and Marie built their first home. Judson had also built a lower room within the home that was hidden away, for him to work on his weapons. Her father Hank and her cousins Michael and Caroline were going to live with them until they had places of their own, and they would work for the vineyard. The house was going to be quite spacious, with each addition they had planned to make space for everyone. It was going to be the most beautiful vineyard Marie had ever seen as it climbed up the mountain. She dreamed of one day building small buildings where others could come and stay with them to enjoy the views—family, friends, or visitors, it didn't matter—she wanted to share her dream. It would be a place of peace where others could find tranquility, but it would also serve to calm her inner hunter when it grew challenging. Judson had also built an outbuilding for an actual forge to continue with metalwork for the town, as well.

Part of their agreement when choosing to stay in the town was that everyone had a part to play. The Blackstones' part would be threefold: to inform the town council if they sensed black magic, as it would not be allowed, to inform the town if other hunters showed up in the area unannounced, and to provide weapons for the town's use. Judson and Marie had agreed.

One day, at the base of the waterfalls, Marie sat reading through her family's journal once more. Content to put it away for a time, whether she found out the secret of the book or not, she wanted one last viewing. Dante was out of the picture—she hoped for a long, long time—and she had her chance to start over and define who the Blackstone hunters would be from now on. Running her fingers gently over the metalwork on the front, she stuck her finger into the depression in the middle, where it appeared something should fit.

An idea struck her, and she pulled out the dagger Judson had restored for her that had also belonged to her family. Examining the metalwork on the dagger, she realized that instead of them being the same pattern, they were each an exact mirror copy of the other, except where the book had a depression, the knife had a round stone set in the middle. Anticipation bubbled up in Marie. Could the key have been with her all along? Was it that simple? She placed the dagger face down on top of the book's cover and gently pushed the interlocking metal together like a puzzle. The stone on the knife fit snugly into the depression on the book. Unfortunately, nothing happened. Frowning,

Marie tried it a couple more times, but the same result remained. Nothing.

She had taken her shoes off earlier and dipped her toes into the cool refreshing water of the pond. Dipping her hand into the water, she stirred it around her fingers. It wasn't warm enough for a dip at the moment, but she hoped to swim in it someday soon. Turning her focus one last time to what would become just a family heirloom, she pulled the knife free and ran her finger over the colorless stone; it was such a curious stone—she had no idea what it was. This time, when her water-moistened finger moved over the stone, it flickered with color. Marie gasped and almost dropped the thing.

"Do you need water? Or this particular water?" Marie wondered aloud.

In a bold move, she cupped her hand and brought a trickle of water, dripping it right over the stone. It glowed a bright blueish-green and actually absorbed the water containing it. Not knowing what else to do, she pushed the face of the dagger back into the metal work on the book and watched the two click together like a locking mechanism. The book hadn't been locked, but it unlocked pages that had not been there before—secret pages. It had now become a more personal diary, with grave details about the hunters and their powers, how to use them, how to contain them, how to not pass them on to human offspring, and how to control them and use them for good.

"I knew there was more to you!" Marie practically shouted in her excitement.

"More to what?" Judson asked, climbing up the pathway to where she was, carrying a picnic basket.

"My book! I figured it out!" She showed him all she had discovered. "Now I just need to read it all."

"Well, I have no doubt you will do that and more. Is there a section for you to add your own experiences so far? You should continue to document things for future generations of hunters."

"Yes, you are right. I have much to document so far. I also was thinking about the inscription on the dagger: Choose Yourself. I could see where one—a hunter specifically and in our case, Dante—would think it to mean choosing yourself above all else. But I believe it to mean I can choose for myself who I am to be."

"I believe you are right," Judson said with a big smile. "And have you?"

"I have!" She returned his big smile. "Did you bring me lunch?"

"I did." He placed the basket on the ground next to her and sat down. "How is Rachael adjusting?"

"She has decided to continue her training with the Luna Coven. She didn't feel she was ready to take over her coven, and they have since assimilated into the Lunas here, dropping the Stronghold name. It seemed like the best decision on all parts. I think she's happy. Plus, she's been busy with Ahote, from what I can tell." Marie winked at him with a devilish smile. "I can think of someone I'd like to be busy with." Marie flung her arms around Judson's neck.

He took a minute to admire his woman. But when she winked saucily, he laughed, then added, "I'm glad she is doing well."

Marie barely let him finish his words before she planted her mouth on his, kissing him senseless and taking control. They broke apart moments later.

"Should we have lunch?" Marie asked, quickly recovering.

"I'd like more of that first, though, please," he said breathlessly, pulling back from her strike attack.

He grabbed her around the waist and lifted her closer to him. Judson tenderly traced her lips with his own, keeping it light, teasing. Marie moaned and parted her lips for him. He wasted no time taking advantage of her open mouth and deepened the kiss, filling it with passion for Marie and their new life together. When she broke for air, she leaned her forehead against his.

"I love you, Judson Carter Blackstone."

"I love you too, Marie." He put her down and stepped back, still holding one of her hands. "There is something I've wanted to do for a while now, and since we are settled a bit more, I feel it's the right time."

"Oh? What's that?" Marie asked coyly, thinking he wanted to take their loving a bit further there at the falls.

Judson got down on one knee and raised a ring from his pocket. "Marie, my love. I know we are already married in the eyes of God, but we have never married publicly in the eyes of man. Will you do me the honor of marrying me once again, so I can proudly proclaim you my wife in front of our new friends in our new life?"

Tears streaming down her face, Marie was taken aback at the thoughtful sincerity of the man she had already chosen to be with for the rest of her life.

"Yes, I will."

Here in this new life, armed with new information and new support, Marie took a deep breath as she looked deeply into Judson's eyes. This was what she had always wanted. This was a new era for the Blackstone family . . . the dawn of the witch hunters.

Read more about the history of the witch hunters, coming January 2019. Also, you can discover Marie's descendants—the modern-day Blackstones—in *Reawakened* (A Havenwood Falls High Novella), available now.

ABOUT THE AUTHOR

Morgan Wylie is an award-winning and *USA Today* bestselling author with several genres published, from YA fantasy to adult paranormal romance and other things in between. Morgan published her first novel, Silent Orchids, one year after moving across the country with her family on a journey of new discovery. After an amazing three years in Nashville, TN, and the release of two more books, Morgan and her family found their way back to the Northwest, where they now reside. Still working every day with great optimism, Morgan continues to embrace all things: "Mama," wife, teacher, and mediator to the many voices and muses constantly chattering in her head . . . where it gets pretty loud!

You can find her and news on her books at the following:

MorganWylie.net
 MorganWylieBooks on Facebook
 @MWylieBooks on Twitter

ACKNOWLEDGMENTS

First off, I'd like to thank my amazing husband and my eight-year-old daughter, whose patience and support allows me to keep doing what I love to be doing, which is writing.

Next, I'd like to thank Kristie Cook, who had the amazing dream of creating Havenwood Falls and inviting others like me to come and play in her world. And thank you for the use of your characters the Beaumonts, the Petrans, and others; they were invaluable to my story.

Also, thank you to Kristie and Liz Ferry for your editing insights and expertise! Also for your patience as I attempted to challenge my thoughts and words from today's speech back into the 1800's.

I'd also like to thank Randi Cooley Wilson for the use of the Bishop boys, E.J. Fechenda for the mention of Elsmed, Amy Hale for the use of Lawrence Mills, and all the other authors whose characters made a brief appearance as a part of the wagon train. And to all my Havenwood Falls family, thank you for your tremendous support and encouragement. I'm thrilled to be in this adventure with you!

And thank you, readers! Whether this is your first introduction to the Blackstone family or you are a Blackstone veteran, thank you. Your support and time is most appreciated! And stay tuned for more from the Blackstone family in the future! Thank You!

REDEMPTION'S END

ERIC R. ASHER

~ A Legends of Havenwood Falls Novella ~

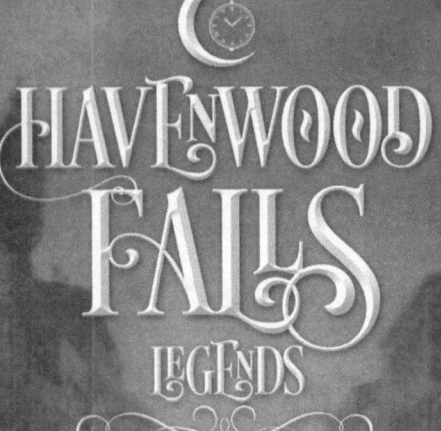

HAVENWOOD FALLS

LEGENDS

REDEMPTION'S
END

ERIC R. ASHER

Sometimes there is magic in the steam.

CHAPTER 1

"*H*ow can you stand the noise in here?" Charlotte asked.

I kept my eyes on the seemingly random array of tiny gears and screws under the magnifying glass in front of me. Trying not to give myself away, I screwed the top back onto the flask in my left hand and slid it under the workbench.

"What noise?" I asked. I pulled another lens over my larger magnifier and carefully screwed one of the cogs back together. Only then did I turn away and look up at my wife, not missing the subtle frown and crease of her brow above her light brown eyes.

"No need to hide your flask," Charlotte said. "Even if I hadn't seen your clumsy ass trying to hide it, it smells like a still in here. I'm sure that's just what our customers want to see—you drunk, Gregory."

I sheepishly held out the bronze flask to Charlotte. "Just testing."

Somehow Charlotte managed to take a long swig out of the flask without breaking eye contact. The woman knew me too well, and I loved it.

"Who are you making that automata for?" Charlotte asked, indicating the detached body, limbs, and tiny gears strewn about the workbench. When it was assembled, it would be an intricately animated dancer. Now it was, admittedly, a bit of a mess.

I took the flask back as she handed it to me, narrowing my eyes and taking a small sip. The slightly sweet moonshine burned its way down my throat before settling as a fire in my gut. "This one's just for the shop."

"Another bauble without a buyer," Charlotte muttered. "You need to finish those watches. At least until we find out there's a fence in town for some of our . . . less legitimate keepsakes, as I don't think the bank will accept stolen art. We can afford two more loan payments on the shop with what we have in cash. Maybe. We've barely been here a year, and the town has been here longer than that. I don't want to leave a bad impression on the banks."

I pinched the bridge of my nose and took a deep breath. "I know."

"Sure," Charlotte said. "What you really mean to say is that you find working on those pocket watches boring. And I understand that, I really do. But you aren't getting paid by the city again until you finish the conservatory. And that's if those contraptions will even work."

"They'll work," I said. "They have to. With all the creatures . . ."

"Species," Charlotte said, correcting me.

I nodded. "With all the species coming here, the town needs protection. Werewolves and vampires are peoples' neighbors in this place, but I don't think they fully understand the threat a fae can represent. Especially the Unseelie fae."

Charlotte settled into the workbench beside me. It used to be we could share the workbench, like one giant communal space. But if I was being honest with myself, I'd grown sloppy in my old age. There was a method to the chaos, and I always knew which screws went with which part and what springs I'd removed from which frame, but to the casual observer, it was pure chaos.

But beside me, Charlotte's workstation was pure order. She could chisel and carve wood, building the most intricate locks and puzzle boxes you can imagine, from the picture in her mind. There were a few things I could build from memory. I preferred to draw things out ahead of time. So in addition to three dozen jars of screws and fifty different trays of tiny parts, my workspace was littered with paper.

"You sell many more of those puzzle boxes," I said, "I won't need to worry about fixing those watches, or selling moonshine."

The front door—a thick heavy thing with a great deal of intricate carvings—swung open. Some of the patterns were subtle, but if someone had grown up around the tinkers' guilds, they were sure to recognize a few. And if they had grown up in the company of pirates, they were likely to recognize the vague outline of the crossbones formed from old iron.

Theodore, my apprentice, glanced back at the hinges as he crossed the threshold. He'd let his sandy brown hair grow to the point that he looked more like some of the soldiers I'd known in the east than the neatly groomed young man I was used to.

"You finally got the hinges to stop squeaking? They didn't even whisper."

The door snapped closed a moment later, and welcome chimes sounded. While I may have been able to fix the squeaking hinges, I was still having trouble regulating the volume of the chimes. They thundered to life, playing a quick four-note arpeggio that one might mistake for a thunderclap.

Theodore threw his hands over his ears, but by the time he managed to cover them, the chime was already done.

"Sorry about that," I said.

"What?" Theodore asked, slowly lowering his hands.

"I changed my mind," Charlotte said. "I think you should focus on fixing that damn chime."

"All in good time," I said, shooting her a crooked smile.

I stood up from the bench, carefully lifting the leather apron over my head. It held nearly as many tools as I had strewn across the workbench. "Ready for a little hike?"

"I'm ready to learn how to run those stills," Theodore said.

Charlotte slowly raised an eyebrow. "I believe what Theodore means is that he'd like to learn how to run the stills without blowing himself up."

I frowned slightly and nodded. "As I said."

I hung the apron on a small rack sunk into the wall. I pulled a discreet lever, capped with a polished walnut handle, and the entire rack sank into the wall, only to be replaced by a display of some of Charlotte's finest puzzle boxes.

"How cold is it today?" Charlotte asked.

"You haven't been out?" Theodore asked.

Charlotte shook her head. "Haven't needed to yet. Living above the shop is rather convenient like that."

"I'd say it's close to sixty."

"Take your coat," Charlotte said, eyeing me as I circled around the workbench very much without my coat.

"I don't think that's really necessary," I said.

"It doesn't matter if you think it's necessary," Charlotte said. "Take your coat."

I blinked at my wife, and while I pondered arguing for a moment, I instead hurried to the back, grabbed my coat, and joined Theodore in the front of the store. "We'll be back in a few hours."

"If you're not," Charlotte said, "I'll assume you're dead."

Theodore laughed, but he shut up when I shot him a cutting glare.

I rolled the cuff of my coat back and checked the watch sewn into the lining. It would likely take a half hour to hike to the stills if we didn't run into trouble. That would give us two hours before we needed to head back. "I'll take you out for a fine dinner tonight," I said.

Charlotte harrumphed. "As long as you're not cooking it, it should be fine indeed."

I leveled my gaze at her. "Charlotte."

She grinned at me and shooed us out the front door. I sighed when the chimes sounded again as the door closed behind us.

"Let's get on with it then," I said.

Most of the town had gravel streets now, but a few places tended to get muddy enough to trap a wagon wheel. I glanced back at the shop as my boots crunched in the rock. When we first opened the store, it had been my decision to simply put up a sign that said horologist. Charlotte protested, saying too many people wouldn't realize that we even sold watches, much less puzzle boxes and automata. As usual, she'd been right. So below the word horologist, we now had gilt lettering that said, "Timepieces, Music Boxes & Gifts."

I took a deep breath and smiled at the brick façade lined with rich lumber. It had long been our dream to leave our old seafaring life behind and open a shop, and it gave me hope that life would be good in this new town.

"You okay?" Theodore asked, pulling me out of my thoughts.

"I'm excellent, son," I said, pulling my coat a little tighter against a chilly breeze. "Into the woods."

CHAPTER 2

$\mathcal{T}$he town had come a long way in the months since Charlotte and I moved in. Or had it been a year now? I tended to lose track of these things when I was focused on my work. It was easy to let the days slide by, exchanging one set of dangers for another. From the outside, frontier life looked softer than life on the seas, but they were both hard.

I helped design some of the buildings here. Others were a bit more what I would call clunky. Inefficient architecture and designs that served no real purpose other than a rural Main Street aesthetic I'd seen a dozen times before. I supposed that was well and good. Most people wouldn't want their town to look like a square box. What truly set the view apart were the mountains—soaring, majestic things that reminded me of the white-capped waves in a squall.

My gaze lingered on the conservatory we'd been repairing on the back of the inn. The structure was mostly a framework now, as we had to pull the glass down to get to the root of the problem, and I doubted anyone would realize what I'd hidden there. It had taken some convincing to get Mihail, the inn's owner, to let me include the ward designs, but that wasn't the kind of thing you did without permission. Or, at least not without partial permission. This was especially true when the owners were vampires. They may have understood the threat of other vampires, and even hunters, but I suspected they hadn't had dealings with the darkest side of the Unseelie fae like Charlotte and I had.

The rock and dirt of the streets gave way to trees and the meandering creek. Theodore and I followed the old creek north into the mountains. In the distance, I heard the faint crashing of the waterfalls.

There was something both reassuring and threatening about the more remote parts of the woods. It would take some time to reach the stills, as they were deeper into the wilderness, closer to the falls. I was pretty sure Theodore felt the same way about our isolation. I caught his gaze flickering from one side of the path to the other, trying to locate whatever wildlife was bouncing around the trees above us. It was early in the day, but not much sunlight reached the forest floor, leaving us in a surreal world of shadows.

WE HADN'T RUN anything through the stills in a couple weeks. Not only because I was behind on the projects and repairs in the shop, but because the heavy rains in the springtime tended to wash out the path around the creeks. And a small footbridge that only spanned half of the raging current of water wasn't much good to anyone. I wasn't too happy about the delay occurring right after we replaced the still Theodore had destroyed.

We spent most of the walk in silence, only the sounds of the forest keeping us company along with the crunch of underbrush beneath our boots. The kid may have been young enough to maintain a conversation during the more difficult parts of the hike, but I wasn't nearly so young as him. In some ways, I supposed I was jealous of his easy stride up the side of the mountain, but I'd never want to live through those years again. Charlotte and I were building a new life, in what I hoped was a safer place. We weren't exactly spoiled for choices.

I slowed as we crested the ridge, and a small spiral of steam curled up from the shack that stored our stills. In the year since I'd set up, no one had bothered the operation. I didn't really know if it was simply because our neighbors were all good people, or they understood the dangers of the still, or perhaps the smells were overwhelming to those with enhanced senses. In any case, the steam meant someone had been here, or was still here.

That wasn't to say I'd never seen anyone in the area before, and I was nothing if not cautious. I slid the sleek form of a small pistol out of a hidden pocket in my coat. From another pocket, I pulled the strange clip of ammunition and cylinders that gave the gun its name: the harmonica pistol. It wasn't until I slid the ammunition home and cocked the gun that Theodore realized what was in my hand.

"What are you doing?"

"Someone's here," I said. "And I'm getting ready to greet them."

"Oh," Theodore said. "It was me. I pulled the mash and fired up the stills yesterday. I just wanted you to see that I'm not an idiot."

I slowly raised an eyebrow. "I told you not to touch these things without me. That's not a complicated instruction, is it?"

"It's fine," Theodore said, biting off the words. "Yes, of course I understand. But I've been following you around up here for six months, and you haven't let me touch a damn thing."

I frowned at the anger in Theodore's words.

"No," I said, "and when you didn't listen? We lost a still."

The boy had always been patient, but perhaps he was reaching the end. He was recently in his twenties, and I had a fuzzy remembrance of being that age myself. I took a deep breath, trying to will my frustration away. But Theodore had managed to blow one of our stills up, and it could have been him, if he'd been standing too close. I didn't want to be the one to explain that to his parents, or any part of his family.

"What time did you start yesterday?" I asked.

"About noon," Theodore said, some of the anger bleeding out of his words. "I made sure to mark it."

I nodded and started toward the plain cedar door, considering the idea I should put a lock on the shack. I slid through the doorway, sweeping my pistol around the room before releasing a breath I hadn't realized I'd been holding.

"What do we have?" I asked as I hooked the pistol into a loop on my vest and checked the pressure on the still. Theodore had obviously put an adequate amount of fuel in, but not enough to cause a rupture. It was still good on water, which meant as long as he had a proper mixture of corn, sugar, yeast, and water, this batch of moonshine should be just fine. But something didn't smell quite right. It smelled too mature, too rich. I frowned.

"I did it just like you always told me to. The only thing different is the stream was a little muddy."

"You put muddy water in the still?" I asked, unable to hide the disgust in my voice.

"Of course not," Theodore said. "I went a little farther upstream. Where the pond is."

"The pond?" I asked. "You put water from the pond in here?"

I hadn't explained to him exactly why that was a bad idea. He didn't know what Charlotte and I knew. I bit my lip and thanked the stars that the stills hadn't blown up again. That didn't do much to alleviate the slightly more concerning thought that the stills could blow up in our face now.

"Shut the fires down," I said. "Whatever we have, we have. We need to shut this down now."

"I've done it before."

"Kill the fire now. We'll lose the whole still. Again."

Theodore didn't ask me to clarify. We went about our business, throwing the lever to cut off the airflow around the fires underneath the still. He pulled another lever to drop the tray of charcoal out from underneath and slid it into a fire pit in the corner of the shack.

I turned the nozzle on the collection barrel and whistled when a clear stream of moonshine splashed down into my copper mug, with one small side effect. A subtle golden light glowed from the normally crystal-clear liquid.

"What is that?" Theodore asked.

"There's something I have to tell you about that old waterfall, and the pond you took this water from."

I took a deep breath through my nose over the copper cup in my hand, surprised to find the usual burning aroma of fresh moonshine, but there was something else. The water Theodore had used had imbued it with something more. I pondered the mug for a moment, before deciding I'd lived a good life and took a sip.

I winced at the ungodly sear, but exhaled slowly as the burning left and a slightly sweet aftertaste remained. I ran my tongue across my teeth and sighed.

"That pond is where we harvest the aether. It's in the very waters. Whatever placed it there, of which I'm fairly sure was a magic beyond anything I've encountered before, also holds it there. It doesn't seem to be anywhere downstream. It stops at that pond."

Theodore blinked at me.

"But it's a pond," Theodore said.

I shrugged. "You've seen the power sources that fuel some of the automata. I've been filling vessels here for almost a year, and it hasn't diluted at all. Whatever it is, I think it might be more closely related to some of the strangeness around this town than any natural phenomena."

"Like someone put it there?"

I nodded. "There are a few beings I've heard of with the power to do it."

There was a time Theodore would've asked me more questions. Or he would have scoffed at my mention of supernatural things creeping along in the night. And something stalking the woods in broad daylight? Unthinkable. But we'd all seen things. Some of the families of the town had been open with Charlotte, and even a few with me. We knew there was a great deal more to our little town than one saw on the surface.

I took another sip, frowned, and looked down at my copper mug. Warmth flooded through me, sliding into my arms and down to my toes. That one sip felt more like a misguided night in my youth spent curled around a bottle of rum.

"I think this might be a little stronger than usual," I said. "Might even make the vampires happy."

Theodore frowned and stared at the stills for a moment, quite probably contemplating the still exploding. The kid had gotten lucky the first time. I was glad he hadn't blown himself up, or the new still.

"Old man, are you there?" a voice shouted from outside the shack.

I muttered under my breath, fairly certain the man would be able to hear every word. "Let me do the talking. I don't want you going and getting shot. Or worse."

CHAPTER 3

I raised my voice and said, "I'm here. And I have Theodore with me."

"You going to ask me in?"

"I thought that was just a legend," I said.

The voice on the other side of the door chuckled, and light flooded the shack as Roman, one of the Bishop brothers, stepped inside. Charlotte thought the man was handsome—debonair was the word she'd used. I knew his ilk. I suspected if he lived long enough, he'd have far less savory dealings than running moonshine. We'd have used him as bait on the galleons we once sailed.

"You're not so skeptical as most," Roman said, brushing dark hair away from his ocean-blue eyes. "But I already told you, I am no vampire."

"You hear stories," I said. "I suppose you heard our whole conversation?"

Roman hesitated, and I suspected he was pondering whether or not to play dumb in an effort to use the information as leverage at some later date. I rather thought he'd make a great politician someday, and I wasn't particularly fond of politicians. After a time, he nodded.

"Many of us in town already know about the pond. But I must admit, we hadn't thought about making moonshine out of it."

I barked out a harsh laugh. "That's because most of you have a better sense of self-preservation than my apprentice here."

Roman looked at Theodore and studied him for a moment. I took a deep breath, forcing myself to remain calm despite being in the presence of a creature I didn't fully understand. He wasn't entirely human, of that I had no doubt. Roman turned his attention back to me, his gaze boring into mine. "Have you thought about my offer? In all my years, I haven't met a bootlegger that could make a moonshine like yours."

"There are plenty of moonshiners out there that can do better than me." I held out the copper mug.

Roman frowned at it for a moment, and then apparently decided that he too had lived long enough. He sniffed at the rim of the mug before draining it in one long gulp. I studied Roman's face, watching his subtle frown lift slightly and the crease of his brow relax.

"Not bad?" I asked.

"You could sell this at every bar in town."

"We only have one bar."

"For now," Roman said. "I know you're not earning enough to keep that shop running. How many of the people who live here even know what horology is?"

I bristled at his words before muttering some rather inappropriate curses at Roman.

He smiled. "I was just trying to make a point."

Roman took a deep breath and settled onto a stool near the door. "Charlotte has been more open about your financial situation. She seems willing to entertain me handling distribution."

The liquor was clearly beginning to affect Roman, and that surprised me. He sighed and crossed his arms. He looked more relaxed than I'd seen him since I'd known him.

I crossed my arms, mimicking Roman's pose. I knew he'd spoken to Charlotte, and perhaps he thought he'd been subtle about it. That irritated me. But the simple fact of the matter was that we needed the deal, and I might be able to use it to get Roman's unwitting help.

I nodded. "I do have a condition. Two actually."

Roman inclined his head.

"Keep everyone away from the conservatory tomorrow. And if anything happens to me or Charlotte, you'll treat Theodore as you would me. With respect."

Roman's lips curled into a smile. "You're a brave man to demand what can be taken so easily."

"Make the deal," I said.

Bishop studied my hand for only a moment, then reached out and exchanged grips. "You'll be making some serious coin off of this, old man. You made the right choice."

"Be in the conservatory at daybreak," I said. "Make sure it's cleared out. I'll have a contract drawn up."

"Of course you will. See you around, Theodore." He paused at the doorway. "I understand there's an Unseelie fae that's taken some issue with you. Maybe they heard about your agreement to install the wards and didn't much like it." With that, Roman Bishop left.

I blinked at the empty doorway.

"You said yes," Theodore said.

"We need the money, and I imagine the Bishops will be more discreet than a lot of runners would be. I'm somewhat more concerned how Roman knew about the wards."

"The good news is he probably wants you alive," Theodore said. "You'll be his new supplier, after all."

I harrumphed. "We shall see."

I wondered if there was more to Bishop's warning, if something from our past had caught up to us.

Theodore pursed his lips, but said no more.

"Fill a few jars," I said. "We'll take them back to the shop. There's work to be done. We have to prep the wards for the conservatory, and we only have until sunrise to finish them."

The trek back may not have been any longer, but it was most assuredly more effort carrying a few large jugs of moonshine. Theodore had bound four of them together and stuffed them into a large sack. Almost every step he took, I worried that he was going to overbalance and tumble down the mountain. Or worse, break a jar.

Once we were back onto the relatively flat roads, the walk wasn't nearly as strenuous. My boots thudded on the wooden walkway outside the shop, and I pulled the door open to let Theodore in first. He shuffled past, careful not to smack the doorframe with the load he was carrying. The door had barely closed behind me when the thunderous chimes announced our arrival.

Charlotte grimaced and raised an eyebrow.

"I'll get to it," I muttered, glancing back at the calamity of chimes.

"Of course you will."

"Theodore knows about the aether," I said.

"Well, it's about time," Charlotte said. "He does have a key to the store, after all."

"He also ran the pond water through the still again," I said.

Charlotte's other eyebrow rose to join the first. "I confess I'm rather surprised to see both of you alive."

"The batch is surprisingly good," I said.

"You *drank* it?" Charlotte asked.

"It's not like it's the first time," I said. "We've been swimming in that pond before, before we realized what was."

"That wasn't distilled into a concentrated form," Charlotte said. "Lord above, that could have killed you both."

Theodore slowly untied the satchel after setting it on the workbench. His gaze flicked between me and Charlotte, and I suspected he was wondering if it was safe to speak.

"We're getting low on the vessels for aether," Charlotte said. "I checked the safe upstairs, and it looks like we only have a few left."

I grimaced before nodding. "The conservatory ward has to go up at daybreak. We should have enough vessels for the morning. Roman Bishop is going to draw everyone away from the conservatory. I'll have those defenses installed whether the innkeeper's agreed to it or not."

"What are the defenses?" Theodore asked.

"My great-grandmother used to call them wards," Charlotte said.

"Protection against the Unseelie fae." She glanced at me. "I assume we're telling him everything at this point?"

I nodded. I didn't really see a point in keeping anything else from Theodore. If he was going to live as a human among the monsters, he needed to understand.

He needed to be ready.

CHAPTER 4

"*W*hy is Roman Bishop going to help you with this?" Charlotte asked. "The Bishop boys have never seemed very fond of you."

I harrumphed.

"What have you gotten us into?"

"Nothing. I took Roman up on his offer to distribute our moonshine. That's it." I patted one of the jugs on the workbench. "And he's planning on selling this new aether brand at a premium. We may yet get out from under that banker."

Charlotte frowned, her lips just barely turning down at the edges. She was considering my words, and probably weighing the benefits of working with the Bishops against the weight of our debts. It was much the same argument I'd had in my own head.

"So be it." She nodded. "We need to do something."

"I know," I said quietly. "It's why I said yes."

Charlotte sighed.

"So what exactly are we doing tonight?" Theodore asked as he walked back into the room. He'd left for a short while after I'd told him it had been his girlfriend, Betsy, who had designed the wards. "And what do we need to do at the conservatory in the morning?"

A slow smile spread across my lips.

I exchanged a glance with Charlotte. Something that I'd truly come to enjoy about being in a relationship as long as we had been was that much communication could occur in just that glance. I couldn't really explain it, whether it was the tilt of the eyes, or the body position of the other person, but it was like we could carry on entire conversations without speaking a word.

I wanted to be sure she agreed with telling Theodore everything, and when she blinked once, slowly, I knew she did.

I turned my attention back to Theodore. "This place is a haven for people, and creatures, that are different from much of the world. And while most of the folks here may be the peaceful sort, we all have histories."

"What do you mean by histories?" Theodore asked. "I mean, we've all known some bad people . . ."

"These aren't just bad people," Charlotte said. "Settlers are going missing."

Theodore frowned slightly. He'd heard the rumors, stories of some of the stranger creatures that had been sighted around the town. People still liked to share stories around the campfire, even when those tales had more truth in them than the listeners may have known.

"There are Unseelie fae nearby." I let the words hang in the air, waiting for Theodore's reaction.

Theodore frowned. "What can we do?"

"Fae can die if exposed to iron," I said.

"Is that what we're doing at the conservatory?" Theodore asked. "Ironwork?"

I shook my head. Charlotte held up one of the aether vessels. "You've seen these before."

Theodore nodded.

"Gregory has designed them to work as a power source. And they can power a great many things."

"Combined with iron and wards, it makes for an effective defense against the Unseelie fae. That's what we're setting up in the conservatory. I think we can shield the entire town with three strategically placed wards. The inn, the saloon, and the meeting hall."

Charlotte glanced at me and frowned. "But we have concerns. The wards are fae wards, and if the fae themselves can be poisoned by iron, I worry what might happen. Will the iron cancel out their magic, or render it too weak to be useful? We'll test it tomorrow."

I studied Theodore for a short time. "We won't know until we try. It's better than anything we have right now. Charlotte can provide an amulet to the innkeeper that will offer protection to even an Unseelie fae should they choose."

Charlotte nodded. "You might want to call Betsy over for dinner. We have a lot of work to do tonight."

BETSY WAS one of those strange people who loved to cook. She had her hair pulled up into a braid that didn't look so different from Charlotte's, other than its jet black color. I'd suspected Betsy was something more than human the first time I'd met her, as even Charlotte had commented on her ethereal beauty. But it was also the only reason I could come up with as to why in the world she would be running around with Theodore, a brash young man most would consider far less attractive than Betsy.

"Disgusting," Charlotte said, eyeing the giggling couple as they worked on installing a handful of our smallest vessels.

"We used to be like that," I said.

Charlotte harrumphed. "Maybe in your head," she muttered.

"Maybe."

I scraped up the last bittersweet bread from my plate before picking up everyone else's dishes and taking them to the wash bucket in the back. It was more of a trough, I supposed, just a bit cleaner than what you'd let the horses drink out of. I let the small stack of dishes clink to the bottom where, if I was being honest, they'd probably soak for several hours.

My boots thudded on the hardwood floors as I made my way back to the workbench and settled in beside Charlotte. She was putting the finishing touches on one of her intricate gift boxes, more or less a bribe for the Petrans, the owners of the inn, for letting us work in the conservatory. For a moment, I didn't focus on my work; I just watched Charlotte. She moved with the deft motions of someone who had practiced their art for a very long time. There was no uncertainty as she slid fragile bits of wood into a baffling alignment that would only open when someone inserted one of the aether pendants, or broke the box open entirely. She fiddled with the lid and tightened the ratio on the wooden gears used to withdraw the locking bars.

"Pass me that pendant, would you," Charlotte said, "if you're just going to stare?"

I smiled and slid the slightly luminescent pendant closer to her. Her fingertips brushing mine, she took the locket and placed it on top of the puzzle box. The faint glow of the trapped aether etched its way across the box until the polished crystal she'd inlaid in the wood burst into life, and the mechanism inside clicked. The faintest echo of wood sliding across wood preceded the lid of the box slowly creeping open. Charlotte smiled at her handiwork, and I shook my head.

"That's a fine gift," I said. "Are you sure you want to give it away? I don't know if we have the finer?"

"There will always be more boxes. I think more might sell with the aether pendants. It's attractive."

"I'd certainly buy one," Betsy said. "My mother loved puzzle boxes."

"We can take a small one," Theodore said. "Leave it on her grave?"

Betsy gave him a smile and patted his shoulder.

I pulled the spring-loaded lever off the shelf behind the workbench. It had a long empty space in the middle, almost like a lathe that I would use to turn wood, but this was something quite different. Once the lever was securely mounted to the workbench, I pulled one of the folded iron plates out from the hidden drawer beneath the workbench. Some tinkers I'd known would go so far as to create hidden panels all across their shop, but I generally found that hiding something under the table was good enough.

The plate itself was mounted to a cylinder, and when its twelve sections were folded together, it looked like little more than the head of a walking cane. An unbalanced and perhaps ugly cane, but a cane nonetheless.

I pulled the lever, which struck the mechanism at the center of the pole, causing the plate to fan out and the small receptacle to become exposed. I slid one of the aether vessels into the pipe, not so unlike loading a bullet into a rifle. Once it was seated, I released the lever and let the plate slap closed once more.

"Are you bringing that one?" Theodore asked. "It looks like the ones you use in the automata, just bigger."

I shook my head. "It's similar, but it's not the same. This one will fit into the pipes that run along the conservatory. You remember the broken pipe you pointed out last week?"

Theodore nodded.

I pulled the cylinder off the lever and held it up. "This will fill that gap, and the aether will flow through the ward etched into this plate."

"You really think that gadget will power a ward?" Betsy asked.

I nodded.

"Where in the world did you get a fae ward?" Betsy asked. "Those aren't exactly common knowledge. Although, not so uncommon around here, I suppose."

I blinked at her. She'd given it to us. Was this a less-than-subtle way of telling us not to tell Theodore? I glanced between the two.

"Yes, I know she gave you the ward," Theodore said, exasperated. He turned to Betsy. "Is this really the time for more mischief?"

She grinned at him.

"It's not active when it's collapsed," I said, returning my attention to the ward. "Only when we install it will it activate."

"These aren't weapons," Charlotte said. She eyed Theodore for a moment. "They won't defend you from what's out there. You've seen them. Around the still, near the old mine."

Theodore nodded. "The man of shadows."

"So dramatic," Betsy said.

CHAPTER 5

It took more effort to keep our work clean as the night wore on. We needed precision in the assembly to allow the wards to work. When Theodore's head started to fall forward and his grip became loose on the ward he was working on, Betsy snatched the ironwork away.

My gaze may have been a bit too sharp, as she gave me an odd look.

Betsy glanced at Theodore, and then back to me. "Did you expect it to burn me?"

I blinked at the question.

"You've been good to Theodore," Charlotte said. "You've been good to us. There is no quarrel here, only the insatiable curiosity of a tinker."

I narrowed my eyes. "I can tell she's keeping secrets."

Betsy grinned. She glanced at Theodore, who was now half bent over on the workbench and snoring. "I like this town, and I like the people that have come here. I want no harm done to them."

I ran my finger across the rune etched in one of the plates that formed the ward. "You must like us if you've offered your family's magic."

Betsy didn't respond. She only offered a small smile, then elbowed Theodore to wake him up. He woke with a start, almost falling sideways off his chair before Betsy caught him.

"What did I miss?" Theodore asked before releasing a wide yawn.

"Wordplay and shenanigans," Charlotte said. "The usual nonsense."

"Are you still playing this game, Gregory?" Theodore asked, eyeing me.

The question rankled. "It's not a game, boy. It's simply a concern for Betsy's well-being, and ours. Fae magicks can be quite dangerous, to both the user and the target."

"You could be a politician with words so smooth as that," Betsy said.

"No, he couldn't," Charlotte said.

I snapped the last pole out of the levering mechanism and studied the panel on the back. Theodore had done the metalwork on parts of this one. The grooves fit together perfectly, so no man, or creature, could fit so much as a hair into the grooves to pry open the aether chamber.

"It's good work," I said. "Damn good work."

"I think we're done," Charlotte said. "Let's get packed up and ready to go."

"How many do we need for the morning?" Theodore asked. He gestured at the array of five plates and columns.

"We're only installing one," Charlotte said. "But take them all, in case we have issues when we try to install it."

"All of them?" Betsy asked. "Doesn't that seem a little excessive?"

"No," I said. "Charlotte's right. We haven't tested this on a structure as large as the inn and the conservatory."

Betsy nodded, apparently agreeing with the thought to some degree.

I looked at the clock on the wall, a mass of exposed gears and springs. We had about two hours before daylight. "If you want to, you're welcome to rest here. Or we can rendezvous in the morning."

"There's plenty of room in the guest room upstairs," Charlotte said.

"Let's just stay here," Theodore said. Betsy wrapped her arm around his and nodded.

"Until the morning then," I said.

"You're being too hard on that girl," Charlotte said, her voice barely above a whisper. "She has done nothing to us. She has done nothing to our friends. If she was a threat, we would've seen some semblance of it by now. No creature is so patient as to sit among their prey for a year."

"But—"

"No," Charlotte said. "You approach everything as if it's a threat. And sometimes you're right. But you've also alienated some of our greatest friends, and befriended some of our greatest enemies. And I think it's made you paranoid, Gregory. Theodore is a smart boy. I'm telling you, we should trust her until we see different."

"She touched the iron tonight," I said.

"Yes," Charlotte said. "She's clearly not an Unseelie fae sent to infiltrate our clock shop."

I harrumphed, but the sheer level of sarcasm in Charlotte's words made me cringe.

"I'm not saying you need to apologize," Charlotte said. "All I'm saying is you could be a little more subtle in your suspicions. Not everyone is out to get you. No matter how much you deserve it," she added with a small laugh.

I grumbled and pressed a small button on the side of my end table. A mechanism inside started to turn, and the old woven cable that led up to the suspended lanterns above us slowly closed and snuffed the light with an old iron half sphere.

"That sounds a little squeaky," Charlotte said. She elbowed me in the ribs.

"Woman. You'll be the death of me." I rolled closer and snaked my hand across her waist. She settled in next to me, and I kissed her, lightly at first, until she responded.

A moment later, she pulled away and cracked one eye open. "Don't even think about it. Two hours of sleep is barely enough as it is."

"We're too old for this," I said with a small laugh.

Our short sleep came and went far too quickly. It felt as though I had barely closed my eyes, barely drifted off, before the gentle buzz on my nightstand grew into the dull calamitous roar of my bell alarm clock. It didn't take much to get dressed, as we hadn't really bothered to get into night clothes. Changing into something soft and warm sounded much more appealing at that moment than trudging our way across the square to the conservatory.

"Get a move on, then," Charlotte said. "You can put some coffee in that contraption of yours."

I nodded and started down the stairs with heavy, sleepy footsteps, surprised when I reached the bottom and found Theodore and Betsy waiting for us at the workbench. They almost looked chipper, which I found unusually irritating.

Theodore slid a mug of coffee toward me, and Betsy clinked the copper vacuum flask down beside it. "No time for breakfast. Let's go."

"There's always time for breakfast," Charlotte said. She pulled the basket off the counter behind her workbench and held out a scone she'd made the day before. You could almost say there was an art to eating leftover scones. They tended to turn into rocks, but if you soaked it in coffee or tea for just a moment, it made for a quick and easy snack.

I frowned at the small sea of crumbs the scone left in my mug before dumping everything into the copper vacuum flask. Charlotte took a few sips of coffee and added hers to the thermos as well. I figured that would be enough to get us through the morning.

"Let's find out if these Bishop brothers are worth their word," I said.

"If they hear you say that," Betsy said, "it's not their word you'll have to worry about."

"I've dealt with sharper blades in my day," I said.

"Your day was quite a while ago," Theodore said. "Charlotte might have to abandon you to the old folks soon."

Charlotte choked out a laugh. I gave her an exasperated look.

Betsy hefted one of the leather sacks that held the wards and the mechanics. I grabbed the other. Charlotte was better and faster than me with any gun, her vision sharper even now than I think mine had ever been. I'd rather her hands be free to take care of any issues that might arise than to be tangled up hauling around more tools.

"Let's get this done."

CHAPTER 6

*C*rossing the square so early in the morning was almost as uneventful as I'd hoped. There were more people out than I'd expected, but maybe that was part of Roman Bishop's plan. While I'd normally be focusing on some of the newer unfinished buildings going up, that morning found me glancing down every alleyway and checking every shadowed doorway. Would an old Unseelie fae be hiding behind one of those doors? I suspected they had never really come after us in earnest. And what rush did they have, really? Time wouldn't move the same for an immortal.

"We aren't alone out here," Betsy said, hurrying forward to step up beside me.

"I can see that," I said.

Betsy grimaced. "I can see more than you. I can feel more than you. And you know it. We're being followed."

My first instinct was to look over my shoulder, but my survival instinct told me not to do something so obvious. "Can you tell who?"

"No," she said. "I can only tell what."

"You're no fae," I said under my breath. This probably wasn't the best time to grill Betsy about what she really was. But it might've been the best time to actually get an answer out of her, if she was worried about her own safety as well as ours. Or at least as well as Theodore's.

Betsy cursed under her breath. "I'm not."

"Of course you aren't," Charlotte said. "We've seen you handle iron like it was an inert piece of wood."

"We don't have time for this," Theodore hissed.

The total lack of curiosity in the boy's voice surprised me. I glanced back at him for a split second. "You already know." There was no accusation in my voice; it was simply a statement of fact.

"Of course he knows," Betsy said. "I'm a halfling. A halfbreed. Whatever horrible term you want to apply to me."

I blinked. I hadn't expected her to admit it so freely. A million things ran through my brain at once. With effort, I tamped down the rampaging questions in my head and asked the one that mattered. "What's behind us?"

"One fae, I think. It's hard to tell with all the iron we're carrying."

I took a deep breath and made a mental note that iron did affect Betsy, but it didn't seem to damage her physically.

The rest of the walk was far more tense. It felt longer, but nothing came from the shadows. No doorway creaked open as we passed, and nothing ambushed us from the alleys. We made our way past the most recently finished building closest to the end of the square, and as we turned the corner, the skeleton of the conservatory came into view. It was all copper and brass pipes with framing that housed a magnificent greenhouse. But now that we'd torn part of it down again, it was just dirt and metal and hope.

"Come," I said. "We may have a chance to test this far sooner than I would've preferred."

I made my way over to the pipes that would serve as the irrigation lines. I absently noted that the wood for the flooring had been delivered far earlier than had been expected. That wasn't necessarily a great thing, as the weather might take its toll.

The satchel slid off my back, and I gently laid it next to the support in the middle of the conservatory. My gaze lingered on a patch of dirt that had clearly been dug up and repacked, but it was out of the way, and not my concern at that moment. To the untrained eye, the support may have looked like a simple metal beam propping up the bulk of the structure. But there was a small section about five feet off the ground that had what appeared to be a solid iron band wrapped around it. I held up one of the aether vessels to a small indentation in the plate, and the mechanism behind it clanked. The plate fell, revealing the recess that would hold the wards we'd mounted.

"It looks like Bishop kept his word," Charlotte said. "I don't see anyone."

I nodded. I could hear the surprise in Charlotte's voice, and it very much echoed my own. Roman struck me as someone who might keep his word to the letter of the law, but he also might twist the spirit of it like a fae.

I placed the pipe into the recess, and a small knob set inside rocked perfectly into the indentation on the bottom of the pipe. I twisted it so the ward plate would be facing out. Once it was balancing on its own, I reached back for the tool bag, realizing I'd left it too far away. "Theodore, palm wrench."

Theodore rooted through my pack for a moment, and then handed me a device that didn't look much like a wrench at all. It was flat and slender, and slid easily into the recesses of the opening in the beam. It took me a moment fishing around in the darkness, but eventually I felt the metal slide over the valve that would let me adjust the mechanism inside.

Two turns lowered a piston from above and secured the pipe on top and bottom. I pulled the palm wrench out and handed it back to Theodore.

"It didn't open," Betsy said.

"Not yet," I said, pulling the larger aether vessel out of my pocket. This one wasn't massive, and it wasn't camouflaged to hide the glow. I reached inside the pole and snapped it into the receptacle that I'd mounted and sited a month before. It burst to life, and for a split second, I could see the aether tracing the wires that led to the ward's mount.

I snatched my hand back, knowing that had I left it in there, I had a real risk of losing it. Two seconds later, the plates snapped out, far faster than anything we'd seen in the workshop. The iron clanged together, forming a circle for the light tracing the ward and bursting into brilliant life before fading back to a dull glow.

"It works," Charlotte said.

"Is that confidence I hear in your voice?" I asked, grinning at Charlotte.

Theodore helped me raise the iron cuff until it sat in place, concealing the plate. I placed the aether key on an indentation higher up the band, and the locking mechanism clicked home.

We stood silently for a moment.

"And it doesn't bother you?" Theodore asked. "You're sure?"

"I told you it wouldn't," Betsy said. "I wouldn't lie to you, Theodore."

"What have you done?" a voice hissed from somewhere behind us.

CHAPTER 7

I turned, snapping my gaze to the area I thought the voice had come from. Behind us, a slender form waited. I'd only seen him this close once, with his sword nearly at my throat as I escaped into one of the old mines. It seemed to be one of the few places he wouldn't follow. The man of shadows.

"Driscoll," Betsy said, her voice verging on a growl.

At first I thought his eyes were locked on Betsy, but as he shifted, and the wind caught the tails of his finely tailored jacket, I realized he was staring at the ward.

"What have you done?" Driscoll asked. He pointed at Betsy. "You would give these unevolved monkeys fae magicks? I can sense it behind the iron. Behind the inferior power of the witches."

"But can you see my friends?" Betsy asked.

"I see you well enough, halfbreed," Driscoll snapped.

"That wasn't my question."

Driscoll froze, his eyes darting around the construction area. "I should strike you down for this."

A slow smile crawled its way across Betsy's face. In the end, the expression was more like she had bared her teeth at Driscoll, and the effect was terrifying.

"It's working," she said, turning her back on Driscoll.

"You can't see us?" Theodore asked her.

"A side effect I'd hoped the wards would give—a shield to anything that lives inside these walls."

"They're still here," Driscoll said. It wasn't a question.

I came to realize that Betsy had deliberately tipped him off to the fact we were still standing here. A power play? Something more? The girl perplexed me, and the loyalties of any immortal always concerned me.

Driscoll's sword sang as he unsheathed it, a narrow blade that looked as if it could be bent between two fingers. But I had little doubt about the deadliness of that edge, or the fae who wielded it.

"You're weak," Betsy said. "And this town will defend itself against your will. Abandon your vendetta, and leave these people in peace."

Driscoll's face curled into a snarl. "You go too far, halfbreed." He charged.

Charlotte raised her rifle as the Unseelie fae closed on us. Betsy produced two short blades not so unlike the razor-thin sword wielded by Driscoll. She played her role well. Well enough that it unnerved me. But this was what we wanted.

This was not what Driscoll expected. He barked out a primal scream as his sword slid through the air toward Betsy. It didn't get far. As soon as his hand hit the threshold, the finger he had extended at the tip of the blade snapped back in a terrible crack. Surprise lit Driscoll's face for a second before he crashed into the invisible wall created by the wards. The faerie stumbled, catching himself in an obscenely graceful dip. He frowned and looked back up at Betsy. "You're a fool if you think that will keep me out."

"Then come in," Betsy said. "If you can."

An unnatural calm settled over Driscoll's face. "I will tear this house down, girl. And these people will know it was you that brought their end."

Clouds shifted above us, and as the shadows moved across the world, the shadowed man went with them.

"Did that go well?" Theodore asked. "Was that really bad?"

"Bit of both," Charlotte muttered.

"He issued you a challenge," I said, turning to Betsy.

She nodded and looked to the sky. "He'll return at the same time tomorrow. And he will keep his word."

I cursed. "How likely do you think it is he'll attack us before then?"

"Driscoll is known to be deceitful," Betsy said. "It is certainly a possibility."

"Then we stay together," I said. "You two come back to the shop with us. You can help me finish the wards before we all die horribly."

"Who could resist an invitation like that?" Charlotte asked. "I'll even serve you some stale bread for your last meal."

Betsy gave us a small smile as she slid her daggers back into her sleeves. Theodore just gave us a nervous laugh.

I pulled one of the portable wards out from the inside of my leather jacket and turned it over in my hand. "I would have liked to have tried this."

"I'm afraid you'll have your chance," Betsy said. "But I'm not sure you really want it."

WE WERE WALKING AWAY when I heard the first of the voices behind us, people returning to the inn from whatever distraction Bishop had set up. The construction workers would be back at their tasks without realizing what had happened, or what had been added to the conservatory.

I let out a relieved sigh as we crossed the threshold into our shop. It had been a long time since I'd fought any sort of battle. I didn't like the idea of going head-to-head with an Unseelie fae. If it had to happen, I was glad Charlotte was with me, and Theodore, and most especially Betsy.

"Thank you, Betsy," I said. "The ward clearly works."

She inclined her head.

"I thought Driscoll would use magic," I said. I had a sneaking suspicion he could cut us down without much effort.

"Most of the bloodthirsty fae I've known prefer to cut you open with their swords if they can," Betsy said. "Make no mistake—we insulted him, and it's going to get ugly."

I felt the reassuring weight of the clip for my harmonica pistol in my left breast pocket. It wasn't as portable as a revolver, and some would say it was not as reliable, but I'd come to know it quite well, and the ammunition was easy to manufacture.

"Even if the bullets fail," Betsy said, "the shields won't."

It was unnerving the way some people, and especially the fae, could read a human so easily.

"You and Theodore can make more money selling arms to the city," Charlotte said. "You wouldn't have to worry about what my crotchety old husband needs you for."

"Crotchety?" Theodore asked. "Is that a new term for cheap? Penny-pinching?"

"It's a new term for unemployed," I said slowly.

Betsy grinned at me and turned her attention to Charlotte. "I know we could. I know that would be a nice life for Theodore. But I have no desire for war."

"War?" I said.

Betsy remained quiet. And again I found myself wondering just how long she'd lived. How much she'd seen. And what she didn't tell us.

"When I was young, and lived in another place, there were wars. The humans rejected the half fae, and the Unseelie made to wipe us out. Not drive us from our home. They sought genocide. And it is why I help you now."

I often thought of war as the realm of man. As though humans were the only ones stupid enough to encourage the wholesale slaughter of their own people. But the more knowledge I'd gained of other beings, faeries and werewolves and things I once thought nothing but tales for children, I was coming to realize we were not unique for killing in this world.

"I will make you a thousand shields," Betsy said. "But I will not make your weapons. I will not give you a blade to pierce the heart of another, or a bullet to steal the life of a stranger.

"The journeys in past lives of the people who come to this settlement brought much darkness with them. There are darker things here. And there are darker things coming."

CHAPTER 8

"We need to get back to the mine," I said, rooting through the cabinet drawer that was now depleted of its usual load of ore. "I don't think I have enough to make the vessel for the meeting hall. It's not going to be enough to shield the town."

"Are you mad?" Betsy asked. "Driscoll's going to be watching for you. You think he won't be watching the mines?"

"We have to take that chance," I said. "He might be watching the stills."

"And if you're wrong?" Charlotte asked. "You think you'll dissuade him with what's in your pocket? You don't even know if that will work."

"What?" Betsy asked.

"Gregory carries the clip you etched for his gun."

"I am well aware of what I placed on it," Betsy said. "That old ward will prevent the metal from rupturing when he fires. What he chooses to do with what comes out of that barrel is of no consequence to me."

"Even if it changes the bullet?" Charlotte asked.

Betsy nodded.

The front door creaked open, and the clock chimes boomed into life a moment later.

"Are you open?" A slender man asked as he stepped inside. "I've heard you sell very fine puzzle boxes, and strange figures that can move on their own."

Charlotte's irritation flipped over to her smiling salesman persona in a second. "Automata, yes, of course we do. Is it a special occasion? A gift for a lady you're courting? I'm Charlotte, by the way."

"Lawrence," the man said, ignoring her other questions, instead staring at the wall of puzzle boxes and various watches we'd made and occasionally plundered over the years. "Lawrence Mills."

"Mills," I said. "You're one of the founders."

He nodded and gave me a small smile. "I heard you were taking action."

"Heard from who?"

"Mihail, at the inn. A few of us know of your past with the Unseelie. Some might wonder if you are . . . more worried than you need to be."

"Probably where Roman heard it then," I said under my breath, letting Lawrence's words slide off my back. I raised my voice a bit. "Best to be prepared."

Lawrence eyed Betsy for a moment, looked like he was going to say more, but remained silent. He stepped closer to one of the displays on the far side of the room.

"The automata are mostly in the cases," I said, inclining my head toward the wall of tall glass cabinets. "I'm not sure what your budget runs, but they're more expensive than most puzzle boxes."

"Gregory," Charlotte snapped. "That was rather rude."

I blinked. Some of the social niceties escaped me in my old age.

Lawrence held his hand out in a placating gesture. "It's fine," he said with a laugh. "No insult was taken."

"You see," I said. "Perfectly reasonable young man."

Charlotte turned slightly and scowled at me so Lawrence wouldn't be able to see.

"Are you shopping for a lover?" Betsy asked.

"Yes, and no. I'd like something that our grandchildren's grandchildren will still be able to enjoy long after we're gone."

Charlotte smiled and turned to the wall of puzzle boxes, pulling down a gold rectangular box. It was one of my favorites, with the mechanisms partially exposed, but hidden in intricate geometric patterns that surrounded a circle set in the middle.

"Oh, Christine would love that," Lawrence said, taking the box from Charlotte.

Charlotte held out a pendant. "This is the key. Placing it on top will start the lock opening."

Betsy turned to Charlotte. "Why don't you let Theodore and me take care of the shop? That delivery isn't going to wait."

Lawrence didn't seem to find anything strange about this conversation. And I rather admired Betsy's penchant for subtlety.

Charlotte nodded. "Of course. That's a wonderful idea. Come, dear."

We made our way into the back of the shop. Charlotte went straight for the armoire that was far more than it seemed. She opened the front of the massive piece, and at first glance, it appeared to hold nothing but sweaters and neatly folded trousers. When she pulled a hidden leather lever beneath the third shelf, a second layer opened, one that was partially sunken in the wall. Here were some of my stranger inventions: mechanical armor, swords that could be folded into their own selves, and ammunition that I'd not yet gained the confidence to test.

Charlotte pulled a pair of vambraces off one peg. She handed me the thicker one, and wrapped the other around her forearm. The front of the leather had what appeared to be random gears stuck to it, with a large gap in the center. But they weren't random—everything had a purpose. I handed her one of the cartridges from the inside of the right hand door, which she snapped into the opening on her vambrace. I did the same with mine, enjoying the satisfying click when everything locked together. I designed them for utility, and there were several different attachments we could use with the armor. The choice of shields seemed prudent for the day, but I also took the time to hand

Charlotte a dark gray metallic cartridge. It was expandable, and held small bolts almost like a crossbow. In one accessory, we now had something to defend ourselves, and attack if needed.

Once we'd gathered up all we planned to take, I hefted the pack onto my back. It was unlikely anyone would steal the rudimentary mining equipment we'd left in the old caves, but I didn't want to hike all the way up there only to find we had nothing to help extract the ore.

I heard Theodore complimenting our patron's choice of puzzle box as we made our way out the back door. I exchanged a smile with Charlotte.

"He has some sense about him," Charlotte said as the door snapped closed behind us. "That will be useful to you."

"He's already quite useful," I said.

"I mean more useful than ruining your batches of moonshine, and trying to blow himself up."

"Fair point."

We made our way across town and followed the stream for a while. I waited until the sounds of the hammers, crashing boards, and what bustle there was in the town turned to nothing but a whisper.

"You're right," I said.

"About Betsy?" Charlotte asked.

I nodded.

"Of course I was." Charlotte lowered her voice. "What else could she be?"

"You mean your family didn't pass down ancient fae wards from generation to generation? I thought that was a regular dinner conversation for most families."

Charlotte blew out an exasperated breath. "At least you can admit when you're wrong. Watching Theodore twist his words up and ignore logic altogether, just so he doesn't have to admit he was wrong, is truly a spectacle."

"I know," I said. "But he means well."

We followed one of the rough mountain trails close to where the stills were at. Or at least close to where the path to the stills branched off. This time we continued on, climbing higher, making our way toward the Great Falls.

The sound of the falls crept up on us. You could hear them all the way from the town if you listened close enough and the birds were quiet enough, but it was different in the woods. It was always there, a little rush, the echoes of the stream winding through ancient rock. But the sound grew as we rounded a boulder, and the mountain split open before us.

Water crashed down into the pool at our feet, sending a fine mist into the air. It was a place you didn't want to be in the chilly months. My eyes trailed up the slope, half taking in the beauty, and half looking for Driscoll.

CHAPTER 9

"*L*et's get down there, then," Charlotte said.

I led the way off what to the naked eye looked like a ledge, but below the rounded face of a rock was a fractured stone that worked very much like an ill-formed staircase. When I first heard about the cave, or more like when I first stumbled onto it, I hadn't realized just how valuable it was. Some folks would be taken with the fancy gemstones and a few veins of precious metals found deeper in the cave system, but that's not why I was here. I was here for the strange ore. I'd tried crafting the aether vessels from gold and silver, copper and bronze, but they all failed. Some alloys lasted longer than others, but most couldn't survive the heat.

Aether itself didn't give off much heat, if any, but when used in devices like we concocted for the wards, it did. It wasn't what I thought of as natural heat, but one able to melt metal as it was while leaving flesh and wood untouched. I found it peculiar enough that I tried building a vessel out of wood, but the aether would seep through and eventually escape no matter how much I polished and sealed the outer layers. Only the ore in these caves mixed with iron seemed able to hold it. I only wished I knew what it was.

Down in the pool at the base of the falls waited boulders the size of horses. They sat in a pattern, spiraling out from the center of the falls. It was an ill-defined pattern, and I supposed many folks might not even consider it a pattern at all, but I'd spent enough time in the woods and streams to know that it wasn't natural.

"Something's above us," Charlotte said. She followed these words up with a small laugh, and her nonchalant approach sent a bolt of adrenaline down my back. It was a simple way to throw your enemy off, to not let on you knew they were there.

"Get in the cave," I said.

"I plan to," Charlotte said. "Of course, I have an old fool in front of me slowing me down."

I gave her a tight smile. We raised our voices, shouting to each other with the intent of seeming oblivious to whoever was watching. But we weren't oblivious. I'd seen the shadow now, near the top of the waterfall.

I waited until we rounded the back of one of the large boulders, which hid us from the eyes above. And I hissed, "Run!"

Sprinting across wet stone was a good way to break your body, but here it was even riskier. You get your foot caught in the wrong place, and the rivers swell, the waters would swallow you whole. Of course, the more obvious threat today was a bit more immediate.

Our boots splashed in puddles and echoed around the sunken pool. We'd almost reached the edge of the waterfall when I saw the shadow move above us. It was either a madman flinging himself to his death, or a faerie gifted with flight.

"Dive!" Charlotte shouted.

Next thing I knew, she'd pushed me forward. As I tumbled into the shadowed cave entrance, I saw the sword flicker through the waters above my head. Charlotte pulled the lever on the side of her vambrace, and a shield exploded out from the sides. She used it to batter away the sword before diving over me. Charlotte grabbed my wrist and yanked me toward the shadowy cavern. It was a small opening, but I'd sunken enough iron into the entrance to deter most fae. Nothing tried to follow us past the waterfall. The falls parted, and a snarling face appeared with water running down its ears and nose.

Driscoll eyed the entrance to the cave, then flung himself back through the waterfall.

"He really doesn't like us much," Charlotte said.

I barked out a laugh. "Come on."

THE LANTERNS I'd left inside the cave several months before waited on a rickety wooden table. I remembered bringing Theodore here once and how he worried the lanterns wouldn't light with so much moisture in the air. That was before I showed him the fuel wrapped in the oiled leather pouches. I dropped two jagged white chunks into the lantern base and added a little water. We waited a few seconds before striking flint across the face of the lantern. The gas caught fire. The reflectors hooked on the little lanterns focused the light and pierced the shadows. Charlotte slid the mount of a lantern into her vest, and we made our way into the narrow section of the cave.

If I'd been much larger, the cave would've been impassable. As it was, the lantern on my own vest scraped against one wall while my shoulder blades scraped against the other. The passage was wider near the floor. I supposed I could've gone through on my stomach, but the cave had a tendency to take on water. And that seemed like a stupid way to die.

"I think I need to feed you less bread," Charlotte said. "Or we'll have to come up here and pry you out of this cave one day."

I didn't argue. She was right.

We only spent a few minutes in the narrows before the cave mercifully opened wide. It wasn't long before we could walk shoulder to shoulder without bumping into each other or the side of the cave. The glow of the lantern light glinted on some dusty metal in the distance.

"Looks like the equipment is still here," I said.

"Really, Gregory, who is going to climb into this mess and figure out how to drag that equipment out of here?"

"There are other passages through here. You never know if

someone will find an easier way. We've dug a fairly deep channel into this mountain now." I shined my light at the timbers supporting the entrance to the tunnel I'd carved out over the past year.

The tunnel sloped downward and our conversation trailed off. Keeping our footing required more effort than at the relatively flat entrance to the cave. Theodore and I had carved wide rough steps into the steeper parts of the slope while leaving a smooth, almost ramp-like expanse to our right. It was down that ramp we let the heavier tools slide.

"Why don't you just leave all these at the bottom of the ramp?" Charlotte asked.

"Because if there's a cave-in, we'll lose all of our tools. It would be bad enough to lose the effort of digging this place out. Losing all our gear as well would take much longer to replace."

It wasn't long to the bottom of the curved tunnel, but it always felt significantly longer than it was. It was more damp than the mine above us had been. Part of it was cool and dry further in, until we finally reached the wall we'd been mining ore from.

While we didn't leave much equipment in the mine, we did leave the boilers at the bottom of the shaft. When they were filled with water, they were far too heavy to move. There was just enough of a trickle running down the ceiling that I was able to set up a sluice to refill them while we were out. Now one of them was overflowing, and I was glad I'd added an overflow release to keep the fuel below dry.

Charlotte lit the fire under the boilers while I studied the ore lodged in the wall. "I think we can stay on this vein that Theodore and I started." I ran my finger along a reflective gray streak embedded in the wall.

"You've gone deeper than I thought you would," Charlotte said. She pointed at the wooden support beams above me. "You're really stretching this out. You're going to need to get more lumber down here, and I don't think we can afford to hire anyone right now."

"Quite sure we can convince Betsy's friend to help us again. I never saw the man last time, and I suspect there's a very good reason for that."

"Fae?"

"That would be my suspicion."

Charlotte nodded. "It makes sense. Who else could have gotten timber in without being seen? Or at least without piquing someone's curiosity or leaving an obvious trail through the woods?"

I took a deep breath and turned back toward Charlotte. "The boilers ready?"

"Almost. The smaller one. Larger won't be ready for some time."

A few minutes later, the first hiss of steam punched through the release valve of the smaller boiler. I slid one end of the braided hose over the nearest valve and ratcheted a clamp down to hold it in place. Charlotte picked up the bigger end. She took what looked like deformed pickax heads out of the bag we'd dragged down and started attaching them to a belt that ran around the digger. Another minute and we were ready to start.

The fires turned the room into something more like a hot spring. What had been relatively dry had now been saturated by the steam emanating from the boilers.

"Ready?" I asked.

Charlotte pulled a pair of goggles down over her face and rolled out the leather mask hanging beneath them. It would keep the worst of the debris away from her face, and protect her lungs all at once. She nodded.

I opened the valve on the boiler, and the hose spasmed. The braid expanded and fattened as the superheated steam rushed down. A cloud of white spewed from the side when Charlotte threw the lever.

The handheld digger roared to life, and Charlotte leaned into it, placing it against the wall where I'd indicated the vein of the gray ore.

What had been a quiet cave with nothing more than the hiss of fires became a deafening cacophony of machinery, broken stone, and crumbling ore. I grinned as I watched Charlotte work. She wielded the digger with more familiarity and ease than Theodore ever could. When the larger chunks of ore fell from the wall, I checked the clumps closer to me so I could scoop them up and drop them into a wheeled cart.

We stayed at it for another fifteen or twenty minutes before the digger clanged against something hard enough and deep enough to stop the sleeve of spinning pickax blades.

"Whoa!" I shouted.

Charlotte shut the valve, and the digger wound to a stop, the steam spraying from the side of the machine. I closed the valve on the boiler.

"What was that?" Charlotte asked.

"Looks like a large deposit of ore," I said, leaning in closer and adjusting my lamp so I could see the dented metal in the light.

"I don't think we're getting that out with the digger."

"I don't know if we're ever getting that out," I said. "And certainly not today."

Charlotte looked down at the ore loaded up in the small wheeled cart. "You think it's enough?"

I nodded. "Let's get back to the shop."

"Let's see if that wagon will float first," Charlotte said.

"I'm a little worried about that," I said with a nod. "This is a lot more ore, but I can't tell exactly how much metal is in each rock." I cursed. "I should've just built the pulverizer up here like I'd planned to."

"Of course. That would've been so subtle. I'm sure no one would've noticed you hauling all that equipment through the woods."

"Yes . . . Well . . ."

"We can load some of it into the packs. Just to be safe," Charlotte said.

"There's too much equipment in the packs," I said.

"Well," Charlotte said, "let's leave some of it here. At the bottom of the mine. It's not likely to flood this week, and no one's going to find it."

Charlotte made a lot of sense. She tended to be more levelheaded when I got frustrated and worried that one of my plans wasn't working out exactly as it should have.

I nodded. "You're right. We have to keep Driscoll away. Let's go."

CHAPTER 10

e propped the digger up so the blades wouldn't be resting on the ground. It may have been an unnecessary precaution considering the steel they'd been forged from, but I wasn't so sure about the mount of the blade itself.

"We used it to dig ore out of a rock wall," Charlotte said. "I'm sure it can survive sitting on the ground."

"Probably," I said, "but I'd rather not take the chance."

We finished clearing out the leather sacks we used for hiking and started dragging the wagon back up the ramp. The harness I had fastened around my shoulders and waist had actually been one of Theodore's ideas. Before that, we'd been dragging the wagon by hand, and every trip had been exhausting. I wouldn't say that hauling a load of ore was easy, but a great deal of strain had certainly been lifted by Theodore's addition.

"The question now," I said, taking a deep breath as we reached the top of the mine once more, "is whether or not Driscoll is waiting for us."

"Check your armor," Charlotte said. "We don't want to be caught unprepared."

I nodded and went about doing just that.

We reached the entrance to the mine, and I frowned at the overarching barrier of iron. I silently hoped we wouldn't need our armor, and stepped outside.

I dragged the wagon deeper into the waterfall, until we were nearly out the other side. This was the best place I'd found to lower the wagon into the waters. I undid the harness and pulled one of the sacks of ore onto my back. It was heavy, but not unbearably so. Charlotte did the same. Once we had a good length of rope tied to the edge of the wagon, Charlotte started back along the ridge. I slowly let the wagon slide into the waters, grinding my teeth as the corner went under, and blowing out a breath when the ballast tanks dipped for only a moment, keeping the wagon afloat. It vanished through the edge of the falls as Charlotte pulled it toward the other side.

I yanked the harmonica pistol out of my jacket and removed the ammunition from my vest. The two pieces slid together with a click, and I hurried around the bank to meet Charlotte.

She dragged the wagon through the water, maneuvering around boulders and small whirlpools until she finally reached the sloping bank we could use as a ramp on the other side.

"You have it?" I asked.

The look on her face told me that she had it, and that I was, in fact, an idiot for asking. Old habits, I supposed. You work with an apprentice long enough, and you just assume everyone needs a little help.

Charlotte had the wagon out of the water before she let out a long sigh. She slid the pack off her back and let the stone-filled leather crack down onto the small pile of ore. I did the same, awkwardly shifting the straps around my harmonica pistol.

"Did you see something?" Charlotte asked, eyeing the pistol.

I shook my head. "I don't want to fumble with it if I do see something. Just wanted to be ready."

Charlotte tapped the dark gray box on her vambrace. It was her way of telling me she agreed, without actually telling me she agreed.

I fastened the harness to myself again, and we started back down the trail. For the steeper parts of the woods, Charlotte pulled on the rope from behind to keep the wagon of ore from running me over. It was a little awkward in the rougher areas of the trail, and for the most severe parts, we both got behind the wagon. There were a lot of stupid ways to die in the woods, and getting run down by an ore wagon was particularly dumb.

I stared at the shadows to the west. The sun was high enough now that a decent amount of sunlight penetrated the canopy, but the shadows it cast were misleading at best. Every crack of a branch sent my eyes roaming toward the deepest parts of the woods. Charlotte studied the canopy, something you needed to do when you were dealing with an enemy that could fly.

"What's Driscoll's issue with this town anyway?" Charlotte asked. "Is it really just because he's at odds with the Court of the Sun and the Moon?"

"Around here, that's like saying is he really just at odds with the sheriff," I said. "Going against the rule of law in any city is bound to get you in trouble."

"Of course," Charlotte said. "That's why you have a license to produce liquor. All your moonshining is aboveboard."

"Of course," I said with a small laugh.

A twig snapped nearby, and I froze. Something was close, something big.

"You need not fear me, Gregory," a voice said from the shadows, so smooth and silky that I distrusted it immediately.

I started to unhook my pistol from my vest, but Charlotte's hand shot out and interrupted me.

"It's Orna," she said.

"The wood elf?"

The shadow of a tree moved, and a large deer strode into the clearing, and upon its back sat a creature of impossible beauty.

"Orna . . ." Charlotte whispered.

"Orna?" I said, raising my eyebrows.

"Peace, mortals," the woman said, her voice lilting as if sung by the finest bard, the sunlight caressing alabaster skin that betrayed no human imperfections.

"What do you want of us?" I asked, my voice throaty and gruff compared to Orna's.

"I have driven away the Unseelie stalking you in these woods. You bring my goddaughter into danger."

"Goddaughter?" I said, unable to keep the surprise from my voice.

"Betsy?" Charlotte asked.

Orna inclined her head. The deer moved with her, as if it too agreed with Charlotte's words.

"Yes, Betsy is the name she has taken for herself in this life. The name she has chosen to share with the mortals. No harm will come to her."

"We would never," I said.

"I do not believe you would intentionally harm her, or allow harm to come to her, but now comes the Unseelie known as Driscoll. And that is an unfortunate turn of events. Should my family come to harm from your meddling, I will hold you and Driscoll responsible. The consequences will be immediate."

"Betsy is her own person," Charlotte said as Orna started to turn away. "We don't control her decisions. Her willingness to help us was a kindness. But it does not place the responsibility on our shoulders."

Orna paused and tilted her head, slowly turning back to Charlotte. "I have lived through days where I would have struck you down for such words. And perhaps there is some truth in your words, mortal. But there is more truth in mine. You will be held responsible."

Orna turned in earnest, and the deer began to pace away.

"Then help her," I shouted after her. "Stop Driscoll. Is it not your duty to stand against the Unseelie?"

She didn't turn around again, but her voice echoed through the woods and whispered through the leaves. "You have much to learn of the fae."

The deer crossed into a shadow, and Orna was gone.

Charlotte took a deep breath and turned to me. "That was new. What did we get tied up in this time?"

"Nothing much. Apparently just a minor fae who rules over the woods in this area. Still better than morgens."

Charlotte barked out a laugh. "Let's get back. The longer we stay here, the more likely it is Driscoll will come back."

I nodded and leaned into the harness.

CHAPTER 11

*H*eading back into the town was truly a relief. We dragged the wagon to the back of the shop, and I pulled up a small lift we'd installed on the rear deck. Footsteps sounded in the kitchen before the door creaked open.

"We were getting worried," Theodore said. "You've been gone quite a while."

I glanced at my watch and frowned at Theodore. "We've been up to the mine, acquired the ore, and journeyed back to town. I rather think we made excellent time."

"Did you see Driscoll?" Betsy asked as we crossed the threshold into the shop.

"We did," I said. "Thankfully, we lost him at the entrance to the mine. Although I'd say that was one of the less interesting parts of our trip."

"I saw him in town, too," Betsy said. "Walking toward the conservatory."

"If you saw him," Charlotte said, "it's because he wanted you to see him."

I nodded my agreement. "Boilers ready?"

Theodore nodded. "They're set, and the rock crushers are ready to go."

"Good," I said. "Start loading the ore in. As soon as you have it sorted out, get it in the crucible. We're going to try casting the vessels. We don't have time to form them by hand."

"Time before what?" Betsy asked.

"Time before Driscoll comes after you, and then your godmother comes after us."

"What?" she said, unable to conceal the surprise in her voice.

"The more interesting part of our trip," Charlotte said.

"You saw Orna?" Theodore asked.

I smiled. "You've been sharing a lot with him."

"That's none of your business," Betsy said. "It's none of hers, either."

"I'll be sure to remember that when she tramples us with her *deer*," Charlotte snapped.

"You're welcome here," I said, "but the least you can do is forewarn us."

"How am I supposed to forewarn you of something I'm unaware of?" Betsy snapped. "Most of the fae won't intercede in mortal affairs, but you can rest assured they'll take revenge. They thrive on it."

Theodore, apparently being the wiser of the two of us in that moment, dragged the wagon back through the kitchen and out into the workshop where the crucible and the rock crusher waited.

"Perfect—" I started.

"Shut it," Charlotte said. Her voice was just as cutting as Betsy's, only I didn't understand where the anger was coming from. "Leave her alone. She's good as family to us, as much as Theodore is, and I'll not have you talking down to her."

My anger flared for a moment, but I stifled it with a deep breath. Charlotte was right. Betsy was sticking her neck out for Theodore, for us. How could we do any less?

I ground my teeth together and slid out of my tool-laden vest. I let it drop with a loud thud to the workbench as I stormed through the doorway, more angry with myself than Betsy. "I'm sorry."

As I followed Theodore out into our second workshop, I heard Charlotte telling Betsy that I didn't always handle stress very well. She was right, but the comment rankled.

The workshop in the back of the building wasn't as neat and polished as the workbenches that the customers saw. Here there was almost always a fine layer of dust on things, but it wasn't from lack of use. It was the powder created from pulverizing rock, along with shards left from working with glass and metal. The scent of hot metal and burning coals filled the air, the small steam engine whirring as it pumped air into the fires.

The shop felt like home. Sometimes even more so than the home we kept above it.

"You okay?" Theodore asked.

I nodded. I picked up some of the larger chunks of ore and placed them in the chute of the rock crusher. The metal and stone clanged against the steel slide.

Theodore pulled the brass lever down that opened the gate for the steam. The piston started up, bits of ore rattling into the crusher as our conversation was drowned out by the calamity of the machine.

We continued like that for a few moments, feeding the raw ore into the machine and gathering the crushed remnants on the other side.

There it mixed with water before running down a sluice. The concentrate separated until we were left with rock containing the metals we needed, and a lighter, more fluid mass that carried smaller flecks and shards of the gray substance. Theodore funneled this into a barrel. Once we had enough, he loaded the smaller remnants onto the wagon with the barrel and dragged it toward the back door.

I turned to watch him go before starting to shut down the rock crusher. It would take a while for heat from the steam engine to dissipate. In the meantime, we could start smelting the ore.

Once I was satisfied the fires were out and the rock crusher was on its way to cooling down, I followed Theodore into the back.

The furnace may have been attached to the shop, but it generated far too much heat to keep it indoors. Perhaps it would've been possible if we had a large barn, or other open area, but as it was, I didn't want to burn the house down.

Theodore flipped open the metal disc that sat on top of the furnace. Inside burned a fire hot enough that it glowed like the sun.

The long tongs we used for loading ore into the crucible were unwieldy and hard to handle. I'd come up with a solution to use it with wicker baskets. We lowered it into the crucible where it burst into flames and let the ore settle to the bottom.

"We can get more in here," Theodore said. "Probably at least another quarter of the load."

I shook my head. "We don't need that much."

I grabbed a hook and used it to pull the heavy lid closed. Theodore turned the valve, and airflow into the furnace increased, sending a small burst of flame out through the hole in the center of the lid.

"You want to do anything with the barrel now?" Theodore asked.

"No," I said. "We have all we need for the vessels. Let's focus on that."

"How do you plan to cast these?" Theodore asked.

Most of the work we'd done with the vessels for the aether involved crafting them by hand. That took time, more time than I was willing to risk with Driscoll in town.

I pulled two pairs of wood blocks out from underneath the workbench beside the furnace.

"You can't get the details of the vessels chamber with that," Theodore said.

I handed Theodore one set of blocks and said, "Look inside."

Theodore cracked the block open, and his eyes widened as he stared at the intricate web work of copper and iron. "You think this will work?"

"The theory is sound. And what better time than now to test it?"

"I don't know," Theodore said. "Maybe about two weeks ago before we really needed it?"

I barked out a harsh laugh and said, "You make a fair point. Ore from the cave will form a bond with the copper."

"An alloy," Theodore said, nodding his head. "And the iron has a higher melting point so it should help you keep it shaped."

"That's the theory," I said.

"Aren't you worried about weakening the wards?" Betsy asked as she stepped outside the shop and joined us by the furnace.

I glanced between her and Theodore before nodding. "Do you think it will impair the aether itself?"

Betsy frowned. "I honestly don't know. The vessel you're building, it is not a solid structure."

"I'm hoping the alloy will have enough of the ore's property to conduct the aether."

Betsy nodded. "I suppose we'll see soon enough."

"Let's get them ready," I said.

Theodore put the mold back together, and set it into a square metal box partially filled with sand. I handed him the second mold, and he did the same.

"You think those channels are wide enough to take the alloy?" he asked as he studied the points we'd be pouring the molten metal into.

"Should be fine," I said. "Let's fill that up with sand and get ready to pour."

Betsy studied the furnace and the box we were using to cast the vessels. "I think I'll just wait inside."

I leaned toward Theodore. "I think she's smarter than us."

"Oh, I have no doubt about that," Theodore said.

The door clicked closed behind Betsy as Theodore finished leveling the sand off around the molds.

"Grab the tongs," I said as I picked up the hook and moved toward the furnace.

"You want me to pour?" Theodore asked.

"I can handle this." I pulled on thick heavy leather gloves. The padding inside of them was enough that I could barely move my hands, but it provided an adequate level of insulation from the heat of the forge.

Theodore hurried to put his own gloves on. Once he was ready, I lowered the end into the forge, and hooked the tongs around the crucible.

"Locked in," I said.

"Ready."

He nodded and stepped back, only helping with leverage to get the crucible, now filled with slag and molten ore, evenly out of the forge. Even with our protective clothes on, this wasn't the kind of thing you wanted sloshing over your feet. I'd known more than one blacksmith over the years who had terrible injuries from accidents like that. I'd known some who didn't survive it.

Sweat poured off both of us as the heat of the open furnace filled the area with a stifling blast of air. I positioned the red-hot crucible in the sand and took a deep breath before turning my entire body slightly to line up the spout on the crucible with the opening in the mold. Another moment of focus, and then I levered it forward. Liquid metal slid from the crucible like a river of heated butter. It spat steam into the air as it slid into the mold. It only took a few seconds of pouring before the opening at the other end of the mold bubbled molten metal up in the sandbox. I carefully tilted the crucible back into a sitting position.

"Let's get the other one," I said, grabbing the tongs close to where they were connected. I could feel the heat through my gloves now, a good sign that I was done handling the tongs. With the crucible positioned, Theodore stepped away. I repeated the pour before emptying the crucible into a small round pocket at the edge of the metal box. Once the extra metal cooled, we could knock the slag off and would have all the metal we needed to make the rest of the vessels later.

CHAPTER 12

"Turn the forge down," I said. "We shouldn't need it now."

Theodore stuck the crucible back on top of the forge before he released the tongs. Those he hung back on the metal hooks, with the heat safely out of the way.

Theodore straightened his back with a start and turned to face me. "Are we going to get aether in those?"

"It's already in," I said. "It's the only option I could think of that would allow us to do the casting."

Theodore looked back at the box of molds. "What if it would've ruptured?"

"I suppose if it had, we likely wouldn't be talking about it right now."

"If this works," Betsy said, walking back outside to join us, "you've only provided the town protection against one threat. I don't believe these wards will dissuade a great many of the other things that threaten the settlement."

"And I thought I was the optimistic one," I said.

Charlotte let out a low laugh as she followed Betsy out the back door. "The biggest threat to this place right now is Driscoll," Charlotte said. "Whether the people who live here know it or not."

Betsy nodded. "There's more you don't know. Driscoll is Unseelie, clearly, and he wears that fact proudly. What you don't know is that he is vile even by the standards of the Unseelie fae. Many years ago, Driscoll's sister was exiled from this place. A faerie of the wood, exiled to the desert. You understand what that means?"

I exchanged a look with Charlotte. I had some idea of what the consequences might have been, but not enough.

"No," I said.

Charlotte shook her head too.

"It is a slow death," Betsy said. "Taken away from the magicks that sustained her, she would have starved. Some of the old tales say it took months, and some say it took years. But there's one thing all of the stories agree on. Driscoll found her before she died, but he was too late. He may not be at odds with the Court of the Sun and the Moon directly, but he is at odds with anyone who trespasses on the land where his sister lived. The mere existence of this town has awakened a monster that you do not understand. And that monster knows what you did to the Unseelie fae of the Caribbean."

"We get the wards in place," I said. "That's our priority."

"He's had time to study the conservatory," Charlotte said. "He's seen the wards work. He likely already knows what we're doing."

I looked down at the molds at our feet. "He might know, but he'll be too late to stop us."

The molten metals cooled quite quickly once they were in the mold. Without the heat of the forge to keep the temperatures above the melting point, the metal regained its form in moments. It wouldn't be cool enough to touch with bare hands until we quenched it.

"What do you want to do?" Theodore asked. "Drop them straight in the bucket? Or crack the molds and inspect them first?"

"Just drop them right in the buckets. We don't have the time to worry about small imperfections in the castings right now. There's no point in inspecting them too closely."

Theodore nodded.

I picked up the wooden block with my padded leather gloves, undid the small clamp holding the two halves closed, and let the vessel inside fall into the water. It hissed, and steam exploded from the top of the bucket as the metal sank to the bottom. Theodore did the same, and we waited for the frenzy of activity to slow. The boiling waters became a slow stream of bubbles as the steam cleared enough we could see the bottom of the steel bucket.

I reached in with a short pair of tongs and grasped the first of the vessels. I held up a small cylinder and frowned at the coloration. The webwork of copper we'd used to frame everything out had held up fairly well, but as it melted, it created something that almost looked more like Damascus steel than the uniform coloration of the vessels we'd crafted by hand.

"It looks good," I said. "It should be functional. But give it a few more minutes to cool down, and we can try it in one of the wards."

"So soon?" Theodore asked.

"Yes. I doubt that aether would be affected very much by letting it cool down more. If it wasn't destroyed in the mold, it should be working."

"Let me see it," Betsy said.

I held the tongs out to her, but instead of taking them from me, she plucked the vessel off the end before I could so much as shout a warning about the heat.

I blinked at her.

She rubbed at the gray and copper cylinder.

"Wow," I said, watching as she cleared the soot and remnants away. Beneath was a brilliantly polished core.

"I can still sense the aether," she said. "But it is odd. I sense it as if it is a blankness. As if it has dulled my senses. I don't know if I will ever grow accustomed to that sensation."

I frowned. "I don't want these wards to affect you. I want them to affect the Unseelie. Are you sure you'll be okay when we activate this web of wards?"

Betsy nodded. "The aether in this vessel has no purpose. The wards give it purpose. My family has used wards similar to those for many years. We will be safe."

"One day you're going to tell us how many years," Charlotte said, crossing her arms.

Betsy gave her a small smile before holding the vessel back out to me.

"Is it safe to touch?"

"What he means," Charlotte said, "is it safe for him to touch?"

Betsy released a small laugh and nodded.

I took the vessel from her outstretched hand and felt the warmth rising in my palm. It was not too hot, and the temperature evened out just before it reached uncomfortable levels.

Charlotte stepped closer and studied the vessel in my hand. "It's beautiful."

"I didn't expect that," I said.

"Get the gun," she said, looking into my eyes.

I nodded. "Theodore, it's time for us to test this."

"Finally!" Theodore said, hurrying into the shop.

"I only hope we won't need to use it," I said.

Betsy took a deep breath. "That is a noble thought. But Driscoll is fond of threes. He will not come alone."

CHAPTER 13

The heavy clank from inside the workshop told me Theodore had opened one of the safes. It was an odd thing to work on something for so long without testing it.

"We came here to escape this life," Charlotte said.

I grimaced and took the oak case from Theodore. "No rest for the wicked."

I set the case on the workbench near the forge and threw the latch to open it. The hinges were whisper quiet, and they gave up their contents without protest. Inside was a nest of leather and velvet and steel.

An oddly shaped gun waited in the beautiful case Charlotte had made for it. Of all the things I'd thought to do with the aether, I must confess, I didn't expect it to be crafted into a weapon.

"Pirate stories again?" Theodore asked.

"I don't believe that was a story," Betsy said. "There is much truth in Gregory's words, and Charlotte's."

I ran my finger down the bronze inlays on the side of the pistol. At first glance, one might think it was just a contemporary revolver, but it was far more than that. I slid the polished cylinder out and frowned at the single hole drilled inside it.

"Pass me the vessel," I said. I knew I'd been lucky to only lose one still since we discovered the aether. Theodore's mistake was one that I'd made myself, unaware of the power hidden in those waters. I hadn't told him just how lucky he was. And now we were casting the stuff in fire and metal.

Theodore sanded off the last vestige of the mold we used to cast the new vessel. I took it from him gently and slid it into the cylinder before closing the gun.

Betsy cursed when the small glass window on the top of the barrel began to glow, dim at first, but increasing until it became as bright as one of the lanterns the townsfolk would carry at night.

"Not particularly stealthy," Charlotte said.

"It doesn't need to be," I said. "It only needs to kill a fae."

"You're telling me you were pirates?" Theodore asked.

I placed my thumb in an indentation beneath the barrel and drew it back slowly. About the time the movement reached the cylinder, a satisfying click sounded.

"There aren't real pirates anymore," I said. "They're dead or imprisoned."

"We're just shopkeepers and moonshiners now," Charlotte said.

Theodore narrowed his eyes.

"They've killed fae before," Betsy said.

"And we'll kill them again," I said, leveling the pistol at a thick area of scrub brush. I moved my finger to the trigger and let the hammer drop. A narrow beam of light rocketed out of the end of the gun, leaving no recoil in my hand but a strange feeling in my heart as I stared at the smoking ruin of the bush.

"Shit," I muttered, frowning at the weapon in my hand. I crouched and studied the bush. The damage that beam had done to the wood was terrifying. It had cut a hole clean through it. The aether gun wasn't something I'd want in an enemy's hands.

Charlotte rubbed at her ear. "Not as loud as a pistol, but that whine was one strange sound."

"I think the more important fact," I said, "is that we're not all dead."

Betsy pinched the bridge of her nose. "Humans. It's a wonder you live as long as you do."

"Do you have any weapons?" I asked.

"Of course," she said. "Half human, so only half an idiot."

Charlotte grinned at Betsy while Theodore awkwardly shuffled his feet.

"Still coming to terms with this whole thing?" Charlotte asked.

"It's fine," Theodore said. "She's just never been this open about it with other people. It's . . . odd."

"I get it," I said. "It's a big secret that only the two of you have known as long as you've been together. And now we know. It changes things."

"It changes nothing," Betsy said. "I will be with Theodore as long as he needs me, or until he dies. It is as simple as that."

"I felt much the same way about a cat I once had," I said.

Theodore's anxiousness fractured into a smile. "Shut up, old man."

"Get your armor, your shotgun, and whatever iron-rich blades you have laying around."

"Here we go," Charlotte said. "Now he's going to say we're going to stop Driscoll here or die trying."

I blinked. "That's absolutely not what I was going to say."

"Uh huh."

"Dammit, woman," I grumbled.

"Told you," Charlotte said, turning to Theodore. "Get your supplies. We have to hurry."

"We must seal the last two wards before Driscoll can destroy the mounts," Betsy said. "If he saw what you've done at the conservatory, he may now know what he's looking for."

"Then like Charlotte said," I said, "hurry."

I studied the holster that Charlotte had strapped to her waist. The aether gun fit neatly into the old cracked leather. I smiled at her.

Charlotte pulled a thin shawl over her shoulders. It hung low enough to conceal the guns, but it still left her vambrace exposed. Normally I'd consider that an issue, but today it could mean the difference between life and death.

The thought of the sleeve or some other piece of clothing getting caught on that vambrace and slowing down one of the iron bolts that weapon could throw was sobering at best. It was always good to think positive before battle, but I'd never been able to convince my brain to do that. I always thought of what could go wrong, what we could plan for, and what we could fall back on.

That paranoia may have been why we were still around. We'd spent time at sea, as what some would call pirates, and Charlotte and I had survived more than one battle. Engagements at sea were different. You were less likely to be surrounded, and it was easier to tell where your enemies were headed. Chances were, they were either trying to sink your ship, or board it and take it.

But now we were in a town. Surrounded by wilderness on all sides. Many different people had come here for various reasons. But that wasn't my real concern. On land, it was harder to find your enemies' target, unless you yourself were that target. We suspected Driscoll was trying to stop our placement of the wards. But we didn't know for sure.

But if we were right, that could mean one of Betsy's friends, or even her fae family, could have let slip the nature of our work. But what if it wasn't someone from her family? What if it was someone who was already seated in the Court of the Sun and the Moon?

"Bishop," I said, turning to Betsy as she came back down the stairs with Theodore. "Did you tell Bishop?"

"About Driscoll?" Betsy asked. "No."

I frowned and looked away. "How else could Bishop know? Who else would've told him?"

"That's neither here nor there," Charlotte said. "Stop your worrying and straighten your back."

I pulled my vest closed and double checked the clasps on my vambrace. As I had the harmonica pistol, I kept the shield cartridge loaded on my wrist. Charlotte opted for the bolt thrower, but she was always more mindful of offense than defense.

Once I was satisfied I had everything locked down, and had

dropped the remaining vessels into the pouch at my waist, I made for the back door. "Let's get this done."

We walked out of the back of the shop, the entire time Betsy's warning about Driscoll preferring threes echoing in my mind. I led the group south to Main Street. It had been a long day, and I doubted we would have sunlight for more than a couple more hours.

The streets were busier now, both with workers hammering away in some of the newer buildings and those local residents who had been here since the town was founded not so long ago. We headed east, along the same road that would take us to the inn, only that wasn't our destination that evening.

Or at least not our first destination.

One thing every town needed was a saloon, and our small town hidden in the wilderness of the Colorado territory was no different. People liked to joke that the saloon was the first building to go up when the settlement first started, but it wasn't really a joke. It literally had been one of the first buildings to be erected.

It was also where we met the first of our opposition.

CHAPTER 14

"inker," the slender face said as its owner stepped off the wooden deck and onto the gravel street. "We have business."

"He's my business," Betsy said. "If you take issue with that, you can speak with the Court."

The newcomer bared his teeth, contorting his face into a rictus grin that looked anything but human.

"Gregory and Charlotte Trent," the faerie said. "You carry with you a power that does not belong to humans."

"It's distilled from the power of witches," Charlotte said. "It is the very power of humans."

The fae curled his lip and looked down at Charlotte. He stood close to a foot taller than my wife, and nearly that much taller than me, but Charlotte didn't back down. She stared the fae down as her fingers traced the outline of her vambrace.

"Your reputation precedes you," he said with a small inclination of his head. "I am Cathal, brother to Driscoll and seeker of stolen magicks."

"It's my right to protect my home," I said. "It's every one of our rights. Now step aside."

"You are a fool," Cathal said with a humorless laugh. "You do not sail upon a galleon in the seas to the south. You are not armed with mighty iron cannons, loaded and prepared to do battle with the morgens. What hope have you?"

"Theodore, take him," I said.

"No!" Betsy said. Whether she'd meant to issue a warning, or something else, it came too late.

The weapon Theodore wielded looked like a crossbow to those not familiar with it. It worked much the same, but it had the ability to fire three bolts at once. Hit a man in the chest with that, and he'd rarely get back up. Hit a fae in the chest with three iron bolts, and he'd die screaming.

Cathal barely raised his right arm, causing the fabric of his sleeve to billow out and catch the iron bolts. In one violent motion, he snapped his arm downward, and the bolts clanged against the gravel.

"Fool," Cathal muttered. "You think every fae in this town hasn't heard of your inventions? You think the fae of the Caribbean would not tell of your slaughter of the morgens? We will have your blood for theirs."

I almost growled. Cathal knew more of our history than I would've suspected. He knew more of it than Theodore knew, which meant at least some of his knowledge hadn't come from Betsy, and I let that small sliver of trust I had in her grow just a little more.

Cathal stepped toward Theodore, continuing his diatribe as he drew a slender blade sheathed at his waist. I hesitated to call it a dagger, but it wasn't quite long enough to be a short sword. The weight of the harmonica pistol felt good in my grasp. I'd been in enough firefights to learn how to control my movements, even when our lives were on the line.

The cartridge slid home with a satisfying click, and I raised the barrel. There was a time when I was more noble and I probably would've warned Cathal, but I'd grown impatient in my old age. Or perhaps I'd grown more cautious.

I pulled the trigger smoothly, and the light from the ward on the clip shone almost as bright as the burst of fire from the end of the gun. It was a good shot, taking Cathal in the shoulder. But where the iron should have crashed into his body and sent him to the earth, instead it ricocheted off into the air.

The fae looked back at me, his eyes wide before he dashed behind Theodore and I lost my shot. I expected the fae to take Theodore hostage, but instead he sprinted past us, dodging behind a carriage full of wary onlookers.

"He ran," Betsy said, the disbelief plain in her voice.

I stared after him. He was fast and moved with a sublime grace that I only saw in the supernatural creatures I'd encountered, and extremely seasoned fighters. "He could've taken us."

The world shimmered, and Cathal vanished. It was as if a thin veil of water had run across my vision, and then it was gone.

"What the hell was that?" Charlotte asked.

"A misdirection," Betsy said. "He can hide himself through magic. It's a skill some of the older fae have. I'm surprised you didn't encounter it when you battled the morgens in the Caribbean."

I frowned. "We've seen similar things, but nothing quite so comprehensive. I could've sworn his very footsteps vanished."

Betsy shook her head. "That's unlikely. Too many sounds for him to mask at once. And here," she said, gesturing to the calm crowds walking around us, "it would appear he hid our altercation from the townsfolk."

"Fine," Theodore said. "Gregory and Charlotte are pirates, and crazed fae are trying to kill us. Why don't we stop thinking about it and hurry up to get the shit done?"

"Theodore's right," I said, hurrying toward the back of the saloon and rummaging through a pocket on my vest. I pulled a pair of goggles over my eyes and clipped an aether lens to the side. I glanced at Charlotte. "Why didn't you take a shot?"

"And tip our hand so early?" she asked. "You're smarter than that, dear."

I gave a sharp nod and focused on the saloon. While the other buildings we were warding were still under construction, or at least repair, the saloon had already been here. And since I didn't really know where everyone's loyalties lied, I didn't dare tell the proprietors what we were doing. That meant the ward for the saloon needed to be installed outside, or we would have to break in. Certainly a possibility, but also a good way to get killed.

Sixteen across and four down, I counted to myself as I ran my hand along the bricks. At the end, there waited a brick where the mortar had been chipped away. We'd wedged a bit of painted wood into the gap that was textured to look like mortar. It would decay faster than the actual stone, but to the casual observer, it was virtually identical.

I cursed when I realized the new rain barrel that had been placed out back was slightly in the way. "Help me move this."

Theodore came around to my side of the barrel. He put his shoulder into the edge while I twisted at the top. We didn't need to move it far, but even half a foot made quite a ruckus. Once we were done kicking up dust and grunting with the effort, I took a deep breath and looked around. I was happy to find no one had their attention on us.

I stuck the edge of the metal bar into the groove that should've been mortar. I wiggled it around a bit, the metal scraping and squealing against the brick before the wood gave way. I grasped it between my fingernails and pulled. The brick behind it fell into a slant, and Charlotte pulled it out before I turned back. I grabbed the second brick from on top of it and one from beside it to reveal the mount we'd installed in the wall.

"It's not going to work as well as the pipes in the conservatory," Betsy said.

"Just watch our backs," I said. "We'll deal with it if it fails."

Theodore rummaged through the leather sack he'd had on his back. He pulled out one of the pipe-mounted wards, very much like what we had installed at the conservatory.

"Slide it in," I said. "Keep the narrow end to the east."

Theodore glanced up and frowned.

"Pointed at me," I said.

Theodore nodded and leaned forward.

"Hold it steady," I said as I docked the pipe. Once it was stable, I pulled the small lever hidden behind one of the mortared bricks. It clicked and sent the gears turning, which caused the small piston to slide into the top of the ward. I nodded in satisfaction as the plates slowly spread out.

"Looks good," Charlotte said. The last segment of the plate expanded, and the ward glowed. Something crashed inside the saloon. Loud enough I could hear through the wall, and large enough I could feel it in the bricks as I slid everything back together.

"Sounds like we may have surprised some fae inside the saloon," Betsy said.

"Let's move," Charlotte said. "If that's what happened, we don't need to be out here when they come to investigate."

We shifted the barrel back, and Charlotte kicked at the dirt to hide the signs that anyone had moved it. We hurried to the east and rounded the corner of the block before I heard raised voices behind us.

"Get onto the street," Charlotte said. We crossed over the square, and it was a straight shot to the meeting hall.

We were halfway across the square before anyone really noticed us.

"I'm sure that's them," someone said from behind us.

"They look busy," someone else said. "Let's just leave them alone."

I glanced back and saw some of our recent customers. Charlotte caught me looking, and our entire group slowed down. She turned to face whatever was behind us, her hand sliding toward her vambrace.

I gave a tiny shake of my head, and her hand fell away.

"Oh, we didn't mean to bother you," the woman behind us said.

"We just wanted to thank you for the beautiful puzzle box," the man said.

"It's no trouble, dears," Charlotte said. "We're just looking for one of our friends, and I am afraid we don't have much time to talk. But I appreciate you telling us. It was very kind of you."

"Of course," the man said. "Thank you again."

I inclined my head as we parted ways. "What was their name again?"

"You are terrible with names, Gregory," Charlotte said.

"Almost as bad as Theodore," Betsy said. "That was Lawrence and his wife, Christine. Come now. We must hurry."

Apparently our hurried manner was enough to turn away the usually polite townsfolk. The crunch of gravel in the center of the town square gave way to a patch of grass. Our footsteps fell quiet until we reached the next street, and the meeting hall.

The core of the building was simple enough, but that wasn't my focus. That wasn't our goal. On either side of the squat building rose the framing of a beautiful expansion. By the time they had the meeting hall completed, it would rival some of the nicest buildings I'd seen in my travels.

"Come," I said, "to the left. Down the alley, and we're nearly there."

The alley was a narrow thing, not so much due to its own nature, but due to the fact they had stacked lumber and various building supplies all along it. Once we cleared the edge, and the walls were open, we stepped into the skeleton of the new construction.

Once we were on the north side of the meeting hall, we were in the shadow of what many called Mount Alexa. Something about the woods on the north side of the town always unsettled me. It was an odd thing, as technically the woods where my still resided was in the Northwoods, but it was nothing like that looming form of Mount Alexa. Perhaps it was Orna, ever keeping a watchful eye. Or perhaps it was something more ominous, something we mortals couldn't understand, and maybe never would.

We wove between the precisely cut wooden supports of the new expansion. It wasn't the wood that interested me. It was the massive iron beams they'd used as the main supports. It gave me pause, knowing that a building that would harbor fae intermittently would be partially constructed of iron. Perhaps it had been intentional? I couldn't say, but it would work for my purposes.

"Here," I said, kneeling down near the center of the rear construction. The middle of the iron column had what appeared to be a welded plate over it. But that wasn't it at all. While I had made the cuts at the conservatory, I'd recruited Theodore to prepare the installation at the meeting hall.

Our packs thumped down onto the hardened earth beneath the black iron. Theodore opened his pack and pulled out the last of the wards. This one was different. Much as we'd customized the others to fit the bronze pipework in the conservatory and the brass piston we'd installed in the saloon, this one was a darker affair. The post was nearly solid iron, while the plate that hosted the wards was an alloy.

I placed a magnet in the center of the welded plate. The response was instant. I could hear the bolt retract as the magnet pulled on the levers behind the plate. It was delicate work, getting the gears in the proper ratio that a simple magnet could undo the bolts, but Theodore had proven his skill.

I pulled the plate off with ease. Charlotte took it out of my hand while Theodore reached into the void. He settled the bottom of the post onto a slightly raised bolt. It fit squarely in the socket on the base of the ward, and one hard push locked the top of it into place. I slid one long locking pin from the front through the back before reaching behind the assembly and bending the pin down.

"You're sure that's enough to hold it?" Theodore asked.

I fished around in the pocket on my vest and pulled out the last of our new vessels. "I suppose we'll know in a second."

I pulled the spring-loaded panel to the side on the post before sliding the vessel inside. I let the panel snap closed, and a moment later the plate sprang into action. Each segment locked into the one before it until it fully formed the ward and started to glow.

"So far, so good," Charlotte said.

"Why do you always have to say that?" I asked. "Every time."

"Oh, come now," Charlotte said. "Put your silly superstitions to rest. Nothing bad has happened since we retired."

"Retired from being a pirate?" Theodore muttered.

I stared at the ward. And waited.

And waited.

"I don't sense the wards connecting," Betsy said.

"Every. Time," I said as I looked up at Charlotte.

"Check it again," Theodore said. "Is it in right?"

I gave him a flat look.

"We need to get back to the conservatory," Betsy said, wringing her hands. "Driscoll was there earlier."

I cursed. "What if he got to the ward?"

Charlotte bit her lip and shook her head. "No, he can't touch it."

"We need to get back there," Betsy said. "Now."

I took a deep breath and closed my eyes, willing myself to calm down. She was right. We needed to get back to the conservatory and see what had been compromised. There couldn't be another explanation, unless the wards themselves had failed, and I couldn't afford that kind of doubt.

I gave one sharp nod and hopped up to my feet. "Grab your bags. We're going."

CHAPTER 15

heodore tied the flap of his backpack off and slung it over his shoulder. I followed suit, the sweat on my palms causing the leather to grow slick beneath my grasp.

We hurried out the back of the meeting hall construction, hurdling supplies and ducking through the various supports of the new construction.

Once we were out on the road behind it, more of a dirt path really, I started to notice more of the sounds in the city. In the distance you could just barely hear the falls crashing, and I realized it wasn't so much the sounds of the city I was hearing, but the lack of sound.

We hurried east until we reached the edge of the meeting hall, and then we cut south. Charlotte took the lead, as she had always been the lookout when we were on the seas. While my vision had grown worse with age, to the point that I could barely get around without some sort of glasses, she could still spot prey at two hundred yards.

Theodore and Betsy stayed close behind us as our speed increased. The silence bothered me, and the farther we made it through the town square, the more I realized just how quiet it was.

"What's going on?" I asked, my gaze flashing from Betsy back to Charlotte.

"They're waiting for us," Betsy said. "They've already masked the area from the locals. But this is beyond Driscoll's skill. I can still hear you, and you can still hear me. The discipline it would take to make a cloak like this so precise is astounding."

"You're not making me feel much better, girl," Charlotte said. She pulled a lever on the side of her vambrace, releasing the safety on the bolt thrower she now had mounted to it.

I unhooked the strap that was loosely holding the harmonica pistol against my chest. It would be a quick draw and easy aim, and I only hoped it would be fast enough.

We closed on the front of the inn, skirting around its grand façade. We stayed to the west of the building, hugging the wide porch and the turret that rose three stories above us. I glanced up at one of the brick chimneys that crowned the roof, and could've sworn I saw movement.

"Something's above us," I said.

Charlotte nodded, and I suspected she was the only one who had heard me. Once we cleared the side of the inn, the conservatory came into view.

"You'll not keep me from my prey, mortal," Driscoll said. His glare was icy enough to physically cut someone. If he'd been human, I would've said he looked cocky. But most fae I'd encountered over the years weren't the overconfident type. They generally knew what advantage they had, and how to leverage it.

"You here alone?" I asked.

"Only I stand before you," Driscoll said.

I'd once heard a tale that the fae told lies through truth, and I'd seen it and heard it with my own ears more than once. I turned my body slightly toward the inn and drew the harmonica pistol in one swift motion. The trigger clicked back, and the hammer dropped. The boom that followed would be enough to draw a crowd if the fae weren't masking everything we were doing.

But that hadn't been my point.

The shadow on the roof danced away from the bullet, and while I was quite sure no fae could move so fast as to dodge a bullet, the rapid motion of the blur certainly gave that impression. But I watched in satisfaction as one of the tiles beneath its foot slipped, and Cathal came tumbling down to the edge of the roof. With one violent swipe of his hand, he broke through the edge of the inn and grasped the hole he'd just created to keep from falling.

Cathal wasn't so slender as Driscoll. His chest was broader and tapered into a muscled waist. He looked down at me and snarled.

"What sorcery have you?" he shouted down. "No mortal can see us."

I let a small smile crawl over my face. I raised the aether magnifier away from the goggle over my left eye. "Apparently humans can do more than you know."

The faerie narrowed his eyes, released his grip, and thumped gracefully onto the earth not twenty feet from the barrel of my gun. "Can your lens protect you from a sword in your gut?"

Charlotte moved out to my right. It was a standard formation we'd used more than once when our ship had been boarded on the seas. I didn't care how good of a sailor you were, there was always a faster pirate, a stealthier ship, and you had to trust someone at your back.

Theodore had been a brawler before Betsy knocked some sense into him. He worked hard, but he'd also made a serious effort at screwing up his life. But it was the side of him that tended toward violence I hoped he'd brought today.

"Brothers," Betsy said. "Leave this place in peace."

"Halfbreed," Driscoll snarled. "Do not spew your talk of peace with me. These people have invaded our lands, people who are wanted by the very courts that govern us."

"He is my mate," Betsy said, stepping closer to Theodore. "You cannot strike him down, without breaking the very bonds of the fae. If you would strike at him, you strike at me."

"You speak of the old laws," Cathal said. "But you are a halfbreed. You have lived your entire life in the shadow of the mortals. You have no comprehension of what you speak."

"So be it," Betsy said. She drew a slender blade from each sleeve of her loose-fitting gown. "Leave now, or you will not leave this place alive."

"Fool."

"Found him," Theodore said. "Tree line to the east. Looks like a bow."

"What?" Driscoll said, his gaze turning to the trees.

Driscoll was almost as fast to turn as Charlotte was to draw the aether gun. The fae had never seen something like that, of that I had little doubt. The dim glow of the aether brightened as Charlotte pulled the mechanism below the barrel back in full. The fae in the woods had to have been a hundred yards away, no easy shot. But the bolt of magic that the aether gun threw had no concern for the wind in the air, or the friction of the barrel, or the head that it destroyed.

I couldn't hear the fae fall, but I could see the gore, and the collapse of the ruined body.

"You know not what you've done," Driscoll snarled as he drew his sword.

"Exterminating the bilge rats," Charlotte growled.

I expected him to talk more—that's usually how it went with the immortals. They fixated on spewing nonsense as they went about eviscerating their enemies. Driscoll had apparently spoken enough words. He moved like lightning, diving back into the webwork of the conservatory and dodging between the brass supports.

The other fae kept his gaze fixated on Charlotte's gun. I wasn't sure if he was tracking the barrel in order to make sure he didn't get his own head blown off, or if he was just lusting after the damned thing.

"How long?" I shouted.

"Less than half," Charlotte said.

I cursed under my breath. From what Charlotte was saying, the aether gun wouldn't be ready to fire for another minute at least. If I was being honest with myself, the two remaining fae could kill us all in that time. But they didn't know we couldn't fire again yet. They just thought we were half-crazed mortals. And that we could use to our advantage.

I pressed the plate on my vambrace, and the teardrop-shaped shield erupted on the back of my arm. It was one of the hardest alloys I'd ever seen, and Charlotte and I had put it up against gunfire and swords and a hundred different weapons. But here, faced with a half-mad fae, I worried just how much it could stop.

I sidestepped to the right, keeping the harmonica pistol leveled roughly between Cathal and Driscoll. They both kept the relaxed stance, which was both infuriating and intimidating. Charlotte and Theodore moved with me. I hadn't spent much time training Theodore on the finer points of strategic combat, and that was a fact I regretted in that moment.

"Theodore, don't!" Betsy shouted.

But Theodore was already moving, closing the distance between him and Cathal. A slow smile lifted the corners of Cathal's lips. I cursed, shifted my aim for Cathal, and fired. The harmonica pistol boomed, and the clip moved one more slot toward being empty. The bullet ricocheted into the air, hitting an invisible force not two inches from Cathal's shoulder. The faerie snarled and brought a rapid left uppercut into Theodore's ribs.

I didn't have to hear the crack to know something had broken. Theodore stumbled forward, aiming a clumsy left-handed blow at Cathal's face. The faerie reared back to strike again, but Theodore smacked the button on his vambrace, and a shield much like mine exploded around his arm. Except unlike mine, the boy had added some very nasty blades to the edge, the longest of which cut into the collarbone of the fae. Cathal roared in pain and spun away.

Driscoll's calm façade fractured, and he moved into action. Betsy broke formation, skirting past me and whispering in my ear, "Fix the ward."

She shoved off me, sending me stumbling toward Charlotte, and closer to the pipes where we'd installed the ward.

Charlotte aimed her wrist and clicked the button on her vambrace. Three bolts shot out, two finding nothing but air, but the third cutting into Driscoll's sleeve. The faerie doubled over, his smug expression completely overcome by the pain of the iron. He ripped his shirt sleeve off as he threw the projectile to the ground. In a motion so quick I could barely follow, the faerie tossed a throwing dagger at Charlotte. She barely had her arm up in time to stop the blade with her own flesh, but instead the razor-sharp projectile sank into the mechanism on her vambrace. There'd be no more bolts flying from that.

Betsy took the opportunity to aim a swift kick at Driscoll's head while Theodore wrestled with Cathal. Cathal grabbed Theodore and threw him to the ground, sending a cloud of dust and gravel into the air. I didn't know much how much more the boy could take, his pained screech cutting into my ears. I'd been hit like that before, and I didn't get back up.

I hurried around Charlotte and slid to a stop before the pipes.

I could see almost immediately what Driscoll had done. He hadn't damaged the ward so much as taken its power source away. The compartment that held the vessel was cracked open and was nowhere to be found. "Fire the gun and throw it to me!"

Charlotte didn't hesitate. She took a shot at Cathal as he raised a sword to bring an end to Theodore, who now lay on the ground, struggling to breathe through his broken ribs. The aether gun fired, and a hole appeared in Cathal's torso. The faerie stumbled backward and collapsed against the inn. It wasn't an instant kill. He was still a threat.

Betsy's sword clanged against Driscoll's, and her words reverberated through my mind. *Fix the ward.*

Charlotte hurled the aether gun at me. I caught it and popped the cylinder out of the side, fumbling to get the vessel out of it as quickly as possible. It felt as though the motion took forever, as Driscoll landed a blow against Betsy and sent her tumbling to the ground beside Theodore. Charlotte pulled the throwing knife out of her vambrace and hurled it at Driscoll.

The thump of blade on flesh was sickening. The lack of expression on Driscoll's face was terrifying.

I finally slid the vessel out of the cylinder and slammed it home in the ward. The plate glowed, and for a moment, my breath left me as a force I didn't fully understand burst through the area.

Driscoll stumbled backwards. He reached out, as if he couldn't see what was in front of him. With the trinity in place, the world was snatched from the Unseelie fae. At least for a time.

Charlotte charged. Betsy held the sword up to her, and Charlotte grabbed it near the hilt. It was a dangerous move, it would cut deep into her palm, but the shortened blade made her strike faster than it would otherwise be. It slid cleanly up through Driscoll's jaw, only stopping when it hit the top of his skull. Charlotte screamed as she bowled into him.

Cathal struggled to his feet, shouting, "Where are you! What have you done!"

The harmonica pistol boomed once, twice, and as the warded projectiles passed through the wall that the aether had created, they turned into something more akin to a flaming cannonball. There were few creatures that could survive an eight-inch hole torn through their chest. There were fewer still that could survive two. I fired two more into Cathal, until his body caught fire and he collapsed on the ground.

I looked over to Charlotte, to my wife, as she wrapped her hand in a length of cloth torn from Driscoll's shirt. I stared at Driscoll for a time, the dagger-like blade gleaming in the cavern of his mouth, embedded in the skull.

"Theodore," Betsy said. "Stay awake. Are you okay?"

"Oh yeah," Theodore said. "Our plan went so smoothly, I hardly got a scratch. Except for all these broken ribs."

He started to laugh, and the sound changed to a groan of pain.

"Is he coughing up blood?" I asked.

"Not that I can tell," Betsy said.

"Good. He'll be fine."

"What about them?" Theodore asked.

"We bury them," I said. "Bury them under the conservatory. With this." I held up the aether gun.

"Are you sure?" Charlotte asked. "That was awfully effective."

"It's too dangerous. We won't need it now that the wards are active."

"You could destroy it," Betsy said. "But I wouldn't. You might have friends that are fae, but you also have enemies of all sorts."

I glanced at Charlotte and met her eyes.

She smiled and said, "Don't we always."

EPILOGUE

*S*urprised to find the front door locked, I tucked the wooden crate I was carrying under my arm so I could reach the keys in my leather vest. It had been three months since our encounter with Driscoll, and while I wouldn't say things had returned to normal, exactly, they had certainly calmed down. But Charlotte and I had both taken to locking the doors more than we used to.

The repairs on the conservatory were completed without much trouble, and what trouble there was Theodore had handled with a brilliant bit of brass work. We'd needed the payment, and Mihail hadn't let us down.

Perhaps most surprising, Roman Bishop had kept his word. Our slightly strange whiskey was now a staple at the local bar, and Bishop was confident he could find more buyers than I could make moonshine for. It was a challenge I was ready to take on.

The door swung open, and I blinked at the feet on the ladder beside my head.

"I was going to fix that this weekend," I said, carefully edging my way into the shop where the gentle tones of a repaired chime greeted me.

"Of course you were," Charlotte said, brushing off her hands as she climbed down from the ladder. She slapped a small tool belt against my chest, and I fumbled to catch it.

"Sounds great." I moved to set the tools onto the workbench before setting the crate beside them. "Mihail said the amulets worked great."

"How did he test them?" Charlotte asked, sitting down behind her workbench.

I shrugged. "Don't know. Don't know if I want to know."

Charlotte leaned forward as I took a crowbar to the wooden crate.

"Are those the bottles?" she asked.

I nodded, levered the length of metal, and pried the top off the crate with a squeal and a pop. The individual bottles weren't so heavy as I pulled one out, and I suspected the crate itself had made up a good deal of the weight.

Charlotte stood up and joined me, sliding her own bottle of smoked glass out and running her finger across the golden lettering etched into the side. She read the words aloud: "Warded Whiskey, The Tinkers' Drink."

I shook my head. "Nice craftsmanship on the bottles. Not a huge fan of the name."

Charlotte blew out a puff of air. "It already paid off a quarter of our debt. Bishop can call it whatever the hell he wants if that keeps up."

"Why don't we have Theodore and Betsy over tonight to celebrate?" I said with a smile.

"Okay," Charlotte said. "Just make sure they come through the front door."

I glanced back at the chimes Charlotte had fixed, and laughed.

We hope you enjoyed these stories in the Legends of Havenwood Falls series featuring a variety of supernatural creatures. The series is a collaborative effort by multiple authors.

Books in the historical Legends of Havenwood Falls series:

Lost in Time by Tish Thawer
Dawn of the Witch Hunters by Morgan Wylie
Redemption's End by Eric R. Asher
Trapped Within a Wish by Brynn Myers
Blood and Damnation by Belinda Boring
Fated Beginnings by E.J. Fechenda (September 2018)
Emeline by Katie M. John (October 2018)
Released From a Curse by Brynn Myers (November 2018)

More books releasing on a monthly basis
Also try the signature New Adult/Adult series, Havenwood Falls, and
the YA series, Havenwood Falls High

Stay up to date at www.HavenwoodFalls.com

Subscribe to our reader group and receive free stories and more!

ABOUT THE AUTHOR

Eric is a former bookseller, cellist, and comic seller currently living in Saint Louis, Missouri. A lifelong enthusiast of books, music, toys, and games, he discovered a love for the written word after being dragged to the library by his parents at a young age. When he is not writing, you can usually find him reading, gaming, or buried beneath a small avalanche of Transformers. Find him at http://www.ericrasher.com/.

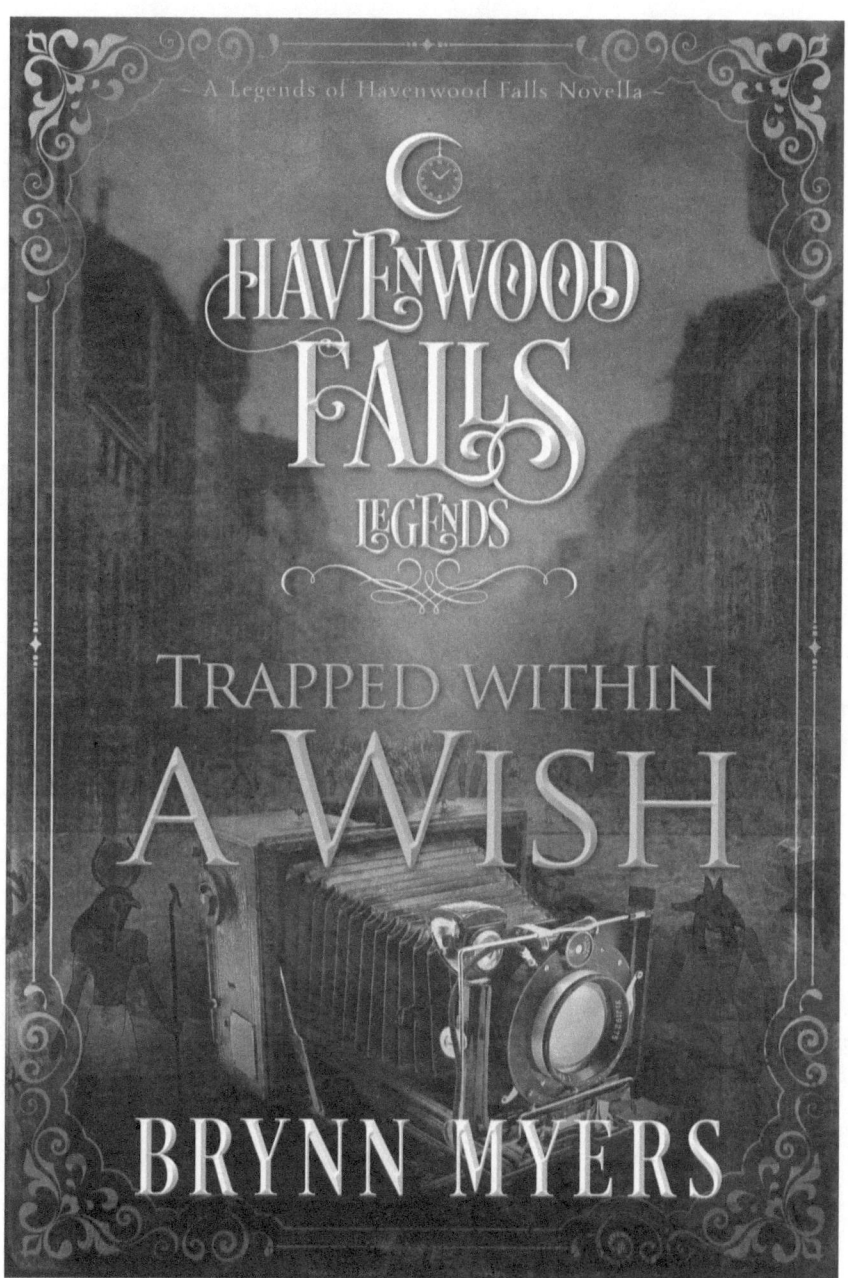

~ A Legends of Havenwood Falls Novella ~

Havenwood Falls

Legends

Trapped Within
A Wish

Brynn Myers

AN EXCERPT

Trapped Within a Wish (A Legends of Havenwood Falls Novella) by Brynn Myers

For eighteen years, Nathan Wade has searched for answers regarding his father's disappearance. Now, in 1920, he receives a letter from Calla Lily Mircea saying she's in possession of some of his father's belongings in a town called Havenwood Falls. Nathan wonders how a field camera lost on an archeological dig in Egypt could end up in a small town in Colorado, but something draws him in. Nathan takes the leap of faith, only to have his world turned upside down when he finds not only the camera, but a hidden treasure within.

Amani lost everything the day she came of age and her true nature was revealed. Now, having been trapped for eighteen years, her only hope is that someone will save her from the hell she's had to endure. When a handsome stranger inadvertently releases her, the wait is over, and the truth of her imprisonment comes to light.

Nathan and Amani are now bound to one another and determined to piece together the past. Someone wanted her gone, and she and Nathan race to solve the mystery that connects them both before it's too late.

TRAPPED WITHIN A WISH

AN EXCERPT

The hallway of New York University bustled with students roaming around—some were on their way to exams, while others were chatting about the upcoming summer break.

In his office on campus, Nathan Wade rifled through term papers, trying to find a student's dissertation on the 42 Laws of Ma'at when the door to his office opened, startling him.

"Is this what you've been waiting for?" Lillian asked as she entered the room.

"I don't know, Ms. Hartman. What is it?" Nathan replied as he continued to shuffle through the stack of papers in his hands.

"Enough with that formal business, young man. There are no students around," Lillian scoffed as she wagged the paper she held in the air. "This came in about an hour and a half ago, but you were teaching, and I didn't think it was important enough to interrupt the class to give it to you," she replied with a sly grin. "And why is he sending telegraphs anyway? Has he forgotten we're in the twentieth century? It is 1920, after all."

Nathan shook his head and chuckled under his breath. "What did Edgar have to say with his antiquated form of communication?"

Lillian reached for the silver chain holding her cheaters and pulled them on to see the words clearer. She read the two words and clicked her tongue in frustration. "Nothing yet."

"Nothing yet, what?"

"That's it. That's all it says." Lillian walked over to her desk and sat down. "I do not know why you continue to pay him to look for your father's satchel—it and the camera are long gone." She shook her head slowly. "I'm sorry. I know that is not what you want to hear, but it's true. It's been eighteen years, son. You have to move past this." Her tone shifted from judgmental to soft as she took off her glasses and let them hang around her neck.

"I can't stop searching and you know why," Nathan said as he stared into the eyes of the woman who'd cared for him after his father's disappearance.

Lillian Hartman was widowed, like his father had been. Before Nathan was born, Lillian and her husband, Charles, had been neighbors and close friends with his parents. When Nathan's mother died of consumption, Lillian became Nathan's surrogate mother. Then, after his father disappeared, she and Charles raised Nathan—gave him a life in lieu of his loss.

When Charles passed away a few years ago, Lillian was in need of a hobby to keep her mind busy. All that unused energy was going to waste, and Nathan was in need of an office assistant, now that he was an associate professor at the university. Lillian was the perfect assistant and the most qualified candidate to manage all of Nathan's pastimes.

"Nathan," Lillian soothed, "the clue to where your father disappeared to is not in that camera. Edgar can search the world over and still conclude what we already know. Sam and the camera are gone."

"I want to know what happened, Lillian. Not knowing is what binds me to this quest."

"But some mysteries will never be unraveled. You simply have to move on."

Nathan bowed his head and whispered, "I know."

"You're better suited spending your energy uncovering the mysteries found in those Egyptian tombs you love so much." She grinned and then threw her hands in the air. "That reminds me. I received notification from Howard Carter's office about an expedition opportunity. I'm not certain how that will work with your current class schedule, though."

Nathan glanced up. "They requested me?"

"Yes," she said, handing him the letter. "Here, read it. It's very complimentary."

"Wow, I didn't expect that," Nathan said as he put on his glasses to read the letter. When he read the last line, he grinned appreciatively. "It is indeed very complimentary, but sadly, I'm going to have to pass on this offer and use my time here to study linguistics in my off time." He sighed. "Maybe they'll ask again, for another dig. I can't imagine there won't be more to come."

"Always wanting to learn more. You always were such a curious boy."

"I received word that new funerary texts have arrived at the Metropolitan Museum of Art. They'll need to be translated, and as you have pointed out, it may do me some good to dive into a distraction."

Lillian picked up a stack of mail from the inbox on the corner of her desk and started to flip through it. As she did, she pulled her glasses back on and examined one envelope with an odd symbol pressed into a wax seal.

"Who uses letter seals anymore?" she mumbled under her breath. "Well, I guess whoever this is from," Lillian said to herself as she reached for her letter opener.

Lillian pulled out the neatly folded letter and read the words, disbelief and shock contorting her face with each word she read.

Dear Mr. Wade,

I'm writing this letter to inform you I am in possession of a camera I believe belongs to you. Inside the top flap of the tattered brown leather case is a tag with this New York address. The inscription reads, Samuel N. Wade. I do hope I've not contacted the wrong person in error and that this field camera indeed belongs to you. When you receive this, please reply to the address listed on the envelope.

Sincerely,
Calla Lily Mircea

"What's wrong, Lillian?" Nathan asked.

"Someone in," she paused to flip over the envelope, "Havenwood Falls has found your father's camera. They even have the bag," Lillian muttered. "I can't believe it."

"Where is Havenwood Falls?"

"According to the postage mark, it's someplace in Colorado."

"Colorado?" Nathan exclaimed. "How in the hell did the camera get there? It has to be a mistake. Egypt to some random place in the middle of nowhere is a bit of a stretch, don't you think?"

Lillian nodded, still trying to comprehend the words she'd just read. Sam's camera had been missing for as long as he had been, and no one, besides Nathan, thought they'd ever see it again. She eyed him over her glasses. "Nathan, I don't want you to get your hopes up."

Nathan took the letter from Lillian and stared at the words on the page for a moment before responding. "It may be nothing, but this is the first lead we've had. I will have to contact this Calla Lily and find out for myself."

"No, you can send Edgar. That is why you hired him, is it not?"

Nathan sighed. "It is, but there is something odd about this letter —this woman's writing. I feel like this is it. This," Nathan paused, "this is my father's camera, Lillian. I have to do this."

"Oh, Nathan," she replied gently.

"Look, it won't hurt anyone. Only another week and classes will be out for summer break. I can go then, and that way nothing will be affected here."

Lillian laid her hand on Nathan's. "This could indeed be a mistake, but I understand what you're saying. I will cover you here. I want you to have peace of mind, and I need you to find closure and put your father's death behind you."

"What if it is his? What if he is alive and has been living in Colorado all this time?"

She pulled him into a hug. "Then I guess that is all the more reason for you to go," she said as she stepped back. "Either way, you'll have an answer."

Nathan nodded. "I don't know, Lillian. I have a feeling I can't shake."

"Well, then let me respond to this Miss Mircea and make the arrangements for you to stay a few days," she said, before she kissed him on the forehead and walked over to her desk.

"This had better not be another dead end," Nathan mumbled under his breath as the gentle clicks of the typewriter sounded in the background.

The week passed by quickly, and Nathan was almost ready to go. Lillian had made all the arrangements with Calla Lily for Nathan to stay at Whisper Falls Inn upon his arrival. She also made sure Nathan's colleagues were aware he'd only be gone a short period of time on a fact-finding mission and would be back before summer's end at the latest.

Lillian thought back to when Samuel disappeared. He'd been working at the excavation site for Hatshepsut's tomb in the Valley of the Kings. Everything was going as expected according to his correspondence, and then one day they received a telegraph stating he'd gone missing—simply vanished, no trace of him found by the other Egyptologists on the dig. The only evidence they had was from a worker who reported seeing him taking a photograph of two young women near the excavation site.

Nathan had convinced himself that his father's satchel was the key to finding out what happened. He'd go on and on about photos, or maybe something Samuel found, and how it could show not only inside information about the tomb, but could also provide clues as to what happened on that day. Either way, Lillian worried about how all of this would affect Nathan in the end. Not knowing left him sad, but hungry for information—a conclusion could leave him broken.

Lillian hoped this trip to Havenwood Falls would confirm the final piece of the puzzle and finally let Nathan accept the truth—Sam met with foul play that fateful day, and the camera and any other belongings were long gone from this world. She typed up the last page for the itinerary and slipped it out of the typewriter wheel with a zing, placing it neatly on her desk. As soon as Nathan returned from afternoon class, she'd let him know the whos, whats, and whens for his departure tomorrow.

The door opened with a click and startled Lillian.

"Finished," Nathan called out as he entered the office. "The only thing left to do is mark the grades and submit them, then it's off to Colorado."

"I've made the final arrangements," she said as she stood. "You'll be taking the train into Montrose, Colorado, and Miss Mircea will meet you there. Apparently, they don't have direct access other than a bus to take you into the town itself, so she's offered to be your means of transportation."

Nathan gave her an odd look.

"Yes, my thoughts exactly, but considering your insistence that you yourself flesh this one out, you will have to abide by the rules set forth by the woman who has the satchel," Lillian said with a slight grin.

"Then I shall take it all at face value," Nathan replied, returning her smile. "Did she say where to meet her?"

"No, only that she'd be there when the train arrived, and she'd be on a bench near the platform."

"Okay then," he sighed.

"Have you finished packing?" Lillian asked as she began to sort the papers Nathan had set on her desk.

"Oh you know, I still have a few things to pack," he replied shyly.

"Nathan Allan Wade. I swear, will you never change?" Lillian laughed out loud. "Go home and get packed this instant."

Nathan grinned, knowing his truth was revealed. He hadn't packed a thing, but he was only going to be gone a few days. Nathan didn't see the point in bringing his dress attire. Instead, he'd settle for his field clothes: a couple of sport shirts, casual trousers, and a pair of suspenders.

"I don't have that much . . ." He relented under Lillian's motherly gaze.

"Nonetheless, off you go," Lillian said, shooing him out the door. "And don't forget to stop by the bank on the way home. You should have plenty of cash with you—enough to last the week at least."

"How about dinner tonight at six at Lombardi's?" Nathan asked as he grabbed his coat and hat.

"That sounds lovely, but only if you've done as I've asked and will be ready to leave in the morning. Your train departs at seven, and you cannot be late," Lillian chided.

"I will not only be ready to leave but will have my bags by the door." Nathan grinned. "I'll pick you up at five thirty," he said as he opened the door to leave.

"Five thirty it is." Lillian waved him out.

Nathan stopped by the bank, as Lillian suggested, and then the library. He needed to grab a book or two to keep his mind occupied on the train. It was, after all, going to take a few days to get to Colorado.

It was five thirty sharp when Nathan knocked on the door of Lillian's apartment. She was always a stickler for being on time, and Nathan knew if he was late, she'd balk over needing to rush to dinner. He adored Lillian and wanted nothing more than to make her happy. They lived in separate apartments, but within the same building. Lillian lived on the floor below his, and as they headed down the stairs, Nathan remembered carrying his father's satchel clumsily down each flight before his dad left for his latest expedition. He'd set it down on the last step and taken Lillian's hand as Samuel told her when he'd be returning. That was the last time he saw his father. It was also the day Lillian became his guardian.

"I want you to order whatever you like tonight, and no scrimping because you're worried about the cost, understand?" Nathan insisted.

"Oh no, you will not," Lillian scolded. "We're going to have a lovely dinner, but it will be on me." Nathan started to protest but stopped when she gave him "the look." "Besides, if you pay, I will assume it is to say goodbye, and I will not be saying goodbye to you, young man. You'll return in a week, and when you do, you can buy dinner then." She winked.

"Deal," Nathan replied as he raised his arm in the air to hail a cab.

"We can walk, Nathan."

"I didn't want you to have to walk all that way," he replied as the car pulled up to the curb. "And you gave no stipulation about a taxi, only dinner."

Nathan opened the door and offered his hand to her.

Lillian clicked her tongue, but didn't argue. Instead, the two rode to the restaurant, enjoyed a lovely meal, and returned home early enough for her to be able to read a chapter in her book before heading to bed. Nathan had left before on excursions, but he always came home. Something about him leaving this time felt different, though. They hugged one another tightly as they said their goodbyes.

"Don't worry. I'll be home in a week," Nathan insisted as he kissed her forehead. "I love you, Lillian."

"I love you too, Nathan. Now be careful. I'll hold the fort down here until you return."

He smiled. "You always do."

Nathan looked back one last time before he headed upstairs.

Find **Trapped Within a Wish** where books are sold.

www.ingramcontent.com/pod-product-compliance
Lightning Source LLC
Chambersburg PA
CBHW032152190626
46814CB00005BA/1958